WICKER DOGS

by D.A. Holwill

Copyright D.A. Holwill 2021

The right of D.A. Holwill to be identified as the author of this work has been asserted by him in accordance with the Copyright, Designs and Patents Act 1988.

First published in 2021

All characters and events in this book, other than those clearly in the public domain, are fictitious and any resemblance to real persons, living or dead, is purely coincidental.

*For all the good people of the small town (not a village)
I've made my home*

and especially for Netty – the best of them

Etching ©Netty Holwill 2021

1

Then...

I awoke at the centre of the stone circle Lord Elias and I raised in happier time. Moonlit figures, disguised by velvet robes, checked I could not escape. Then a whisper from behind a wicker tinner's mask deep within a hood, my beloved Thomas, brought that most dreadful of things – hope.

A single howl pierced the frozen air as they left me on a snow-covered slab.

I tested my bonds and my good left hand came free. The knot, purposely mistied. Thomas's wink was no vain gesture. Another howl in the night, closer this time. I performed the necessary contortions to loose my other hand, pressure forcing me to fumble. I had been tied to that terrible rock too long.

Scarcely had I removed the last rope when I heard a thundering of paws. The hunt were upon me, unrestrained with no master on horseback to whistle them back.

Their master would not wish them whistled back.

D.A. HOLWILL

Now…

'It's beginning to look a lot like Christmas,' Polly sings, a little drunk. 'Everywhere but here.'

It is the first weekend of December and Great Britain is bedecked in tinsel and jolly ho-ho-hoing Santas – apart from the small Devon town of Dourstone Nymet. There, freshly snow-filled streets sport eldritch torches; shop windows and lampposts display definitely-not-Santa-scarecrows; while wickerwork dogs, which can in no way be mistaken for reindeer, punctuate every corner.

'This village is nuts Patrick,' Polly shouts, putting her glasses on to peer through the window. 'Why have we moved here?' She shifts her weight on the box she is sitting on before it collapses.

'It's a town Pol,' Patrick reminds her, remembering to duck under the low doorway that's already left a couple of decent lumps on his curly head. 'Don't ever say village, they'll lynch you. There was a Market Charter from some ancient King or another.' He refills her glass from a fresh bottle of wine.

'Okay, okay… What the hell is that?' Polly screams as she sees movement outside. Flaming torches, borne up the hill by hooded figures accompanying a cart.

'I don't know,' Patrick says, squeezing in close to look. 'I thought it was all over now.'

At 4:30 that morning a group of the fittest and least hungover Dourstonians had pushed a cartload of flaming barrels to the top of the hill where a symbolic scarecrow was thrown on and left to burn through the day while procession after procession of children wrapped head to toe in crepe paper made their way up.

The final, and grandest, of these had finished a couple of hours ago, with another cart of flaming barrels thrown into the embers of their predecessors to burn through the night. Then most of the town headed down to the square to dance the night away in the snow with no coats on.

Between the road closures and the snowdrifts there was no way their moving lorries were getting to the house, so Patrick grudgingly agreed to pay a great deal extra for them to come back the next day. In a gap between processions they tested their newly purchased 4x4's

WICKER DOGS

hill-climbing abilities and unloaded the meagre supplies from its boot before a brief jaunt into town to find food. Since then they have been sitting in an empty room christening the new house with the wines they didn't trust to the moving company. Patrick had suggested they stay in the square for the festivities, but Polly felt too much an outsider and feigned tiredness. That was hours ago, it is midnight and she is still wide awake and drinking.

'Can you hear that chanting?' she asks Patrick.

'Yeah, yeah, that's creepy.'

She wipes the window with her sleeve and sees the grinning face of Mr Punch staring back. Polly cannot bear Mr Punch but at least he's strapped down to the cart where he can't get to her. One of the procession turns towards her but she can't make out any features in the faceless dark of their hood before they turn back to the road.

'Seriously Paddy, what the fuck?' Polly says, the hairs on her skin, already up from the cold, make a valiant attempt to rise further. The previous occupants have not bothered to refill the oil tank, there is no wood for the glorious stove in the fireplace and mains gas remains a Victorian pipedream in Dourstone.

'It's the Wish Weekend Pol, they do a lot of crazy stuff.'

'Wish Weekend? Like wishing on a star? Like the make a wish foundation?'

Patrick furrows his brow and peers through the window where the cart is merging with the fog. 'Wish, as in wisthound, Dad must have told you the legend of The Devil and his dogs.'

'Probably,' Polly sighs. 'He tells a lot of stories.' This is true, Patrick's father is very fond of the sound of his own voice and has a cache of tales for every occasion. Polly has heard all of them more than once in the decade her and Patrick have been together. That doesn't mean she remembers them though. 'Go on then, tell me.'

His eyes light up, like father like son.

'You've heard of the wisthounds right?' he begins.

'Wisthounds?'

'Jesus, you don't listen do you,' Patrick mutters, shuffling on his recycling box. 'The wisthounds, the wild hunt, The Devil's dogs. They're all over Dartmoor, just like Old Nick himself.'

'Really?'

'Yes, folklorically speaking, they're what the whole weekend's about, it's an ancient tradition.'

'Like all the other "ancient traditions" the Victorians invented?' Polly laughs.

'No, this one really is ancient,' Patrick insists. 'Anyway, the story goes like this.' He pauses for effect and takes a mouthful of wine.

'Oh get on with it,' Polly titters. Patrick's flair for the dramatic can be infuriating, but just now it is cute.

'It was a dark and stormy night...'

'Really? Come off it,' Polly mutters.

'Really, that's how it begins.' Patrick reels back in mock hurt. 'Anyway, this particular dark and stormy night, The Devil was abroad, a-hunting with his hounds.'

'His wisthounds,' Polly corrects. 'Hang on, didn't you say they were in Wistman's Wood before?'

'Thought you'd forgotten all about them.' He raises an eyebrow. 'Well, like I said, they're all over Dartmoor. They say they're kennelled at Grimpound too, but that's beside the point, do you want to hear this story or not?'

'I do, I do, sorry, I won't interrupt again.' Polly makes doe-eyes as she sips her drink.

'The Devil swept down into Dourstone Nymet, on a dark and stormy night.' Patrick pauses to let Polly make whooshing wind noises. 'And was moved to a jealous rage for its comfortable position between protective hills. He set his dogs to rip up its crops and murder its livestock before moving on to the townsfolk.'

'Crikey.' Polly makes a mock-scared face.

'Crikey indeed.' Patrick nods. 'But the people were not for turning and they bargained for this place they so loved, with its shelter from the burning Devon winds.'

'Wind doesn't burn,' Polly interjects.

'I'll take you up to High Willhays soon, you'll learn,' Patrick explains. 'They pleaded, with their knees in the mud, and begged The Devil to spare them and their town. He cut a bargain.'

'Two for one on Pedigree Chum in the local shop?'

'Funny, no, but similar.'

'Really?'

'No. They offered to kennel and feed the demonic pack over the worst of the winter. And lo, did he agree to their terms.' Patrick puts one hand over his heart and thrusts the other outward, narrowly missing an oak beam.

'So, Pedigree Chum then?'

'No, wisthounds have rather more rarefied tastes than Fenrir,' Patrick points to an unconscious Irish wolfhound lying in a pool of drool by the stone-cold radiator. They picked him up from Battersea a week ago. Patrick had been reluctant, but in Polly's idyllic childhood fantasies (fuelled by an unending stream of Enid Blyton borrowed from the mobile library) dogs and countryside are inextricably linked, so they had gone to the dogs' home and fallen in love with this awkward scruffy beast. 'So a terrible sacrifice had to be made. Once a year, as autumn turned unmistakably to winter, Dourstonians would leave one of their number atop a hill that marks the northern edge of the parish.' Patrick's voice veers into his best Vincent Price impression. 'The morning after, there would be nothing left but blood and entrails.' He grins a demonic grin. 'You heard them chanting through town earlier, "You feed The Devil's dogs as the cold begins to bite, the first snows of winter stained with blood in the night." Maybe the stories are true?'

'Yeah, but they're not.'

'No, but my dad says back in the dark ages there would have been a real sacrifice made here, a goat or cow or something, but as we've become less superstitious, more genteel, it's evolved into scarecrows, sculptures and lovely bonfires like it is now.'

'Not people then?'

'Not really, no. Probably never was, it's just a story to scare kids, it used to work on me when we stayed down here. Unless…'

'Unless what?'

'Unless nothing, I'm just kidding. It's a remnant of an old pagan festival, a way to prepare for the oncoming cold and dark. Your Christian god didn't make it very far onto the moors until they sorted out the transport.'

At a sound from outside, Fenrir is suddenly wide awake. He scrambles to his feet with an urgent bark, then sits to attention, nose pointing uphill and lips quivering in anticipation.

'That sounded like wolves,' Polly says.

'Bloody idiots,' Patrick chuckles, heading to the kitchen. 'Wolves, in Devon? We're a long way from Dartmoor Zoo here, that's an owl.'

'He's not an idiot,' Polly flings her arms around the dog's neck. 'It's all so new, he's only been with us a week, and we've already dragged him to the other end of the country, new sounds, new smells, fireworks.' He remains uncomforted, sitting to attention, eyes straining wide.

'Have we done the right thing Paddy?' she shouts through the door, still fiercely hugging Fenrir.

'Of course we have.' Patrick laughs, coming back in with coffee. 'It's been a long day. All we saw was some watered-down version of an ancient ritual to ensure a mild winter, give thanks for a good harvest, you know *Wicker Man* type stuff – but with tins of beans instead of Edward Woodward.'

Polly stiffens. She hates that movie. She hates anything with Mr Punch in.

'We don't burn people alive here, everything will seem better in the morning. Come on, let's go to bed and get to work on some kids to put in all these bedrooms.'

'Nice try.' Polly smiles. Patrick knows she doesn't want kids just yet. She will one day, she's sure, but at 28 and a bit she still has time. She wants to settle into their new life before filling it up with sleepless nights and unsolicited vomit.

Keen to explore the new neighbourhood Patrick and Fenrir head outside at first light, leaving Polly asleep: spread-eagled like Jesus across the bed with no room for Patrick to get back in even if he wanted to. His brand new hiking boots disappear into deep snow hiding the pot-holes and ruts of the ancient trackway; as does Fenrir, who barks with joy as he bursts in and out of snowdrifts, liberally covering Patrick in frozen slush that sticks in his neat beard with each leap.

They crest the hill as the sun bursts through wispy clouds. Up here you can see all Devon unfurled. On a clear day (so Patrick's father claims) you can see all the way from Plymouth Harbour in the south to the rugged Exmoor coast. Patrick isn't sure that's true, but it is an impressive sight on a frozen December morning under blue skies.

They make their way up to the site of yesterday's festivities, a large triangular clearing bordered by deep woods on one side, open moorland on the second and the roadway on the hypotenuse. The bonfire still smokes merrily away to one side of the stone circle despite the snow. And in the centre of the standing stones – not actually Neolithic, but a romantic reconstruction dating from the Victorian era, Patrick's father is a font of useless information – stands the cart that passed the house. Untouched by fire, it looks old, dark brown stains across its ancient granite base speak of long years of service, as do deep scratches in its once-brightly-coloured paintwork.

Fenrir barks and pulls at his lead. Desperately scrabbling underneath the cart.

'What is it boy?' Patrick asks, he is trying to bond with this dog, but it remains resolutely Polly's. He is hoping more walks together out in the Dartmoor air will teach him to share.

He pulls his head back out, a cherry red Doctor Marten boot clamped between his jaws.

'Must have fallen off one of the scarecrows.' He laughs, taking it from the dog, who does his best good boy sit in anticipation of having it thrown. Something sharp jabs into Patrick's hand. He winces and licks hot salty blood from the wound; then turns pale and bites back the urge to scream before dropping it and dragging a disappointed Fenrir back down the hill.

What he had thought to be straw peeking out over the leather upper is a jagged bone. Still connected to the bloody stump of an actual foot by frayed sinews of vanished muscle.

2

Then...

I ran. After so long in that tiny cell, it took all the will left at my command to move my aching limbs. Fear, however, proved motivation enough and I found myself sprinting painfully through desolate moorland. The dogs were close on my heels and I had not the faintest idea how to shake them off; all I could do was run. I had not planned on living past this night, but my lack of plan would hinder me no more than my lack of footwear.

Cresting the ridge of a tor, my bleeding foot slipped on smooth rock and I was launched upon the downward slope, falling and rolling faster than the dogs could keep their footing. I bounced from rocks to river, then crawled through icy water to a cave in the bank where I hid in freezing damp, my heart rate slowing. The Dourstone Stickman outfit I wore was of thin garish red linen, easily washed and stitched in time for its next victim – my own design. I hugged myself for warmth, my whole body convulsing with shivers, glad there were none to see my rictus grin as I forced my chattering teeth apart.

Eventually I heard no more scrabbling, nor sniffing, nor barks. The dogs had moved on and I dared venture from my hole. The pleasure of allowing my teeth to rattle freely was short-lived but divine.

I limped my way through drifting snow, legs seizing at every other step, blood-filled footprints leaving an unmistakeable trail. Using the stars to chart my course I aimed north for Okehampton, where I hoped to be able to board a train back to London. But then your face came to me. I could not leave you. With a force of effort I did not know I had I turned around. To die trying would be honourable. To live out my days, having not taken every chance to save you, would be intolerable.

Now...

'I know what they said,' Patrick says, stretching his legs out in front of the Drop of Dew's roaring fire. 'We've been through this enough times already. Tradition, "the first snows of winter stained with blood in the night," Adrian the butcher throws around a bit of offal up there, to scare the kiddies.'

'Exactly, you were just tired.' Polly takes a swig of her drink and sighs. 'We had a stressful weekend.'

'But I know what I saw, Pol,' he continues. 'Pigs don't wear Doctor Martens boots.'

It's been weeks since they started this discussion and there is still no sign of its being resolved.

They have managed to get the much-coveted armchairs by the fireplace – the only comfortable seats in the pub. The rest of it is furnished with rickety chairs, unstable bar stools and pews ripped from the old church – some from before it was gutted by fire, a couple of darker ones from after – that almost, but not quite, match the worm-chewed old beams of the seventeenth century inn. Patrick's amateur archaeologist father swears blind it dates all the way back to the 1450s, he can tell by the chamfering on the purlins.

'You were probably still a bit pissed from the night before Patrick,' Polly continues. 'We did get through three bottles.'

'Yeah, maybe, maybe.' Patrick doesn't like not being able to trust his own eyes.

After his unexpectedly quick return that morning, Polly had immediately dragged him straight back up there with her and Fenrir – who was really enjoying all the walks he was suddenly getting. Somehow, in the time it had taken to get down the hill and back up again, the offending boot had vanished. If it hadn't been for that Patrick might have agreed it was just overactive imagination. But the liberally thrown about pig intestines had not been there before, of that he was completely certain. Fenrir had tried to make himself sick on animal guts on the second visit before being told to stop. He was still scared enough of the possibility he might be sent back to doggy prison that he obeyed any command his new food dispensers gave.

But he had made a beeline straight for the cart that first time. No distractions.

Polly theorised that another dog, or a fox or badger must have taken the shoe, but Patrick would not be convinced. The scene looked staged, obviously, it was deliberately staged to add a little magic to the weekend. But things were not the same, Patrick was convinced, though nobody would believe him.

'Weird village Pat. Why did we move here?' Polly shakes her head.

'Keep your voice down Pol. Town, market charter, remember?'

'I thought you said it didn't have a market anymore?' Polly grins. 'They sold it and made it into an old folks' home and a car park?'

'Yeah, they did but...'

'But what?' She folds her arms. 'No market, no town, it's a village, and you still haven't answered my question.'

'Please don't let anyone hear you say that.' Patrick sighs. 'You know why we're here Polly, you hated London. This is where you come from, this is where I come from, we're coming home for some peace and quiet.'

'I'm not from here. I'm from Appledore, North Devon, by the sea, not this landlocked rain trap.'

'It'll stop raining soon Polly, Spring's not far away. Anyway, Devon's Devon, s'all the same.' Patrick shrugs.

It is definitely not all the same to Polly. This town bears no resemblance to where she grew up. Not that that's a bad thing. Even the Appledore she grew up in is a long way from the picture postcard literary festival town it has become. She grew up on its shield wall of council estates, where her mum was habitually referred to as the Single Black Female despite being what most of the locals still insist on calling a 'half-caste'. Polly's skin is light enough that people just think she has a tan, and when she left North Devon for university she dealt with the uncontrollable hair that gave her heritage away by relaxing it and going blonde.

'And you're not from here either, you're a bloody Chelsea boy through and through,' she reminds him.

'Dad's side of the family comes from here, we still own the ancestral home.' He points out of the window at a large thatched house on the square. 'We stayed here all the time when we were kids. That graveyard's full of Sumners, I've got blood ties.'

He's taken to saying he's from Devon to a very mixed response, but his claim that it's 'all the same' is a dead giveaway. Chagford and Ilfracombe have nothing in common and their inhabitants would beat you to death with the soggy end of your own arm if you dared suggest they did. It's funny really, since when Polly said everything inside the M25 was London, she got a very long lecture on the difference between Croydon and Pimlico with no trace of irony.

It's true though, she hated London and wanted somewhere more rural, less hectic, somewhere she could breathe the air without feeling her throat close up in protest. Coming back to his ancient family seat where Mama and Papa are still occasionally within reach seemed the only way to get him out.

'Second home-owners are second home-owners Pat, whether they bought it as an investment or inherited it.' She raises her eyebrow and her glass.

'Meh.' He looks around to check none of the locals have overheard the mention of second homes on top of the word village.

Polly considers the matter closed, and the upper hand hers.

'Whoa there doggy!' Patrick says, trying to stop Fenrir pushing past. He fails, and the dog takes prime position in front of the fire, blocking Patrick's legs from the heat. 'What have you got now, you great lump?'

'Not sure,' Polly replies, looking at him curiously.

'Hope you don't mind love,' a gentle Devon accent lilts from the bar. 'Us give him a pork scratching, on account of his being a good boy.' A portly, balding man in a green anorak, his remaining hair kept stubbornly long enough at the back to tie in a ponytail, grins toothlessly at Polly in explanation.

'Also, it was a big one, and neither of us thought we could get through it what with our teeth,' his companion, a taller, thinner man with a long beard and thick curly hair, explains, punctuating with a gap-filled grin.

'That's fine, thank you.' Polly smiles back. 'He does love a treat.' She bends down and scruffs the dog's neck, secretly worrying about the strict diet and scientifically designed food she pays such a lot of money for. Wouldn't do to upset the locals, she thinks, we're still Down-From-Londoners, whatever Patrick says.

'Jesus Christ Polly!' Patrick exclaims, sniffing his post dog-stroking hand. 'He stinks! Has he rolled in fox shit again?'

'I think so,' she admits. 'I've washed him three times, all different shampoos, one specially formulated for fox shit, but I can't get the stink out.'

'You'll have to do something,' Patrick says. 'I can't live with him if he's going to smell like that.'

'You want to talk to Lady Mel,' the taller, hairier, of the two men at the bar butts in. 'She'll sort you out.'

'Yep,' agrees his companion, 'does the best dog wash round here. Up at the old Manor house, number's behind the bar somewhere.' He waves at a board where cheaply printed business cards fill gaps between peanuts, scampi fries and pork scratchings. 'Or just go up there, shout in the yard, bang on the door, she's usually in. Got the stink out of my Bentley after he jumped in the septic tank last year. Never thought it would go away.'

'She's a bit odd, but a good sort,' the tall man continues. 'Family are the ancient Lords of the Manor, from Norman times.'

'Earlier an' that, I reckon, I wouldn't think the Dewers'd let them French bastards take their lands off of them,' the barman adds.

'And now she washes dogs,' the other concludes, grinning. 'Bloody well too.'

'Still owns most of the place though don't she?' hairy tall man says. 'You pay your rent to her, same as I.'

'That I do, glad of it an' all.' Baldy anorak nods. 'Anyway, she still lives up the big house, pop round, she'll sort your stinky doggy out. She's always keen to meet blowins, make sure you fit in proper.'

'She's not that bad, you'll be fine.' The other man smiles.

'Thanks,' Polly says, getting up to buy another round. 'Do you two want a drink?'

'Wouldn't say no, thanks very much,' the fatter, balder one replies, his companion agrees.

'And one for yourself barman,' Polly says as he hands her an embossed card, with the dogwasher's details, pulled from mysterious depths behind dusty top shelf bottles.

'Speak of The Devil,' the taller man says as the door swings open, letting a gust of wind howl through the snug. Fenrir stops begging for snacks and hides behind Polly.

'Pink Gin and a...' the newcomer begins, striding to the bar, long silver hair flowing behind her, 'you'll have a small cider.' More of a statement than a question as she turns to a mousy-looking woman peering about her as if terrified anyone will notice her presence. It shouldn't be a problem, the other woman fills the room, casting everybody else as background.

'Yes, thank you.' The mousy woman nods, before spotting Patrick by the fire and giving him a little wave and a smile. 'Hello you,' she mouths.

'Oh, hi Lynn,' Patrick replies.

Polly remembers Lynn. It was her fault their decision to move here had been so quick. They had run into her while walking down the Thames, just past the Tate Modern, one Sunday afternoon. Patrick knew her from his idyllic childhood Dourstone summers. During one of those 'so what are you up to these days?' conversations, they told her they were thinking of leaving London. She told them about this 'perfect place for you, you'd love it, oh you should come back Patrick, it would be amazing, the place hasn't changed you know?', things kind of spiralled and before they knew it they had bought a cottage.

'How are you settling in?' Lynn asks, coming over.

'Oh, we love the cottage,' Polly butts in. 'Thank you so much for putting us on to it.'

'Not a problem,' Lynn replies. 'By the way, have you met...'

'Hello, hello, who are you, why are you here, why don't I know you?' Lynn's companion throws what Polly hopes is a fake-fur overcoat into Lynn's arms before shoving Lynn towards the coat hooks. 'Lady Melissa Dewer.' She sticks out a hand towards Polly in greeting. 'But you can just call me Mel.'

'Dr Patrick Sumner, and this is my girlfriend, Polly.' Patrick interrupts once he has made up his mind between kissing her ring and shaking the offered hand. He attempts the latter, but Lady Melissa merely wiggles her fingers against his before turning her full attention to Polly.

'Girlfriend? So he hasn't made an honest woman of you?' Mel winks, grabbing Polly's hand in both of hers. 'And who's this?'

Fenrir pokes his nose out between Polly's knees and Mel bends down to stroke it, pushing herself further into Polly's personal space.

'This is Fenrir. He's a rescue.' Polly always introduces him as such, to ensure people know she is not responsible for any bad behaviour.

'He's beautiful, aren't you?' she says to the dog, pushing her head against his as he makes happy whining noises and licks her cheek.

Her perfectly tailored purple velvet trouser suit is quickly covered in dog hair, but she seems not to care. 'Yes you are, yes you are,' she continues, in that special voice people have for dogs.

'Sorry, he's a bit stinky,' Polly apologises.

'No need to apologise.' Lady Melissa jumps back up, shaking out her hair. 'Bring him out to see me tomorrow, up at Dourstone Manor, you can't miss it. I'll give him a scrub, special introductory offer.'

'What's the offer?' Patrick interjects.

'You won't find out unless you come,' Mel addresses Polly, not so much as glancing at Patrick.

'Oh, okay, thank you,' Polly says.

Lynn attempts to pick up hers and Melissa's drinks where they stand uncollected, but the barman refuses to relinquish them without payment. She grudgingly hands over her own money before delivering Mel's pink gin and moving to one side, the same side Patrick finds himself on as Melissa interrogates Polly.

'So, how's the estate agent business going?' Patrick asks Lynn, as their awkward silence becomes unbearable.

'Oh, I'm not an estate agent, I just help Jack out showing houses when he's busy,' Lynn explains.

'Oh, okay, and how's…' Patrick tails off, unable to remember Lynn's husband's name.

'Graham?' Lynn says, her eyes growing watery. 'He's, well he's… I'm sorry, I can't…' She turns and rushes out to the garden, snorting with tears.

Patrick remembers Graham now, the four of them had spent the afternoon on the balcony of the Tate Modern, Patrick using his membership to try and impress a girl he hadn't seen in years with its exclusive access. Graham seemed alright, despite spending a lot of time hiding a cigarette behind his back, much to the annoyance of the very posh lady who couldn't prove it to the waitress.

'Is she alright?' Polly asks.

'Oh, yes, Lynn's fine,' Mel frowns at Fenrir, then gives him a wink and an ear-rub. 'Nothing to worry about, still getting the hang of being single. Happier for it, don't get me wrong, but needs a bit of help since her husband disappeared. I'll see you tomorrow then, any time after about eleven should be fine.' She gives Patrick a cursory nod then heads off after Lynn.

'Bloody hell,' Patrick says, slumping back into his chair. 'It doesn't even occur to her that you might not come does it?'

'I don't think so.' Polly agrees, watching as Mel exchanges pleasantries with all and sundry on her way past.

'Don't mind her,' the taller of the two men at the bar says. 'She's not used to people saying no to her on account of it never happening.'

3

Then...

Upon my return to the Manor I found the doors unguarded and unlocked. I raced through its long, wood-panelled corridors ready to whisk you away, mount Lord Elias' best horse and make it to Okehampton in time for that train to London. The sun was just rising, we could make it, get away before the household rose and build a new life. I felt sure my father would forgive me everything if he met you.

But you weren't there.

In your room stood Elias, grinning like a cat reeling in the same mouse it has freed three times already. I sank to the floor and allowed his men to take me out.

They have locked me in the library, and I have spent the time since trying to piece my story together on paper in the vain hope that some impossible string of kindness and coincidence lead you to these pages and know you were loved. For Lord Elias Dewer will surely never tell you of me, even if he suffers you to live.

Now...

'What are we going to do with this? Is it even legal?' Patrick says, pulling a sword from one of the never-ending boxes they are still unpacking.

'It's very important to me Paddy,' Polly says. 'It was my grandad's, might even be worth a few quid.' She has no idea how her grandfather came to own the 1897 pattern infantry officer's sword, he's told her so many different stories: how he fought with it at Rourke's drift; how Blackbeard presented it to him as welcome to the crew of the Queen Anne's Revenge; how he won it from Joseph Bologne, the Chevalier de Saint Georges – the gentlemen fencer himself, in a duel to the very-near-death. Her grandfather had been the first of his family born in England less than a year after his parents arrived on the Empire Windrush in 1948.

Her mum, in a rare moment of noticing Polly, said he'd most likely either picked it up cheap in a pawn shop or won it in a game of euchre at the Bell Inn. Whatever the truth, he had given it to Polly when she won her first university fencing tournament. She was the first of the family to go and he had been overwhelmed with pride.

'Fair enough, we're in the countryside now, we could do with some weapons, pass it here.' Patrick takes the sword, eyeballing a space above the blackened brick fireplace. 'Well look at that, it's meant to be,' he says, and hangs it in prime position above the fire on a couple of nails that could have been driven into the ancient oak beam for exactly that reason.

'We'll leave it there then.' Polly nods. 'For luck. Shit, what's the time?'

'It's just gone eleven thirty, why?'

'Fuck, fuck, fuckity bum, I'm late.' Polly runs from the room; she has forgotten her appointment with the Lady of the Manor.

Weather beaten hound heads peer out from beneath thick coats of lichen atop every granite post that lines the long driveway to Dourstone Manor. At the final pair, on gateposts that mark its end, Fenrir lets out a snarl. A pair of mismatched amber and blue almond-shaped eyes stare across the cobbled courtyard from the darkness of a barn. Slowly, a wolf takes shape around them as it stalks into the yard, sits down thoughtfully and stares at the newcomers. Fenrir strains forwards at his lead, growling, until the wolf throws its head back and looses a short howl, opening its scarred face wide. Such a face, Polly can see millennia of wolf-kind reflected from his unwavering glare and looks away, unable to stare him down.

His pack answer the call without a sound, filling the yard with pacing, staring, very alert wolves. The way seems blocked. Fenrir still pulls at his lead, but Polly is sure he is trying to run away, rather than towards.

'Hello?' Polly shouts, as loud as she dares from as close as the guardians allow. 'It's Polly? We met last night. Are you there Lady Dewer?'

'It's just Mel to you dear,' comes a clipped aristocratic voice from behind the wall of grey fur. 'Get out of the way, you great lumps.'

'Hello, we're not late are we?' Polly shouts. 'It's a longer walk than I thought.' It's a poor lie. The walk was quite short, but because Dourstone's single-file pavements are accented with large planters either side of every doorway – forcing pedestrians to take their lives in their hands on the narrow, car-lined road – Polly had to stop every time one of many enormous, loud, speeding tractors and trailers passed.

'No, not at all, not at all, come in,' Lady Mel says, beckoning them into the sea of tooth and claw. 'Cronus!' she addresses the ancient wolf with the mismatched eyes. 'Leave off them, they're invited.'

The wolves open out into a circle, stalking around Polly and Fenrir as they make their way in, sizing them up to see which might be easiest to eat. Polly is certain it is her; Fenrir is both better defended and a faster runner. Cronus has not yet taken his eyes from Polly's.

'Oh, don't mind them, they're just nosy,' Mel assures her as she bats one away. 'Push them out of your way, they won't mind.'

Polly tiptoes past an old granite mounting block towards Lady Melissa as the wolves pace around like a furry orrery.

'Oh stop it you big silly!' Mel says, grabbing Cronus by his scruff. 'Call them off, you're not funny.' She stares him down until he looks to the ground in deference.

The ring of wolves stop and let out one long inharmonious howl.

Polly and Fenrir freeze.

'I told you, they're invited, now leave them alone!' Mel says, staring them down wolf by wolf. They refuse to meet her eye as their howls become muted whining. 'I said alone, now back to the barn.'

Cronus gives them a nod and goes back to the barn. The others continue to circle, if less enthusiastically. The threat appears to be over.

'Is it entirely safe to keep wolves?' Polly asks, wide-eyed and holding on to Fenrir's lead so tightly she has lost circulation in one of her fingers.

'Wolves?' Mel laughs. 'These aren't wolves you daft girl, they're Alaskan malamutes, close, but a little more vain and a lot less clever.'

'Sorry.' Polly has never felt such relief, these are just dogs. 'I've never seen them before, beautiful animals.'

'Yes, that's about all they have going for them though,' Mel says. 'The Dewers have always kept a pack, the Nymet hunt, long since retired of course. I didn't hold with the hunt even before the ban. Felt they should even the numbers up, give the foxes horses and guns. I've tried keeping other types of dog, but this kind of got out of control. They don't seem to like other breeds, except as a snack. So I run this place as a malamute rescue centre.'

'A rescue centre?'

'Not really, real rescue centres manage to rehome the odd one, I've never had one leave. I felt sorry for one at a dogs home and rescued it, once. Then I heard of another, so I thought he might like a friend. Then people got wind of it, the trend for getting wolf-type dogs got huge and suddenly before you know it, everybody in the South-West Peninsula is abandoning malamutes, I'm taking them on, and I've got this pack.' She waves an arm in the direction of the dogs.

'I had a similar experience with souvenir spoons,' Polly says, 'though with less consequences, and I don't even like spoons.'

'Bit different girl, yes,' Mel says, stroking Fenrir's nose with a blood-stained hand. 'Sorry,' she adds, noticing Polly's look of shock. 'I was preparing their dinner, raw food. No shortage of it round here, I let the poachers take what they want off my land as long as I get a cut. Feeds the dogs, stocks the pub with cheap local produce. Good for the community.'

'Not a problem,' Polly says, glad of the antibacterial wipes in her anorak pocket.

'Now let's take a look at you shall we.' Mel leans down to Fenrir, shaking, hackled up, ready to either fight or run; Polly would put money on the latter. 'Crikey, you are a stinker aren't you?' she says.

Fenrir tries to drop his head, but Mel holds his chin firmly in her wrinkled grip. The malamutes have lost interest and wandered off; Cronus has accepted the new arrivals.

'I've washed him in three different shampoos, brushed him with five different types of brush, sprayed him, scrubbed him, everything, and, while my boyfriend still insists he smells, I think he's fine,' Polly explains.

'Noseblind to your own dog.' Mel nods. 'Very common. Take my lot, because malamute hair is supposed to be odourless I assume they are. Go and give one of them a sniff, go on.'

Polly really doesn't want to go and sniff one of the aloof and disdainful dogs; she doesn't think they would welcome her attention with anything other than a severed limb.

'Go on. Saxon! Come here boy!' she shouts at the fluffiest as five other dogs turn to look. 'Sorry, these bloody dogs all have the same name, I've got six Saxons, four Nanooks, three Greywinds, five Ghosts and a whole hat-full of Skys.'

'Couldn't you change their names?' Polly suggests.

'I could, but you wouldn't like it if I decided to call you Emily just because I liked it more and already knew a Polly would you?'

'No, I suppose I wouldn't.' Polly nods. Mel seems less glamorous in the morning light; shorter even, with her long silvery hair swept up into a bun. Time etched across her in a way Polly supposes took a lot of make-up and a decent pair of heels to hide.

'Saxon. Here.' Mel singles out the correct Saxon with a hard stare and a pointing finger, he briefly catches her eye, half rises, then lies back down again to chew on his bone. 'Ignorant bloody mutts...' she mutters. 'Come with me.' She takes Polly by the arm and walks her over, leaving Fenrir standing confused in the middle of the yard. She grabs Saxon, who comes up uncomplaining, knowing his place in the pack order. He looks at Polly with his odd yellow eyes and lets out a mournful howl revealing a mouthful of chipped, brown teeth.

Mel pushes Polly's face down into his damp furry neck. 'Go on, sniff that.' Polly inhales, trying not to think about what this dank fur has rolled in. It stinks of about five different kinds of excrement, moss and a trace of some unidentifiable fruit.

'Bloody hell!' Polly exclaims, pulling back out as Mel releases her grip. 'That is a stinky dog!'

'See, can't smell him myself.' Mel grins. 'To me he smells of sunshine and daisies all the time. Now, let's get your little fella in the salon.'

They cross the yard into a crumbling old stable, Polly sneezing uncontrollably from a nose-full of filthy dog hair. The very stones of its walls are falling away from the ivy that forces them apart, while gutters hang from wooden boards sanded down to nothing by Dartmoor winds. Bending low to walk through a weather-beaten door that sticks in its frame, swollen from endless rain, she finds a completely fitted out wet room filled with shelves and cupboards of different coloured shampoos, conditioners and detanglers; racks and racks of brushes, combs, clippers, scissors, matt splitters and a host of what could easily be medieval torture devices that Polly doesn't recognise.

'Right, let's do this.' Mel grabs Fenrir, clips him to what looks like a repurposed manacle and begins to spray him with a warm shower hose. For the first time ever he seems not to mind, to positively enjoy the experience. He is impossible to clean at home, he runs from the hose, he will not sit in the bath. Up until this point he has been unwashable without extreme effort. Yet here he is giving his best good boy sit and even lifting his legs out of the way on command. Polly is reminded of the girls at university that could persuade Patrick to walk them home with just a smile and a tactically deployed hair flick, whereas Polly would be lucky if he called her a taxi.

'Good boy,' Polly says. Fenrir pays her no attention at all, gazing lovingly into Mel's eyes as she rubs thick, pink shampoo into his tummy.

'He is a good boy,' Mel agrees, fingering more shampoo in behind his ears.

'Patrick will be pleased when he gets home to a lovely, fluffy, nice-smelling doggy.'

'Patrick?' Mel looks vaguely out of the door where a pair of malamutes slink off from their vantage point back to the barn.

'He's my boyfriend,' Polly explains. 'You met him last night? The new doctor.'

'Oh yes, him, he's a doctor?' Mel's eyebrows rise. 'He's the doctor?'

'Not the one in the Tardis, but yes, he's the new GP for Dourstone.' Polly beams. She is quite proud of Patrick. She knows it's stupid, but having a handsome doctor all of her very own is one of those childish fantasies she never quite got over.

'Is he by buggery,' Mel says. 'I don't visit the doctor's often, might have to come down with something.' She winks and chuckles to herself as she starts sluicing pink goop from Fenrir, who gives a happy woof and wriggle without so much as a glance at his mistress.

'I know we're young, and we've come from London, but we really want to make a go of it here, and Patrick's got family connections. His dad still owns the old barrel-works on the square, old family home.'

'Oh, I know the Sumner family, yes.' Mel looks wistfully up to the ceiling. 'And how... not seen them in an age mind.'

'I think they still come down from time to time.' Polly finds herself in the unusual position of defending her in-laws.

'I don't doubt it,' Mel says. 'I don't make it into town as much as I once did, and I don't remember them being much for socialising when they're here anyway. Usually bring their own company and stay in that big old house with their fancy London friends.'

Polly can't tell if Mel approves of this, but she doesn't think she likes them, and thus, by association, she doesn't think she likes her.

'That's an interesting ring you've got,' Polly says, noticing a glint from her right hand ring finger.

'It's for my condition,' Mel explains. 'Coffin-nails.'

Looking more closely, Polly can see it has been fashioned from three or four twisted brass-headed nails. 'Condition?'

'It's to prevent fits,' Mel says. 'My nanny gave it to me when I was a child and I haven't had an attack since – apart from on the odd occasion it leaves my finger.'

'You have epilepsy?' Polly can't help prying.

'No idea, never been diagnosed, like I said, I don't hold much with doctors. Nanny put the ring on me and it stopped right away, or so she said. So we didn't need anybody poking their nose in. The ring does the job.'

'If it ain't broke,' Polly says, with what she hopes is a friendly smile.

'If what ain't broke?'

'It's a saying, if it ain't broke, don't fix it,' Polly explains.

'Is that pertinent?'

'Probably not, sorry,' Polly apologises.

'Well, I think he's all done now, have a sniff.' Mel hands Fenrir's lead to Polly, who buries her face in his fur to be overpowered with a fruity smell she recognises from Saxon – now firmly identifiable as strawberry.

'That's amazing, thank you so much!' Polly says.

'Not a problem, first one's on the house, speaking of which, let's go in, we'll have a cup of tea. Welcome you to Dourstone properly.'

They walk back across the courtyard where a small detachment of the pack come over to stand solemnly before Polly, looking across at Mel for permission. She nods to them, almost imperceptibly, and they surround her. Fenrir runs back over from the corner he was sniffing, impatient to protect his mistress.

'What are they doing?' Polly asks.

'They can smell it on you,' Mel says. 'Fenrir too, has he been more protective recently?'

'Well, yes, but I assumed it was just because we were starting to bond, I haven't had him long.'

'There is that as well, yes.' Mel nods.

'Smell what?' Polly asks. She has heard of animals able to smell cancer and rot.

'They can smell the baby, you're pregnant my girl. The dogs never lie.'

4

Then…

I met the Lord Elias Dewer two beautiful Devon springtime's ago. Once the railways had opened the wild parts of England to the less adventurous, such as myself, my father wished me to visit Dartmoor and discover its opportunities for the expansion of his business. He believes there is profit in buying up cheap houses on the moors to rent to their newfound visitors. After my elder brother's untimely death in defence of Queen and Empire my father insisted I end my medical training and prepare to take over the family properties. I protested that my sisters were perfectly qualified to look after them, being far more commercially minded than myself, desperate to continue in what I saw as my calling. But Father would not have women running anything, and, despite my being little better than a woman in his opinion, I was his only choice.

Fighting with my father is a pointless exercise, so I packed my travelling bags, left my rooms in Gloucester Square and boarded a train. Not for me the bumping, shaking, and jostling of the crowded coach and horses. The wide plains, rolling hills, winding rivers and bent-backed men wiping sweat from their faces as they work the fields of Surrey, Hampshire, Somerset and finally, Devon, were spread out for my viewing pleasure as I travelled at ease; although the older gentleman who I shared my carriage with did not look up once from his paper to admire the vista.

It is difficult as one passes the cramped terraced houses lining the tracks upon approach to a town not to gaze voyeuristically through their windows. I must admit, I took full advantage of my position to look upon a world I know little of: smiling families, all gathered in the same room, glad of each other's company seem a world away from my home life. We each live in separate homes, and my father would surely have kept it that way from my birth had it not been

Mother's dying wish to keep us together. He sent us out into the world as soon as he was able, his only regret being my elder brother's military service.

A few short hours later I found myself in a coach headed to Dourstone Nymet for its famous Oak Apple Day celebrations. The speed of travel in these modern times amazes me, the miracle of steam transforming this world for the better. Perhaps not for the innkeepers and coach drivers of the old roads, but seeing the industry springing up alongside the railway lines, they will find other, new employment. Things have a way of working out, Father says the markets will find a way. However, my coach journey of just a few miles felt every bit as long as the rail journey. The sooner some successor to Mr Brunel devises an ingenious way to travel the hills and holes between the railway stations of Great Britain in comfort and speed the better.

Now...

'Look at them,' Patrick says walking past the pub window. 'Every Friday they're in there, doing the early shift.'

'We can go in and join them if you like Pat,' Polly says. 'I don't mind.' Fenrir halts in the doorway, pawing at the wood expectantly.

'No, we'll be out all day tomorrow,' he sighs. 'Besides, I'm missing entry credentials for Dad Club.'

Polly hasn't told him yet. She checked, then double-checked, then went to her doctor ten miles away (the downside of living with the local GP is having to travel to see a doctor). She is definitely pregnant against all odds. The doctor told her no pill was 100 percent reliable, and these things happen.

She has no idea how to tell Patrick. He will be so happy, he has been envious of the Friday afternoon dads' pub club ever since they moved here. Telling Patrick would be to remove all choice, making this whole thing suddenly real. At the moment she can pretend it is a mere possibility. Technically she does still have a choice, it just isn't a choice she is brave enough to take. It isn't one she ever thought she'd have to make. As an enlightened, strong, 21st century feminist she is in favour of abortion, a woman's right to choose – in the abstract. In practice all her strongly held opinions have been thrown up in the air. She's always been careful, taking all precautions, and confident that unwanted pregnancies would only ever happen to other people.

And now she has been saddled with one, with a man she loves and wants to have children with. Just a few years too early. And while she vehemently supports other women's right to abort unwanted fetuses, she can't bring herself to do it. Of course she is going to have the baby, she just wanted a little more time being Polly rather than someone's mum, and as soon as she comes clean to Patrick that's it. She'll just be someone's mum, and can abandon any thoughts of restarting her career. She has been trying to work freelance from home since she left London – despite Patrick's insistence she doesn't need to. She used to go about big city firms in a short skirt and a long jacket noticing how inefficient they were and telling them how not to be; touring the facilities and picking up slack was a piece of cake for her. She has been applying that to long-form financial documents, spotting mistakes and putting them right for an extortionate fee, her formidable reputation justifying the expense. She doesn't think a child will allow her the fierce concentration necessary.

She could never make Patrick give up his job, and she wants to be a proper mum, look after her children herself, not palm them off onto paid strangers like their friends in London. Or leave them to fend for themselves like she had to. As soon she was tall enough to reach the stove-top Polly was cooking dinner for her younger siblings. She doesn't resent her mother this, she was always working at least three jobs to keep the rent paid and the cupboards full of meals a nine-year-old could cook.

Although, again, she very much supports a woman's right to have it all, she would prefer to give everything to either one thing or the other. Not tear herself apart trying to do both. She is very aware that she can only really do one thing well at a time and worries this inability to multi-task may make her less of a woman.

'Come on, we'll just have one.' She grins. 'Maybe they'll let you have a go.' She points at a screaming child in the window, its face twisted in nightmarish grimace.

'You don't "have a go" on a baby Pol.' Patrick sighs, opening the door. 'Jesus, I feel sorry for our kids – if we ever have any.'

Fenrir gives a happy little bark and hops over the threshold.

'I'll get them in then,' Patrick says, waving to Jack, Clive, Dan and Delia, the four members of the Dad Club. Delia has claimed honorary membership as the non-biological parent of her and her wife Wendy's baby.

'No, you go and play with your friends,' Polly says. 'I'll get these, is yours a pint of Otter?'

'Thanks love, yes please.' Patrick heads over to the parent and baby corner by the window.

'What are you lot having?' she shouts.

After a flurry of requests, mishearings and changed minds Polly has a line of drinks on the bar, all bought and paid for (including a large tonic water that Polly has to pretend contains gin – the only way to hide her abstinence is to buy the round).

'Can you take these two?' Polly asks Clive as he comes back from the toilet. 'I think I can manage the rest.'

'Sorry,' Clive replies. 'I can manage one, but this thing doesn't grip.' He waves his prosthetic left hand.

'Oh, Christ! I'm sorry!' Polly shrieks, trying to keep the panic out of her voice.

'You're alright, weren't to know.' Clive gives a laugh. 'Lost it to Father's thresher on the farm years ago.'

'Oh no, how terrible.' Polly gasps.

'Could have been worse, I'd have had to be a farmer if I hadn't lost the hand.'

'What do you do then?'

'I'm an accountant, far more respectable.' He pulls himself up to his full height, avoiding one of the low beams with his head as he does so.

'Oh, that's good.' Polly nods enthusiastically.

'It was, until I moved back here to do the accounts for Father's farm. No escaping destiny.' Clive slouches back down.

'And he gets that robot hand,' Dan interrupts. 'Even if he does use it as an excuse to leave the rest of us dying of thirst, come on Clive.'

'Don't rush him,' Jack chuckles. 'After all, he is Titaaaannniiiiuuummmmm,' he sings, loudly and out of tune.

'Not robotic, not titanium. Stainless steel and fully poseable, like an action figure, but thanks for the song.' Clive carries his own drink as Polly ferries the rest across to a grateful reception.

Half an hour later, Fenrir's whines of boredom have flatlined.

'I'm going to have to take him home,' Polly says. 'Are you staying for another?'

'Yeah, I think I might, that ok?' Patrick checks.

'Of course.' She smiles. 'See you lot later.'

'If you leave him here for a bit and then come back, we're swapping with the mums for the late shift,' Dan explains, with a laugh. 'You could make a night of it.'

'I'll think about it,' Polly replies as Fenrir pulls her out of the door.

'Are you two going to get one of these then?' Jack says in a booming home counties accent, thrusting his baby into Patrick's face.

'One day, yeah,' Patrick nods. 'I want to, pretty sure Polly does as well, but she's not ready yet. I respect her decision, after all, it isn't me that has to get all fat and squeeze it out.'

He looks down at the pudgy red-faced creature in his arms. He wants one, more than anything.

But not this one.

This thing, making odd high-pitched whining noises is not his ultimate goal. He wants something that combines the best of him and Polly. In an ideal world it would come out already able to kick a ball about, have conversations and get his jokes, but he knows you have to get through this larval stage.

'Ha!' Clive laughs. 'No I suppose not, don't leave it too late though, I'm not much older than you, and I'm fucking knackered. All the time.' You can tell he's tried to lose the Devon twang from his accent, smooth it into something resembling Jack's clipped BBC vowels, but it's still there.

'All the time?' Patrick asks, ashen-faced.

'All the time,' the four of them chant.

'Might not bother then.' He chuckles, taking a swig of his ale.

'Oh no, you've got to,' Delia says, earnestly. 'We're a man down for the five a side team, do you play?' She hasn't bothered ironing the edges from her accent.

'Football?' Patrick queries, to enthusiastic nodding. 'Yeah, a bit. I don't need a baby for that do I?'

'No, strictly speaking you don't. But it's more fun with kids, and we're called the Dads, so you'd look a bit out of place.' Delia stares him down. He is pretty sure she could take him in a fight, and her lacquered DA hairdo looks sharp, in every sense of the word. His pithy comeback dies before reaching his lips.

'Fine, I'll swap Polly's pills for Polos and get myself a baby then,' Patrick jokes.

'Nice one, good man, prepared to go the extra mile.' Dan slaps him on the back. Another friendly smile delivered with a Devon accent. For all the complaints about the town filling up with incomers, there seems to be a majority of local. 'You're in. I hope you're as good a goalie as Graham, you've a big pair of cherry red Doctor Martens to fill.'

'Nobody mentioned goalie.' Patrick puts his hands up in protest. 'This deal keeps getting worse all the time.' He can't help but remember a smiling man on a balcony hiding a cigarette behind his back, cherry red Doctor Marten boots resting rebelliously on the handrail; boots that trigger a more gruesome memory.

'Well, we can iron the details out later,' Jack says, running his fingers through overlong brown hair. 'Come to the community centre on Wednesday night and we'll sort it out.'

'Cool, I will. Do you mean Lynn's Graham?' Patrick asks.

'Yeah, he left town a while back,' Clive replies. Patrick notices that he is at least as tall as him. Not many people can look down on Patrick at his six foot four vantage point, but Clive might just edge it. 'Vanished in a hurry, all a bit of a mystery.'

'Vanished?'

'Yeah, upped and disappeared in the middle of the night,' Delia explains.

'How come?'

'Well, rumour has it he and Lynn weren't getting on,' Jack adds.

'Graham wasn't the best husband,' Delia says.

'Or father.' Dan rubs at his bald head.

'Nice bloke though,' Clive puts in, pointing with his glasses.

'Brilliant goalie as well,' Jack says.

'Okay, but none of that explains his upping and leaving for no reason,' Patrick replies. 'I met him you know, in London, before we moved here.'

'Nothing does,' Jack explains. 'He didn't say anything to us, we were all out on Wish Weekend, having a few drinks, we'd left the kids with my in-laws, and then Sunday morning he'd gone. Lynn came round to see the missus, said he'd just decided to up and leave. Pain in the arse really, we had a match that afternoon and had to forfeit, couldn't get anyone to stand in.'

'Inconsiderate,' Clive says, grinning under his mop of almost-but-not-quite-ginger hair.

'Yeah, very.' Patrick mulls this over, something doesn't add up. 'And none of you have heard from him?'

'Nope, not a peep,' Delia says.

'I tried to ring him,' Dan adds, 'but it said the number was disconnected. I suppose he just wanted to make a clean break, didn't want to have to explain himself. Kerry – that's my wife – says he'd been a total shit to Lynn. He's probably too ashamed to talk to any of us. Can't say I blame him, I don't have a lot of sympathy for wife-beaters.'

'No...' Patrick agrees.

'Anyway, my round I think,' Clive says, raising his arm to change the subject and flipping the bird to the whole room. 'Fuck's sake Dan, was that you?'

The room collapses in laughter as Clive readjusts his prosthetic hand to a more family-friendly position.

Polly still hasn't gotten over the sheer solidity of the landscape: the magnitude of these ancient hills, topped with their granite altars, a plethora of legends attached to each. She has developed an interest in The Devil's links to Devon, since Patrick told her the wisthound story, and was surprised to find him all over these moors. Tors crowned with abandoned playing pieces from his game of Quoits with King Arthur; the church on Brentor having to be built at the top as he kept stealing the foundation stones; the sustenance he offered the Bishop of Exeter still visible as Branscombe's loaf and cheese, a rock formation on the edge of Sourton common; and a stone on the village green they turn over once a year to keep him away from Shebbear.

She can't help but think all these stories must come from older, darker roots. The Wish Weekend must have been some solemn, dread ceremony before the years chiselled it away into processions of laughing children draped in crepe paper. The world has intruded on this remote community and blurred its origins: intermingling it with Guy Fawkes night, Carnival time and the changing of the seasons until its pagan originators would no longer recognise the cuddly smiling face of their canine deities.

Having all this on her doorstep often leads her to take the long cut home, over the moors and round the outside of town. You wouldn't even know there was a town hidden in this desolate landscape from here. The only reminder of the craggy north coast she grew up on is the rise and fall of hills emulating the swell of the ocean, while shadows cast by clouds rove over the stubbly grass like whales beneath green waves.

'What's up with you now?' Polly asks, as Fenrir comes sprinting across the moor to stand behind her, growling low.

It soon becomes obvious as a sea of grey and white fur swarms over the tor. The pack is out. Lady Mel at its head.

'Halloo!' she bellows. 'Don't mind this lot, they won't do anything without the nod from Cronus. He's the top dog, biggest and bestest in the pack. Only answers to me, and not even me more often than not. The trouble with malamutes is how bloody loyal they are. Only bond once, with their first owners, so if yours is a rescue you'll always be playing catch up trying to get them on side.'

Polly gives a shaky nod.

'Not a problem with Cronus though, he was my first pup, before I started neutering the buggers. Killed all his brothers and sisters – then his dad – hence all the neutering.'

'Oh my god!' Polly exclaims.

'Oh it's a dog eat dog world girl,' Mel says. 'Literally in this case. Anyway, it didn't take him long to beat the rest of the pack into submission and become alpha. We're bonded, he does what I say, and this lot do what he says: as much as any bloody malamute will do what you say, it's in the breed to trust their own judgement – you don't get very far pulling sleds if you just blindly obey the bloke telling you to run across thin ice. Over here you mad buggers!' She waves to indicate the pack, who ignore her. 'There you go, stubborn, like I said. Care to join us for a walk?'

'We're on the way home I'm afraid, got to get back. Maybe another time?'

'Yes, definitely, some time in the week,' Mel says. Cronus pushes his head into her side urgently and howls. 'Okay, yes, we're going,' she adds to the dog. 'Tuesday afternoon, Tuesday's always a good day, used to be market day before. Not any more, pity, great pity, anyway, come to mine about lunchtime, we'll have a bite then I'll show you the moors proper. How about that?'

'Okay, yes, that would be nice, we'll do that. The moors should be emptier once the bank holidays are over,' Polly agrees, though she doesn't think she has a choice.

'Bank holidays? Of course, Easter weekend.' Mel snaps her fingers. 'It's always best when it falls now, right on the Vernal Equinox.'

'Is it?' Polly asks.

'Oh yes, it means all the rites of spring and chicks and eggs and bunnies and stuff actually mean something, not all the rubbish they added on afterwards.'

'You mean Jesus?'

'Yes, ruined a perfectly good feast day with all of that you know.'

'Oh, if you say so,' Polly replies, diplomatically. She went to a Church of England School and, while not being an active participant in its affiliated Church, her mother had taken full advantage of its Sunday School babysitting facilities. A lot of it worked its way into Polly's brain, and while she hasn't attended a service that didn't involve a wedding, funeral or christening for quite some years, she's never really questioned its teachings and considers herself a Christian – mostly.

'Anyway, have you told that man of yours about the you-know-what yet?'

'No, I was thinking I'd tell him this weekend, a nice Easter surprise,' Polly explains. She has only just decided this, after seeing him in the pub with all those kids. He'll be an excellent dad, she's sure of it.

'Good, let's hope he's surprised,' Mel says, turning on her heel and walking into the pack, who grudgingly part to let her through before following behind.

5

Then…

I had barely left my bags in my lodgings when the band struck up. For a small place it is well furnished with inns, I had my pick of seven, though most were booked out thanks to the festivities. Despite our miserable government's recent repeal of the observance of Oak Apple Day, Dourstone, and many other rural villages, continue to celebrate it. The local farmers and employers feel such strong sentiment that workers are given the whole day off on full pay.

Oak Apple Day, commemorating the restoration of King Charles the Second to the throne, seems an odd choice of date to insist on keeping up in defiance of abolition: rebelling by celebrating a return to the status quo. It might be because this particular celebration coincides with the best of the Devon weather.

The serving girl furnished me with a mug of cider as I exited the building and joined the throng. There was a palpable feeling of joy in the air, Summer was on the way, and it felt like it would be a scorcher. Labourers in battered straw hats stood side by side with the silk finery of their employers in the town square.

It was then that I saw him, a fine figure of a man in stove-pipe hat, centre of attention in the middle of the square. A gentleman, like myself, unable to remove the thick silks and coats that itched maddeningly in the afternoon sun. The low-born labourers had no such niceties to keep up, and lolled on straw bales, shoeless and shirtless. I confess I looked upon them with no small amount of jealous longing.

The tall man in the tall hat sought me out immediately.

'Ho good sir, I do not know you I think?' He turned his steely grey eyes to mine.

'No, sir, I am new to the village,' I replied.

'And how do you find our fair town this day?'

It was a friendly correction. The look in his eye suggested that to say village again would not put me in good standing. I bowed my head in recognition of my mistake. This rural community, its townspeople sporting sprigs of oak upon hats and lapels, was already insinuating itself into my heart. I must confess that, in the heart of the city, the sound of accordion and banjo would fill my heart with dread, I much prefer a string quartet, but, in their natural environment, these rustic tunes lighten ones heart. I had been here less than one hour and not yet finished one jug of cider but I meant every one of the next words I spoke.

'If all days are like this then I may never return to London.'

Lord Elias' laugh was a hearty roar, his long silver hair waving about his shoulders as he slapped my back in camaraderie. The clear blue sky, fluffy clouds and warming sunshine, a straw bale seat next to my new friend, a pipe of fine tobacco and seemingly unending supply of delicious cider all conspired to make me entirely forget my beloved London town.

'That's the right answer,' he assured me. 'Now come over here and hide me from that damnable priest.'

'Priest?' I asked.

'Yes, the Diocese has begun to take notice of the moors, now they're so much easier to reach, and my formerly empty church has been furnished with a new incumbent.'

'Oh, is that a bad thing?'

'Not necessarily, but he has not been enjoying our May revels. Probably because the local children have been waking him with their hodening horse every morning.' He gave another snorting laugh. 'Which reminds me, I still owe them.'

'Hodening horse?'

'Oh you are from the city aren't you? How delightful, one of those, over there.' He pointed to a long pole with what could only be a real horse's skull attached, the jaw opening and closing by means of a system of ropes, which a small group of children were delighting in. 'A real one, none of those wooden fakes you get these days.'

I nodded, unwilling to speak ill of countryside customs I was not privy to.

I spent the day in company of Lord Elias, who gave me his full attention, to the exclusion of all others. I admit, my curiosity was *piqued, this extraordinary creature was pleasing to me and I began to kindle a hope he may share my tastes. I have never met anybody quite like him, he has a strange quality – like many landed gentry, only more so – by which the mere idea that anybody would say no to him is alien. Unusually, he uses it to make people happy, rather than the opposite. At least he did then.*

His innate magnetism draws people to him, makes them want to please him, help him, do his bidding. The townspeople had not one bad word to say of him, which is unusual in these uncertain times. A major landowner having the respect and love of his tenants is a rare thing, but he commands it. Sitting watching him speak, rogue drips of cider in his beard glistening in the spring sunlight it was easy to understand why.

WICKER DOGS

Now...

Sitting on top of this sun-drenched hill, surrounded by daffodils, it feels like spring today. What has to be the last snowfall of the season has melted and Patrick has finally taken his bike out. One of his main reasons for moving here was the cycling opportunities. He's always told people he's an avid cyclist, and yes he has an expensive bike, but in London he was a bit scared of the traffic, the other cyclists, and how pudgy he's got in the last few years – Lycra is not kind. Down here, in the middle of nowhere, he is confident he can get out, get fit again and not be judged, hit by a truck or punched by a taxi driver. Since they moved here, that expensive bike has hung on a specially made hook in the garage, waiting for a day like today.

Today is more a day like today than any other today has been. Easter Saturday, rested after the first bank holiday of a long weekend. Patrick is secretly pleased Polly declined his invite; he'd rather get a feel for Devon roads on his own so he can be prepared if they ever manage to get out together. He knows Polly only pretends to be interested in cycling for his sake, but now he's actually doing it she'll have to either admit it was a bluff or get on her bike – it certainly cost enough money, as did its matching special hook in the garage.

It hasn't escaped him that she looks nauseous in the mornings before he leaves for work. Nor how often she refuses his nightly offer of a glass of wine. Some nights she pours their drinks, her own glass containing something that, to Patrick's connoisseur's eye, is almost certainly grape juice. He doesn't want to believe it until she tells him, but he is fairly sure he is about to earn entry to the Dad Club.

Dartmoor cycling is everything he had hoped for, once he got past that first big hill (his calf muscles are not yet ready for such a steep gradient, and the stone circle at the top still unsettles him), gentle rolling hills, beautiful views of an endless expanse of granite and green, and plenty of places to stop and take it all in. Every so often he'll come up against another never-ending uphill, but either low gearing and slower-than-walking pace, or actually getting off and pushing the bike up suffices. There's nobody out here to judge.

'Hello, hello.' A voice calls from the road.

'Beautiful morning for it,' Patrick replies.

'Certainly is, been a long cold winter.' The man is pushing an old, heavy sit-up-and-beg bike ahead of him in entirely unsuitable cycling gear. Patrick bites down his criticism, the man may yet turn out to be a patient. It's quite a hot day, and a thick tweed suit is not ideal for bicycling, despite the bicycle clips above his brown leather brogues. 'We are truly blessed.' Patrick spots the giveaway white dog collar as he raises his immaculate – though not much use in a crash – homburg hat.

'Need a drink Father?' Patrick proffers his water as the newcomer carefully lays out a tartan rug, pulled from his ample saddle bags.

'Got one thanks,' he replies, pulling what looks like a second world war army issue canteen bottle from his bicycle's basket, before sitting on his rug to fill a small clay pipe from a weathered leather pouch. 'You want one of these? I'm sure I've a spare pipe about me somewhere.'

'No thanks,' Patrick's lungs are having enough trouble getting up these hills without filling them with cancer-ridden smoke. The vicar takes a long drink from his bottle before letting out an unmistakeably cidery belch and lighting his pipe; a pipe that Patrick is fairly certain contains more than just tobacco. He checks his watch, it is 10:30 in the morning. 'I'm Patrick, nice to meet you.'

'Hi Patrick, pleased to meet you too. Father Hearne, though you can call me Arthur, Artie if we get along.' He shakes his hand. 'If I'm not much mistaken you're the new doctor round here? Got the wife with the wolfhound?'

'I am, but we're not married,' Patrick replies.

'Sorry, to hear that, I am duty bound by my calling to advise you that you should – as they say – put a ring on it.' He smiles.

'We're happy as we are thanks.'

'Sorry, sorry, none of my business, contractual obligation. And I'm sorry for using the indefinite article to describe your lady companion, I do try to use the vernacular, be cool, down with the kids. Sometimes it just comes off as rude, anyway, it's none of my business.' He blows smoke rings out across the tops of the tors.

'How come you know who we are?' Patrick asks.

'Small town Dourstone.' Father Hearne shrugs. 'Word gets about, especially with a new doctor.'

'Sorry, it's just I didn't think Dourstone had a priest, the church has been burned out since before I was born. Mum and Dad always used to drive to Tavistock for the big church.'

'I don't live in town.' He waves his drink dismissively before taking another long pull on it. 'But I am, technically, your parish priest.'

'Really?'

'Really, it's a team ministry now – cuts don't just affect the police you know – I'm also the parish priest for Throwleigh, Walkhampton and Buckland in the Moor. But I do conduct the odd service in the ruins of St Euphemia's, on request.'

'That's quite the catchment area. Do you get a lot of requests?'

'No, not really. But I do occasionally bring outsiders along to try and convert the local heathens. It's a nice spot for open air worship.'

'Sounds nice, I might come along next time you're there.'

'I'm there tomorrow morning.'

'Okay, then maybe you'll catch me out in a polite lie,' Patrick admits, face flushing.

'Thanks for your honesty. Dourstone's an odd place, especially in the winter, this Spring is a welcome relief.' He spreads his arms to indicate the blue skies, warm sun and feeling of hope in the air.

'How so?'

'People disappear. Did you know Graham?'

'Graham?'

'Yeah, Villager Graham.'

'Lynn's husband Graham?' Patrick tries to confirm.

'Oh, do you know Lynn?' Father Hearne asks, leaning up on his elbows.

'Yes, she sold us our house. But I knew Lynn way back when we were kids; my parents have a house in town so I used to come down all the time.' He stops short of telling this stranger his and Lynn's entire history, not even Polly knows that.

'Oh, small world, she should be along in a minute, I left her at the bottom of the hill, pedalling furiously.'

'Why do you call him Villager Graham?'

'Cos he was an incomer to Dourstone, like you, but he kept saying village, when it's a town. Folks round your way, they don't like that. It's not a clever nickname, but it's what they called him.'

'Oh.' Patrick supposes he should be used to stupid nicknames. He met a forklift driver called Flipper in the pub and expected some exciting story of a terrible accident. It was disappointing to find out that it was because he had big feet. Two sizes smaller than Patrick's own, impossible to get shoes for, size thirteens, but big feet nonetheless.

'Yeah, anyway, he vanished, back at the Wish Weekend. The official story is that he left Lynn, went back up north, but it wouldn't surprise me if the locals killed him for saying village one too many times.'

'Seems a bit much Father,' Patrick says, a cart with a Dr Martens boot underneath coming to mind.

'Yeah, sorry, poor taste, not my best joke. Anyway, let's say no more of it for the present, here she comes.' The Vicar smiles and taps his nose as Lynn appears on the horizon, feet spinning wildly against the lowest of her mountain bike's 36 gears.

'How did you get here so quick? You walked, you pushed that thing up the hill!' She looks exasperated, gracelessly climbing off her bike to reveal sweat stains in the most personal areas of her pink Lycra.

'I told you, it's quicker to walk up these hills.' Father Hearne smirks. His suit is spotless, and not a bead of sweat can be seen upon him. 'Drink?'

'Don't mind if I do,' Lynn answers as she yanks her helmet off and throws herself down on the rug. 'Are you joining us Pat?'

'I don't think so, I need to get some more miles in, I'm a bit out of practice.' Patrick waves his hands in apology. 'Have a good day though.'

'You too,' Lynn replies, with a little smile and a raised eyebrow as Patrick remounts his bicycle and heads off.

6

Then...

Lord Elias suggested he might be able to help with Father's business plans and I jumped at the chance to spend more time in his company. I sent word that talks were going well and while the property plan for the moors might well be possible, I would have to stay to oversee it. Father's reply was eager, he seemed pleased his idea was taking seed, and that I was going to be both working in his favour and not in his immediate presence.

Lord Elias invited me to stay at the Manor and I took up residence in rooms far greater and more ancient than to which I was accustomed. I have visited the great homes of the aristocracy before, don't misunderstand me, but Dourstone Manor is on a completely different scale. Its wings house an endless network of kitchens, meat stores, laundries, dairies and bakeries on one side, and grand reception rooms including the impressive library I find myself imprisoned in on the other: even now I am in awe at its size, the old Elizabethan long gallery converted into a storehouse of all human knowledge. The upper floors are a warren of bedrooms, nurseries, studies and storerooms and beneath ground the extensive cellars open into a whole other world, though it is rare one makes it past the wine bottles. The house blends so seamlessly from one era to the other it is difficult to see where the original Norman (or earlier, my architectural knowledge is poor) castle ends and the many additions and rebuilds begin. Georgian drawing rooms give on to medieval battlements that look down upon a large modern glasshouse finished just weeks before my arrival.

Lady Dewer was a perfect hostess, happy for me to stay in their home, organising the staff to keep my every need catered for. There must be many more than the single manservant I have seen, otherwise why would the kitchens be so large? I maintain they are well trained to stay out of sight, invisible service is the sign of good service after all.

She made me unsure of Lord Elias' nature though, and I briefly considered a return to London – after all he was the only thing tethering me to this beautiful place – and in quiet moments I would yearn for the clubs of Covent Garden and St James. But I had hope, and, despite the apparent happiness of their marriage, in my heart I prayed it was a façade.

Now...

Polly had spent the night trying to empty Cranmere Pool with a sieve. Rather than the curiously named marshy bog she and Fenrir had visited, the pool was refilled, deep and wide enough to make the task impossible. A strange little man had sat next to her, attempting to fashion trusses from sand and excitedly nodding towards a sheep carcass on the opposite shore. Polly could not understand his gesticulations until his speech returned and he explained they could flood the nearby town of Okehampton with a little ingenuity. She had snapped suddenly awake as he began to skin the sheep.

She put the dream down to stress. Why didn't Patrick seem surprised? He should have been, it's a medical miracle, he's a doctor, he knows she's on the pill, he collects them for her from the pharmacy.

'I can't stop wondering about Graham,' he says, as they march down the hedge-lined, pavementless single-track lane to town. 'Where did he go? Why did he run off? Did he run off? Or was he pushed?'

'I don't know,' Polly says. 'I don't really care either to be honest. Look, Pat, are you excited about this baby?'

'Of course Pol. It's all I've ever wanted, you know that. I can't wait.' He hugs her close and kisses the top of her head.

'It's just, well, you don't seem it, really.'

'I am, I am, it's just work, and this Graham thing, I'm distracted. Sorry, I won't be, let's do this Easter fair, after all, I'm drinking for two now, got to have your share – Mummy.' He winks as they enter the square.

Polly has already been down once, she wanted to remember the true spirit of Easter so attended a service in the shell of St Euphemia's, its roof open to the skies and stained-glass windows long emptied. The priest, looking for all the world as if he had just stepped out of an Agatha Christie novel, had stood under a bright spring morning sun in tweed suit, not even removing his hat, and given a long sermon on the death of winter and rebirth of spring. The hymns had not been traditional ones, but rather old folk tunes of hare and fowl, and possibly one murder ballad. Not once had this eccentric priest mentioned the risen lord, and not one of the congregation had spoken up. Polly had not been surprised by Lady Melissa's absence nor recognised any of the other worshippers; bar Lynn – fully cassocked and assisting the priest.

Normally reserved for Church and chocolate sellers, they have pulled out all the stops for Easter in Dourstone Nymet. The centre of the square is filled with a giant wickerwork rabbit, surrounded by daffodils, snowdrops, and cages of its live counterparts for sale to excitable children. Children who will promise to look after them before forgetting they are there while the long-suffering parents shovel shit from hutches every weekend until, all too soon, they have to dig a sad hole in the flowerbed to weeping offspring who have finally remembered their initial enthusiasm. There are also chickens, ducks, domestic livestock of every description, a small band of eager ukulelists playing traditional springtime songs and, right in the midst of everything, Lady Mel and Cronus – still not on a lead.

'Polly my dear, how are you?' she enthuses. 'Have you?'

'Yes,' Polly interjects. 'Last night.' She looks pointedly at Mel.

'Good, good, I'm so happy for you.' And with that she vanishes into the throng, Cronus padding at her heels.

'What was that about?' Patrick asks, craning his neck over the crowds, looking for a friendly face.

'Oh nothing.'

'Did she know before me? About... you know?'

'Well, if you must know, yes. She did.'

'You told a total stranger you were pregnant before you told the father, who just happens to be a doctor?'

'No, she told me, her dogs smelled it.'

'Dogs? Fine way to make a diagnosis, please tell me there was more evidence than that?'

'Of course, I told you all that last night.' This is true, Polly showed him the test results, having expected cynicism and disbelief before acceptance. He had just nodded, said, 'That's brilliant news,' opened the bubbly (sparkling grape juice for Polly) and accepted it with barely a glance at the paperwork.

'Okay, okay.' He smiles. 'Let's not make a big deal of it. We'll have a nice day; we can tell people now yeah?' He looks hopeful.

'Yeah, we can tell people. Why wouldn't we tell people?' Polly laughs nervously. She has plenty of reasons not to want to tell people. She still doesn't know if she really wants to be a mum yet. Realistically she has no choice, but it will change everything. It already has. Telling people is just another step down a one-way street.

An Easter weekend would normally be a lazy debauched affair – bar Polly's Church visits – pottering around the streets of the capital dropping in at pubs and restaurants with friends, perhaps a trip out to the countryside. But now Patrick is watching her every move, making sure she is in no danger. The list of things she cannot eat is depressing, the fact she can't even drink enough to cheer herself up about the things she cannot eat is doubly so. A stupid urge to rebel against the whole thing, get drunk, buy a packet of cigarettes (Polly hasn't smoked since university, and didn't much then) score some cocaine (Polly has never taken anything stronger than paracetamol) anything, wells up inside her. She really wants to want this baby, but isn't sure for even the briefest of moments it is anything other than a parasite sucking her life force away until it rips through her wrecked genitalia and ruins the rest of her natural life.

'Awesome, where's the Dad Club got to?'

'Try over there.' Polly points to a Punch and Judy stall near the church gates, surrounded by a horde of small children. The parents are all wearing an expression brought on by the realisation your kids are laughing at the same dreadful portrayal of abuse you did at their age and you've only just noticed how bad it is. Your only hope is that they learn a valuable lesson when Mr Punch meets his just desserts. If Mr Punch ever does get justice. You can't remember, and it is increasingly likely that Mr Punch is going to outwit The Devil himself and get away with it, laughing into the void for all eternity.

'Brilliant, thanks,' Patrick says, leading her over by the arm.

'That's the way to do it,' comes Mr Punch's squawking voice, amplified by reverberations from the buildings and sending a shudder down Polly's spine.

'Hey, Jack,' Patrick says with a grin, 'I don't need to pretend any more, I can play in goal for you guys officially now.'

'What?' Jack says, confusion spreading over his clean-shaven face.

'I mean we're having a baby.' He spreads his arms wide to indicate Polly in her glowing glory. Well, her sensible lightweight waterproofs and tired expression. It's already been a long weekend, and, this being Dartmoor, it will almost certainly rain in a minute.

'Cool, cool,' Jack mutters, looking around to see where his toddler has got to while bouncing an increasingly heavy baby up and down on a small platform strapped to his hip. 'Pleased for you, really I am. Now you can definitely join the football team.'

'Football team?' Polly rumples her brow. 'What football team?'

'Ah,' Patrick begins. 'I meant to tell you, I just, forgot, you know, what with one thing and another. I'm going to join the Dads' five a side team.'

'Brilliant,' Polly says, the joy of the day threatening to turn into an argument. She makes a tactical decision to withdraw – and be somewhere she can't hear Mr Punch's screech – before she says something she'll regret. 'I'm sure you'll enjoy it, get yourself fit again, like you've been meaning to.'

'Yeah, sorry, I hope you don't mind...'

'Of course, it's fine.' She looks around for an out and spots a malamute tail waving through the crowd. 'Oh, there's Mel, hang on, I need to talk to her. See you later?'

'Yeah, sure, okay.' Patrick kisses her goodbye and watches her stalk off. She is not happy. He did mean to tell her about the football, but it slipped his mind in all the news, and he didn't think it was important. He can't tell her he had already figured out she was pregnant either. She always thinks he's a terrible smart arse, showing off about how he knows everything. He wanted to let her have this, get one over on him, but he's a dreadful actor and surprise is not easy to fake.

He makes faces at Jack's baby, who blows him an unimpressed raspberry before going back to shaking Jack's drinking arm.

'Think you might be in a bit of trouble there mate, sorry,' Jack says, ignoring the child and draining the drink down to a level where it won't pour down his arm.

'Yeah, she'll be right, misunderstanding, not your fault,' Patrick says. 'Any of you lot in need of another pint?'

A flurry of nods confirms it is going to be an expensive round, so Patrick enlists Dan to help him carry glasses before nipping to the Drop of Dew's specially-constructed-from-old-pallets outside bar.

'Did I hear that right Paddy?' Dan says. 'You're having a baby?'

'Yeah, well, Polly is, not me, but yes.'

'Good news, good news.' Dan nods, all the while looking around

WICKER DOGS

the square for the whereabouts of his children. 'Life will never be the same again for you mate.'

'No,' Patrick says. 'I'm beginning to realise that.'

They carry the drinks back over towards the Punch and Judy, where a volley of children's laughter accompanies Judy being flung over the edge of the stage and plummeting to inevitable death.

'Congratulations sir,' Clive says, taking his drink and immediately cheersing it against the other two Patrick is still clutching, covering his sleeves in sticky cider residue.

'Thanks Clive, I take it you all heard?'

'Certainly did,' Delia grins, taking the other pint. 'Well done. Did you mean to do it?'

'Well, no, as it happens. Happy accident, minor medical miracle in fact.' Patrick goes on to explain about the percentage chance of contraception failure in the way only a doctor can until Delia's eyes begin to glaze over. 'But yes. All good news,' he confirms.

'That's great, took us ages. Turned out I couldn't, after a lot of turkey basters and unpleasantness,' she explains. 'Eventually got myself checked out. Explained everything. Then Wendy, that's the wife.' She points across the square to a woman who looks like something from one of D.H. Lawrence's wet gypsy dreams cooing into the front of a pushchair. 'Got up the duff first try. Lucky bitch.'

'Did you want to do that bit yourself then?' Patrick can't help but ask.

'I did, yeah, well, I did up until I watched her try to pop the thing out. I stopped calling her a lucky bitch pretty soon after that.'

'Fair enough.'

'She didn't manage it anyway, too posh to push, bloody Chagford girls, all the same, had to get it cut out in the end.'

'Okay, well. As long as we're all happy and healthy yeah?' Patrick says, deciding not to lecture her on the dangers of Caesarian section and the myth of 'too posh to push' for the sake of diplomacy. Nobody likes a smart-arse doctor.

'Yeah, I'll drink to that.'

'We all will,' Jack strolls into the conversation with a large group glass clink and a cheer. In the background Mr Punch has just murdered an endangered species for stealing his sausages and Patrick has spotted a familiar sit-up-and-beg bike attached to the colourful trailer that makes up the puppet theatre.

7

Then…

It was our custom to stroll upon the moors after seeing to the livestock each morning. Lord Elias tends his pack of hunting hounds personally, directing them with practised whistles and calls wherever he chooses – he trusts nobody else with his dogs. They seem unremarkable, ordinary hounds: brown, slightly dirty, sniffing at everything before marking it as theirs. Would that I had never learned otherwise.

On one of our morning perambulations the weather took its usual Dartmoor turn, and what had been a mere drizzle was suddenly thrown against us with such force as to completely saturate one's left side while the right remained entirely dry. The three of us ran for the summit of a tor, where the rocks form a natural covered windbreak, and there huddled to wait it out. The dogs were unfazed and continued their patrol of the moors, though what they patrol for remains a mystery.

We formed an awkward mass of wool and human flesh in the too-small hollow, Lord Elias pressed hard against my left, the Lady improperly close to my right. I felt my unquenchable desire rise with him so close, could sense he felt the same way – at last. But could he admit to it, in front of his wife, the warmth and damp of whom was pressed hard against my other side? Out of the wind the day was quite hot, the humidity stifling us inside our walking gear. I worried for her health in these adverse conditions. For though I wished her out of my way, I liked the woman – still like, despite all.

After an uncomfortable silence in which I attempted to crush my growing feeling, he caressed my face, the strange coffin-nail ring he wears cold against my cheek, then turned his head to mine and kissed me. His wife smiled and gave a nod as my Lord and I locked in passionate embrace. She encircled us with her arms. She was on our side, she knew of his tastes and did not disapprove. I knew then that I would stay with these enlightened people for the rest of my life.

I had hoped it would be longer.

Now...

'Send in the next patient would you please?' Patrick barks down the intercom. He's more hungover than he'd like from Easter, despite having drunk nothing stronger than coffee on the Monday. It seems the closer to thirty he gets, the longer it takes to get over a good time. He looks at the patient list on his screen and clicks through to Lady Melissa Dewer's notes. There aren't many.

'What's up Doc?' she grins as she walks in, munching an imaginary carrot.

'Good morning Lady Dewer, and what seems to be the problem?'

'Goodness, call me Mel, please, I don't stand on ceremony.'

'Fair enough, neither will I, call me Patrick.'

'Will do,' she says, rubbing his knee as she sits down on the same side of the desk as him. Patrick learned at medical school that it encourages confidentiality if you're both literally and metaphorically on the same side.

'Anyway, what can I do for you this morning?' he asks, moving his knee away.

'Oh, I've just got this cough, had it since Christmas so I thought it worth getting checked out. You can't be too careful at my time of life.'

Patrick peers at his screen to avoid the uncomfortable situation of asking a lady of a certain age exactly what it is. He is surprised. The beaming picture of health looking at him with that strange glint in her silvery-grey eyes belies the passage of time.

'Well, you're doing very well for someone of your age,' Patrick reassures. 'But since you haven't been in for a very long time, I think we should check you out properly, if that's okay?'

'Fine, fine, get the MOT done while I'm here.' She grins. 'Where do you want to delve first?'

'No delving, you're fine, we'll start with that cough.'

'Okay.'

Patrick begins the listening, groping and note-taking that a full check-up entails.

'How are you two settling in to Dourstone then?' Mel asks,

unbuttoning her shirt to reveal smooth, milk-white skin that no amount of moisturiser should be able to maintain.

'Oh fine, just fine,' Patrick says. 'It's just how I remember it, should have moved back earlier.'

'Oh yes, Polly told me your family own the old barrel-works,' Mel replies.

'I forgot you two were spending so much time together. Perhaps I should be asking you how she's settling in?'

'Ha, very good.' Mel chuckles. 'I couldn't tell you, to be honest. That's why I asked.'

'Well,' Patrick explains, 'you seem to have made all the difference. Now she has a friend she's a lot happier. She wasn't happy in London.'

'Not many people are Patrick, but it's rarely the place that makes you miserable, your problems follow wherever you go.'

'I suppose you're right. Anyway, you know all about our big news don't you?'

'Yes, my dogs smelled it on her. I know it sounds weird, but it's true. Yours did as well, but she's not had him long enough to read the signs.'

'I'm a little cynical to be honest, but since it turned out to be true I shan't complain. I'm very happy about it,' Patrick says, breathing on his stethoscope to warm it up.

'I'm glad you're happy, is this the first of your family to be from Devon?'

'No, Polly's from Devon. She grew up in Appledore.'

'T'ain't proper Devon up there, practically bloody Wales,' Mel mutters.

'Anyway, my family are from here.' Patrick ignores the muttering. 'My great-grandfather was a foundling here. Some posh bugger knocked up a serving wench, according to family folklore he was left on the doorstep of the barrel works. The Sumners took him in, brought him up as their own, even gave him their name. They couldn't have children of their own and it's their house Mum and Dad have now, his old shop. Here, maybe it was one of your lot knocked up my great great granny? We could be related!'

'Could be,' Mel replies. 'The Dewers have always been slightly debauched.' She winks. 'We still are, you ask anyone.'

'Aren't you the only one left though?' Patrick immediately regrets asking this.

'Yes I am, and like I said, you can ask anyone.' She looks deep into his eyes, daring him to blink. He sees her push him back over the desk, rip his clothes away and ride him to a sweaty, aching climax before shaking it from his head: he had no idea his imagination was so graphic.

'Anyway, how's Lynn doing? Any idea where her Graham's got to?'

'Oh Lynn's okay, seems to have found Jesus – or she's fucking that priest, I'm not sure. And who cares about Graham?' Mel fixes Patrick's eye with a hard stare – he sees himself bearing down on her, taking her from behind across the desk as she screams his name. 'Probably back to where he came from.'

'Oh, he wasn't local then?' He forces his attention back to the computer screen.

'No, came down from somewhere up north a few years ago on a building contract and got together with Lynn while she was behind the bar at The Bridge.'

'Where's The Bridge?'

'Sorry, used to be a pub, down by the bridge obviously, it's the vet now. I thought you were local?'

'Sorry, been a long time, I'd forgotten it. We never used to go there anyway, wasn't it mostly full of kids from that council estate over the river?'

'Well, you're not really local until you can look longingly at a building that used to be your favourite pub on your way to one that's still there but not as good. And there's nothing wrong with them lot from the council estate, half the old local families had to move there on account of all the second home owners,' Mel explains.

'Yes well,' Patrick mutters, mind now filled with Mel whipping his naked buttocks.

'Like your mate Lynn, she's local, never lived anywhere else. Had her head turned by Graham's funny accent and flowing cash. That didn't last, once he got his hooks in her he lived off her three jobs. Left the kids with her mum every day and went off out to do whatever he wanted.'

'So why did he run off? Sounds like he was on to a cushy number.' The whip drops from mind-Mel's hand as his psychic self reaches another pinnacle.

'She must have cracked, given him an ultimatum, get a job or get out. I think he felt humiliated enough not to want to tell his mates in the pub, so he vanished under cover of darkness. Nothing suspicious. Why are you so interested anyway?' She raises an eyebrow. Patrick flinches, expecting another erotic vision that doesn't come.

'Don't know really. His name keeps coming up, and none of it makes sense.'

'Did you know him?' Mel asks.

'Well, not really. I met him once in London, when Lynn told us about the house. He seemed alright.' He doesn't want to bring up a severed limb that everyone thinks he hallucinated.

'You're probably just distracting yourself. I'd stop worrying about Graham and start thinking about your impending family.'

'Maybe you're right.'

'Weren't expecting it were you?'

'Well, no, it's a very happy accident to be honest.' Patrick flushes red.

'Accident!' Mel snorts. 'Nobody gets pregnant by accident. Certainly not a full grown woman in a long-term relationship. Particularly if she doesn't have a ring on her finger.' She waggles her hand.

'Okay, well, turn round and cough for me.' Patrick changes the subject, slipping his cold stethoscope down Mel's back to a now familiar gasp that makes him blush again.

Polly doesn't care that they're not married. She doesn't want children yet – or didn't, until this happened. She was adamant about those things. She wouldn't deliberately get herself pregnant. And yet, she is so organised. She would not forget to take a pill, certainly not without mentioning it to him and sorting out an alternative. Even if that alternative was just abstinence. The Devon air, however, has not been leading them to abstinence.

8

Then...

Our sodden return from the moors took us through the square at the same time as the new vicar's Easter procession. Elias took great delight in sending his hounds into the solemn parade. The reverend father used some distinctly unholy words in reaction to the dogs leaping at his person and running off with his banners. Lord Elias gave one of his large, hearty laughs and we carried on back towards the Manor without calling them back. He trusted them to make their own way home when finished with the unloved priest.

Once returned, the three of us sat in front of the roaring kitchen fireplace drinking a herbal concoction of Lady Dewer's. I had never felt more at home than in that moment, the three of us, a close-knit unit. Were it not for our growing lusts I would have thought myself surrogate child to the couple – their lack of offspring being an issue they are unable to hide. But we felt like a family, far more than I have ever felt with my blood family.

That night they came to my chambers. I confess I was not prepared for what I learned in the small hours of the night. Lord Elias has sworn me to secrecy on the matter, but since he has condemned me I have no reason to keep my word.

Damn him.

I found, in the passionate throes of the night, that he is not as he seems. Where I looked for his manhood, I found none. His stout frame is a lie, he is slender, graceful, lithe, but wears padding to camouflage the mammalian appendages upon his breast. In truth, the Lord Elias Dewer is a woman. Somehow his charms still wooed me, I have never before desired the feminine, but his manner, his character, had already so seduced me that I surrendered to the flesh.

I count among my close friends many who lie with both men and women. But I have never, never before, desired a woman. And yet I spent that night engaged in erotic pleasures with a brace of them. Elias assured me that while he prefers the feminine touch, one that understands his biology, he would never deny himself any pleasure by refusing someone on grounds of gender. He declared himself to be neither man nor woman, and that the restriction placed on we humans by having to fit into narrow definitions of sex is unfair. He says we are all just people, and that in his long life nobody has ever questioned his presentation as male until faced with his naked body. The Lady agrees with him, and they have many accessories for their games that ensured I was not left wanting.

Now…

Morning sunlight streams through the leaded windows of Dourstone Manor. Lady Melissa suggested they take tea in the morning room before setting out on their walk and Polly was happy for the opportunity of a proper nose around. She is surprised to find the inside of the house in immaculate condition, not filled with crumbling, dusty, horror movie cliches. Clearly the ancient seat of the Dewers has staff. The ivy strewn, cracked exterior must be entirely for show.

 This tea cup is probably worth more than her whole house, Polly considers, sipping from the ancient fine china. She doesn't want to consider how much is tied up in this place: the room's antique furniture – covered in discarded clothing, books and newspapers – could fund the local council for a year. And then there are the display cabinets filled with time-worn knick-knacks and glassware, casually acquired by generations of Dewers then left to the care of invisible feather-duster bearers without a second thought to their intrinsic value. It is only Lady Mel's unmistakeably modern soft black leather suit that reminds her she is not sitting in a Jane Austen novel. There is even a virginal over by the window without the obligatory 'please do not play this instrument' sign so beloved of the National Trust.

 'So you're saying he didn't seem surprised?' Lady Mel asks.

 'Well, not completely no, but then it's what he's always wanted,' Polly explains.

 'Well, could be that, could be.'

 'What else could it be Mel?'

 'Well he is a doctor isn't he? So he's got access to things we don't.'

 Polly nods. 'And?'

 'And. He wants a baby more than anything, you said that, while you don't. At least not yet, correct?'

 'Correct,' Polly agrees.

 'So.' Mel takes a deep breath before explaining. 'It is not entirely unreasonable to suggest that he could be switching your contraceptive pills for some kind of placebo. In order to take your choice away.'

'It is entirely unreasonable to suggest Patrick would do a thing like that,' Polly insists. 'If you knew him at all, that is.'

'Sorry, I don't mean to overstep the mark. You know best, of course. It's just...'

'Just what?'

'It's quite rare for the pill to fail, unless you forget to take it regularly, and you don't strike me as the disorganised type.'

Mel has hit the nail on the head. Polly is not the type to forget things. It was her attention to detail and remarkable memory that led to her being such a success in The City. The niggling doubt that has been waiting, unspoken, at the back of her mind has been given full voice. What if Patrick did this? Such a violation of trust. It would destroy them. But how can she ask him without bringing on the very thing she fears?

'Shall we go then?' Melissa asks, pulling Polly from her revery.

'Yes, yes, of course.' Polly is surprised to find the room completely tidy as they head out. She did not even hear whoever snuck in to clean.

Two hours later Polly is still dwelling on the Patrick conundrum. What if it was deliberate? Could Patrick be that impatient to start a family? Would he do something so devious, so underhand?

No, he wouldn't, he's not like that. Mel is just stirring – giving her the worst case scenario so she thinks things through before it's too late to abort mission. She can't abort, she doesn't even have it in her to kill spiders, let alone a tiny possibility of a person.

Fenrir's head pokes above the swarm of malamutes, he is taller, a darker grey and a good deal thinner. He seems to have joined the pack, running up tors and back down through deep mires with his new friends, tongue hanging out and eyes wide like the primal wolf.

'It's magical here,' Polly says. 'Truly beautiful.'

'Thank you,' Melissa replies. She strides alongside, looking more vibrant, youthful, and alive than she did sitting indoors. A long green wax coat billows about her, hair controlled by strategic placement of a very old, wide-brimmed, brown leather hat. 'You know, the path used to go that way, over there.' She points at an impassable thicket of tree and hedge.

'How?' Polly asks.

'Well, those two rows of trees used to meet each other at the top, with an aisle between, but people started walking round them once they put all those fences and gates over there.'

'Shame.' Polly nods.

'Not really, it stops all the livestock being run over by trucks, so ultimately it's a good thing. But footpaths are like rivers, they meander, change their course. As people's needs change, their routes become different. They are straighter now than ever, even here people are in such a hurry to get from A to B.'

'Here isn't so different to everywhere else,' Polly suggests.

'Oh, I don't mean Dourstone in general, I mean here, specifically. It's a thin place, where this world collides with the other.'

'The other?'

'Oh don't worry, it's just a fanciful tale people once told, fairies and pixies and whatnot. The moors are littered with stories of babies being stolen away and men enticed by beautiful fae. But standing here, looking out at all that...' She indicates the huge expanse of green and grey. 'You can almost believe it.'

'Yes, I suppose.' Polly looks unconvinced.

'Anyway, he seems a lot happier now,' Mel says, pointing at Fenrir, the wistful look in her eye fading.

'He's settling in, getting used to the locals,' Polly jokes. 'It's good for him to have friends.'

'Everybody needs friends Polly.' Mel nods. 'Everybody.'

Polly nods back. It is good to have a friend.

'You should come to our next WI meeting,' Mel ignores Polly's snort of laughter. 'It's alright. We're not all old duffers. Small place like this, you're not even the youngest. Not by a long shot. Come along, Thursday in the church hall.'

'What the hell, why not? I like jam as much as the next woman.'

'Never made jam in my fucking life girl, get a grip.' Mel whistles the pack back from a group of sheep.

Patrick leans back in his chair. It doesn't make sense. Lady Melissa Dewer's medical records, the results of the tests he carried out and the unwanted erotic visions of her still plaguing his mind, would suggest she was half the age she – and those same medical records – profess her to be. It can't just be genetics and fresh Devon air.

And he still can't understand what happened to Graham. His

conversation with Lady Mel asked more questions than it answered. Patrick would like to bring it up with Lynn, but she is always with that priest. He needs to catch her alone. Lynn always gave her heart away too easily when they were kids, Patrick knows that better than anybody.

But why would Graham run in the middle of the night? What scared him so much? Was it the priest? Or is Patrick's creeping paranoia entirely justified? Has somebody killed Graham and left him in pieces on the moor?

And then there is Polly.

Does she want to get married? It's never come up outside of idle drunken conversation. The idea of a huge, complicated day of ceremonies, and the massive fuss his parents would make – both equal and opposite to the fuss her mother wouldn't – always puts them off. Polly has watched her mother go through three marriages, none of which have made her happy. It would be a waste of time, money and effort for a piece of paper neither of them want.

They have been together since university, ten years now. It has not occurred to either of them to not be together since then, and they have never felt they needed a certificate to prove it. The idea of eloping and avoiding the car crash that a big family wedding would inevitably be has come up before, but they always laugh it off. Maybe she was serious? His mother would never forgive him if they eloped. Remaining unmarried and happy has always been their preferred option. He loves her, and has, up until this new suggestion, always believed it to be reciprocal.

He takes one more look at the long expanse of nothing that is the Lady of the Manor's medical record. There is not a single illness recorded, only one other entry for a routine check-up when they first computerised the records. He shuts down the computer, grabs his jacket from the back of his chair and walks out of the building, setting the alarms (the code is written on a post-it next to the keypad, his predecessor assured him it's fine like that) and locking up.

'Sorry to bother you Patrick.' He nearly jumps out of his skin as Lynn pops out from behind the porch. 'But I wanted to talk to you.'

'Hello Lynn, you could have made an appointment you know? I'm not that busy.'

'Oh, it's not medical, can't waste NHS time, I'm not a time-waster.' She is in pink Lycra again, skin flushed red with exercise and a light dew of sweat on her nose, her bicycle leans against the wall. 'We're still friends right?'

'Of course we are, of course. But I've put the alarm on now, so we can't really go back in.'

'I don't mind, we can talk out here, it's a nice day.' She is right, there's some warmth left in the air from a sudden burst of early spring sunshine. Patrick is still not used to the longer evenings, it feels a bit like sneaking out early when daylight finally reaches the end of the working day. 'Is that picnic table still round the back?' she asks.

'Yeah. the nurses smoke their sneaky cigs there, come on.' He blushes as he ushers her around the building, remembering the last time the two of them were here.

'Thanks, I'm not sure what I'm doing at the moment,' she says as she sits on the table, feet up on the bench.

'Is it because of Graham?' Patrick asks, sitting down next to her.

'Kind of, yeah, I've been lonely without him, you know what I mean?'

'I think so, yes, but you've got the kids, you've got your friends…'

'I need a real friend Patrick. Nobody round here believes me, they all think Graham was a…'

'A what?' Patrick asks.

'You know, you've heard what they've been saying, everybody says it, it's not true.' Lynn looks at him with big watery blue eyes.

'So he didn't hit you?'

'No, never.'

'So all those bruises on your records? The ones I've seen?'

'I am just clumsy, honest. Look.' She stands up and pulls her shorts down to show Patrick a series of bruises all over her upper thighs. He can smell her sweat, its familiar tang turning back time. 'And he's been gone months, I did those on that fucking bike.'

'Okay, fair enough.' Patrick puts up his hands in protest. 'Graham was a good one, he seemed it.'

'He was. And I'm not sure what I did to drive him away.'

'I'm sure it wasn't you, he must have had another reason for leaving.' Patrick doesn't want to tell her about the foot.

'Thanks, you're a good friend. I missed you, when you left.' She shuffles and looks down at the lichened paving slabs.

'I'm sorry, life got in the way. I kind of forgot about this place, not you though. Never you.' He looks at her with teenage eyes, remembering the last summer he spent in Dourstone with his parents before he didn't want to spend summers with them any more. Before university, before he began his life proper. He spent its long sunny days and warm evenings hanging out with Lynn. Eventually, after a few too many scrumpys at a market disco, they climbed over the fence to this secluded table and Lynn deflowered him right where they sit. Or he deflowered her, he thinks it was mutual. Either way, they parted on good terms and Patrick didn't see her again until she appeared strolling down the South Bank a decade and a half later.

'Thanks, you're one of the good ones Pat.'

'What about you and Father Hearne?'

'What about him?'

'You're always together, isn't he on your side? Doesn't he believe you?'

'No, even Artie thinks I'm in denial, I am all alone here.'

'Are you and him? You know, there are rumours, it looks a bit...'

'He's a priest Patrick.'

'Yeah, but Church of England, not Catholic.'

'They're still fairly down on sex outside of marriage, especially with a married woman like me. No, Arthur and I are just friends, sorry to dampen all your fantasies.'

'Okay, sorry, sorry.' Patrick waves his hands in apology.

'You're alright, small place like this. Rumours get everywhere.' She leans in a little too close, that nostalgic salty sweat overwhelming Patrick's senses.

'Yeah, yeah they do.'

There is an awkward silence, and Lynn holds his gaze, a faint smile playing around her lips.

'You remember last time we were here?' She blushes.

Patrick nods.

She moves closer and before Patrick knows it the moment becomes a moment and she lunges in to kiss him. The surroundings, the smells and the sensory experience are like time travel, and Patrick briefly forgets himself, leaving it a little too late to pull away.

'I can't Lynn, I love Polly.' He takes her face in his hands, keeping her at a safe distance. 'I'm sorry if I've led you on. Sorry if you're lonely, I can refer you to professionals that can help. I'm not available though.'

'I'm sorry. I'm…' Lynn pulls away, starts crying.

'Don't be, just...'

'I can't believe I did that, it's not like me. But we were so good together back then, you were my first you know? I waited for you to come back the next summer, but you didn't. And you were such a hard act for anybody else to live up to. I'm so lonely, I'm being stupid. Stupid, stupid Lynn...' She starts to hyperventilate.

'I'm sorry, I'm sure somebody else might be able to...' Patrick stops talking as Lynn's breathing becomes harsher, feeling in his jacket pockets for a paper bag.

He can't find one, and she is starting to turn a nasty shade of red.

'Wait there.' Patrick races off round the building and rummages in the boot of his car until he finds his doctor's bag. A further rummage in said bag uncovers a brown paper bag. So simple, yet perfectly capable of saving someone's life.

As he comes back round the corner, ready to do some doctoring, he finds a note on the table.

Please don't tell anybody about this. Not even Polly, I feel so stupid. For the sake of what we once had, I trust you.

Lynn has gone.

9

Then...

Lady Sophia told me how Elias had found her – a spinster maiden, past her prime with no hope of marrying – and discerned her secret. How she had remained unwed was a mystery to him (and me) though it was almost certainly due to her family's financial position. Born to a respectable merchant family, her father had died and left her and her mother destitute from gambling debts. Elias found them with relatives in Tavistock and, unafraid of scandal (the other landowners of the moors know better than to interfere with a Dewer), offered sanctuary. Sophia took his offer, nervously accepting his hand and moving to the Manor with her mother upon their hastily arranged wedding day. Once she had bound herself to him, Elias revealed his secret, and she fell for him completely. She was a woman who loved women exclusively, and could now live without shame, with – to all public appearance – a man whom she loved above all others.

The Manor has been passed from daughter to daughter for as long as time itself. Each has taken on masculine appearance and named themselves Lord. Elias (I cannot refer to him by the feminine birth name he confided to me) inherited from his mother, Lord Hubert Henry Dewer whose domestic situation had been similarly complex. To be part of the Dewer family, in any position, is to be part of a long held secret. I was left in no doubt that to reveal this would be to put myself, and my family, in gravest danger. I would never have betrayed them, they were more to me than my family. I only do so now because I love you above all else and fear they will cast you out without explanation.

They are in need of an heir. This, I realise now, is the entire reason for my situation. I had thought the family line to be passed from daughter to daughter through poor luck, but events have proven that not to be the case. I believed the three of us were in love, but our long nights of passion in Lord Elias' mountainous bed amounted to no more than a spring planting.

As it is, I have given everything I have to this family. Perhaps if I had behaved in more dignified manner, not done the things I did, it would be different. The Dewers have taken over my family properties with a few deft strokes of a pen and Father would surely have my head when he finds out, were it not now irrevocably damned.

Now…

'Evening girls, this is Polly. I'm hoping she's going to be able to join us,' Mel says, dragging Polly into the church hall. 'Polly, this is Edwina – she's the local vet, if you haven't met professionally yet, very useful person to know – Wendy – she does something with phones I think…'

'App development, I'm a coder, if you ever need anything coding.' Wendy grins, butting in.

'Nobody needs anything coding dear, we're not at war any more,' Mel continues. 'This is Susan, this is Kerry, and I think you already know Lynn.'

'Hey Polly, how's that house treating you?' Lynn asks, with a smile.

'It's still perfect, thank you so much. Hello everybody.' Polly replies, waving nervously to the ladies sitting around the sagging trestle table. A lopsided corkboard hangs against the whitewashed wooden walls, weighed down with decades of unnoticed notices. The hall has the look of a temporary building that achieved permanent status by virtue of not being quite awful enough to replace. Wires peek out from peeling cable routes clinging to a water-stained ceiling. A bucket sits beneath the darkest stain catching drips.

'Oh, speaking of houses, do you know if Clive's dad is going to get planning permission on the big field Mel?' Susan cuts in, her unmistakeable Bristol accent much louder than her diminutive stature would imply.

'I bloody hope not.' Mel pulls up to her full height, chest thrust forwards. 'We've had quite enough shitty houses going up recently.'

'Isn't that a little hypocritical?' Wendy jibes. 'From Dourstone's biggest landowner?'

'Funny,' Mel replies. 'Maybe you and Delia could go and rent from Clive's dad instead? I've never made a profit on my land. Any money that comes from it goes straight back into the upkeep, farms, houses, shops, all of it. For the community.'

'I know, sorry, sorry, I'm just pulling your leg,' Wendy says.

'Whereas your Clive's bloody dad,' Mel says, 'no offence Susan love.' She pats her on the shoulder. 'He's just looking to get a quick profit since he can't make that farm work any more. I should never have given them that land, bloody useless family. They were supposed to work it for the good of the whole community.'

'Clive's family have had that land for the last two and a half centuries Mel,' Edwina interjects. 'Are you using the royal I?'

'Yes, yes, sorry. It's Dewer land, well was, before "we" gave it away in perpetuity, for services rendered,' Mel explains. 'We never asked for anything in return, and this is the thanks we get.'

'So it's not Dewer land any more then?' Susan smiles.

'No, but I've never cared who thinks they own the land, as long as it's being used for the good of the town. Not quick money, not second homes, not more empty shells sucking us dry.' Mel stares Susan down. 'We never enclosed our land back when all the other lords and ladies did, never squeezed the commoners to nothing, always helped. Dourstone moor is still for the poor, for ever more, like the rhyme says. Put your sheep on it if you want. Need an allotment over in my old kitchen garden? Just ask, the Dewers've never said no and I never will, you've got rights.'

'I'll have a word with Clive's dad next time we're there.' Susan gives in.

'Don't bother yourself, I'll do it. We've got plenty more unfinished business.'

'Anyway, welcome Polly!' Kerry butts in.

'Sorry, sorry Polly yes, I know, you thought there'd be more of us.' Mel laughs, back on subject. 'This is just the hardcore, the management committee if you will.'

'Mel is bigging us up a bit there I'm afraid,' Edwina says. She is one of those tall, awkward women who seem to be permanently hunching in apology, with an accent that suggests she once had a pony. 'It's just that the rest of them only come if we've got a film on, or something fun. Tonight's pretty much just business so you've only got us.'

'I think I've met most of you in the pub at some time or another. My other half is going to play football with your menfolk,' Polly says.

'Oh, you're Patrick's wife,' Susan pipes in. 'Clive is so looking forward to getting the team back up and running.'

'They're not married,' Mel says.

'Oh, sorry.' Susan makes an apologetic face. 'No offence.'

'None taken, we're happy as we are,' Polly explains. The room looks at her as if it is an alien concept to not want to be married.

'Good for you,' Kerry chimes in, banging a pudgy fist on the trestle table and almost upending it. 'It's bloody over-rated if you ask me.' Her red face bursts into a grin under a mass of brown curls.

'Nobody did ask you,' Wendy says, a half-smile playing across her olive-skinned face, 'but if I was married to Dan I'd probably agree.'

'You're lucky you're not Wendy, he's obsessed with *Bake Off*. All he does now is cook, our house is brimming over with new pans and dishes that look the same as the pans and dishes we've already got. Every day he's testing a new recipe, I am being constantly force-fed cake. I don't even like cake, the kids are going off it – they're teenagers now, they want to go vegan, he don't want to bake vegan. Our card got declined at the garage the other morning because he'd put us over the limit buying flour. We've already got a cupboard and a half filled with different flours, but no, he needed this one. It's special. Last month it was muffin cases. I know men get obsessions, and I'm lucky it's not a worse addiction, but if it was booze or drugs he might at least be fun.'

'Thank you for the insight Kerry,' Edwina says. 'But we've got a lot to get through so let's get on with it. First off we've got May Day to sort out. Also it's a bound beating year and Whitsun is a week and a bit before Oak Apple Day. Do we want to move one and do them both on the bank holiday weekend? Or do we have three separate bashes this May?'

'Bound beating?' Polly asks, suddenly aware of how little she knows of local customs, and how much difference forty odd miles can make.

'I forgot we had a foreigner in,' Mel says. 'Susan, you're not local either, see if you can answer this one.'

'Okay,' Susan begins, aware as always that as Dourstone's Chinese community (although she has never been further east than Folkestone) she and her children are the town's small nod to ethnic diversity – unless you count Doctor Sharma who locums for Patrick, which nobody does. 'Once every seven years, the people of Dourstone Nymet "beat" the children of the town around its boundaries in order to make sure they know where they're from.

Miser Sue and her horse lead the parade, and the stick man brings up the rear to "beat" any lollygaggers.' Susan's use of air quotes puts Polly's mind at rest as to whether anybody actually gets hit with a stick.

'Very good, extra points for use of the word lollygagger there girl,' Mel says. 'Now, how are we going to organise all this?'

'I vote for combining,' Edwina says, pausing from fiddling with hair that is somewhere between straw and pink bailer twine in both consistency and colour to stick her hand in the air.

'These are the ancient and proper traditions of this town and need to be respected. I don't like any watering down of Oak Apple Day, we're about the only place left in the country that upholds it. That means something to me, even if it doesn't to you blowins,' Mel retorts, rising from her chair. 'Once upon a time, the revels of May would go on all month long, with Robin Hood plays, dancing, drinking and good times right through.'

'Well, that's all well and good…' Edwina replies, and the arguments of rule by committee begin.

An hour later they have broken for a cup of tea and a biscuit to allow tempers to calm.

'How are you doing? On your own I mean,' Polly asks Lynn, not wanting to pry but unable to help herself.

'I'm fine, getting used to it now.' Lynn smiles. Polly spots scar tissue on Lynn's arm before she notices her looking and rolls her sleeve down.

'Do you know where he is?' Polly asks. 'Aren't you worried he'll come back?'

'What do you mean?'

'Sorry, but Mel's told me about him. What he did to you. I'd be scared he might come back if I didn't know where he was.'

'He won't come back. I don't think,' Lynn answers, watching the other women across the hall. 'You're lucky, you've got a baby on the way, man who loves you. He doesn't hurt you does he?'

'Patrick? Hurt me?' Polly laughs. 'No chance. He wouldn't hurt a fly. It wouldn't even occur to him.'

'Yeah, I remember, he's one of the good ones. Hang on to him.' Lynn looks at the floor. 'But men are like dogs, they can all turn on you, just like that.'

'Oh, God, sorry, I didn't mean...'

'No it's okay. I mean, obviously it's not entirely, I'm a bit of a mess, and very jealous of you. I've been left all on my own with two screaming toddlers. But I'm still better off without him.'

'Anything I can do?' Polly smiles, realising how lucky she is. 'Anything, looking after the kids – I'm going to need the practice – I can send Patrick down, make sure your house is safe, secure. Just in case.'

'Thanks, I mean Mum's only round the corner, and Mel's loaned me a couple of her dogs for protection. But a man about the place would be useful. Can he put up shelves?'

'No, sorry. He's not really very practical, but he's a reassuring presence,' Polly says, wondering if Mel's dogs would turn on her, as they drift back to the table.

'Is it always like that?' Polly asks Susan, once the meeting is over and those who have not gone home have retired to the Drop of Dew.

'Yes, pretty much.' Susan nods as she takes their drinks over to the big table by the window. 'You get used to Edwina, she's just a bit bossy. Ex-boarding school head girl, used to telling people what to do, and them jumping to and doing it.'

'So nothing like Lady Mel then?' Polly grins.

'No, it would never occur to Mel that she had to tell people what to do. They usually just do it.'

'Just a cosy four then?' Wendy smiles as Polly and Susan hand out the drinks.

'Looks that way,' Susan replies. 'Kerry doesn't trust Dan not to have electrocuted their teenagers – deliberately, Edwina doesn't trust anybody to do anything right – especially not Jack, and Lynn is terrified her mum will stop having the kids if she pushes it too far. We're lucky.'

'I'm not.' Wendy shrugs. 'I'm here because I know Delia will have used me being out as an excuse to have her bloody parents over, and I'm not dealing with that. They have enough trouble coping with Dee being a lesbian, let alone her being "shacked up with that thieving gyppo," I heard him on the phone once. Tosser.'

'Are you a gypsy?' Polly asks.

'No idea, but he's a racist. I'm from Chagford as far as I know, but I tan easily and I've got long black hair. That's enough for him to make pikey jokes at me all day long,' Wendy replies.

'I know the type,' Polly replies. 'There were plenty like that back home in Appledore.'

'Oh are you…'

'A well-tanned white girl? No, I'm afraid not. I am – according to my grandfather – the proud descendent of a Barbary pirate, marooned on the North Devon coast.' Polly laughs.

'And is that true?' Wendy raises an eyebrow.

'Well, sometimes Grandad claims we're all descended from Copinger the Cruel – despite all legends claiming he was a white Norseman. And sometimes he says he tunnelled all the way from Tobruk to Torrington under the ocean when he was a desert rat in World War 2. He's also been known to say he's an African Prince in hiding for his life from a murderous uncle who stole his crown. And very occasionally, but not often, he lets it slip that he's a first generation Jamaican immigrant. Grandad likes a fanciful tale.' Polly likes them too.

'But you look so…' Susan begins.

'White?' Polly replies. 'I know, it's the straight blonde hair. If I leave it alone too long it goes back to afro, and I really don't. I know I shouldn't but it's easier especially…'

'Especially in Devon?' Susan fills in the gap. 'Don't worry, I have days where I wish I could change my face too, but it's not an option.'

'Sorry.'

'Don't be, you're alright.' Susan raises her glass in solidarity. 'There's a lot of not-a-racist-but pricks about here. Like Wendy's father-in-law.'

'Mother-in-law's no better.' Wendy begins her tirade afresh. 'And we're not "shacked up," as they so delicately put it, we're married, proper job married, church and everything. Just cos they don't think it should be allowed. I told them I did...'

'Yes, we all remember Wendy, no need to go into it,' Mel interrupts. 'It was Christmas dinner, and Wendy decided to call her in-laws a pair of bigoted old cunts before pelting them with pigs in blankets, and now Delia has to sneak them in when she's out.'

'Don't think she should have anything to do with the tossers any more...' Wendy grumbles.

'We know how you feel, but it's blood isn't it? Genetic ties and whatnot,' Mel explains. 'It's not that simple.'

'Bloody is.'

'I'm not having this argument again Wendy.' Mel's face turns dark as she stares the girl down. Wendy backs off, a flash of something, maybe fear, visible for just a second in her eyes.

'Anyway, Polly's bloody lucky not having to sort out childcare yet,' Susan says, clonking her drink down.

'Be difficult, no family in town, married to – sorry, not married, living with – a doctor,' Mel says. 'You'll need friends.'

'Ta-da!' Wendy reaches her jazz hands across the table. 'Welcome to the WI, best baby-sitting network in town.'

'Certainly is, and you're welcome to borrow Clive anytime you like.' Susan grins. 'I love him because he gets tired easily and is happy to stay at home with the kids while I get out and get wasted.' She drains her glass, and indicates everybody else's. They all shake their heads, looking at their barely touched drinks.

'It's true, Clive is happy to do it, we all dump them off over there,' Wendy whispers while Susan is at the bar. 'He's a good egg, reads them stories, plays games with them, sometimes I think he's a bit developmentally challenged like, as if he hasn't grown up, prefers hanging out with the kids, you know what I mean?'

Polly thinks she does.

10

Then…

Come the first snow of winter, as I was beginning to think Dourstone held no more secrets, Elias told me the darkest of them all. The wisthound ceremonies. I did not want anything to do with it, but Lord Elias told me it was necessary if I wanted to be a part of his life, and I so did. Dourstone seemed a veritable paradise on earth; what was the odd sacrifice in return for a place with such heart?

Of course I had come across the local legends of The Devil and his dogs but they seemed to be inferring they were true. I thought them quite mad, but did not argue. They were so kind, and, as I said, I was falling for the place as much as the people. I have never felt so accepted as I had been by this pair of pleasure-seekers. We were a family. Nevertheless, they were women in body whatever they were in spirit, and I am a man of needs.

Now...

May Day had been fun. The folk group hired to play traditional reels in the square were interrupted by locals who decided to 'borrow' their instruments for an impromptu singalong of popular songs with the words changed to be dirtier, though not necessarily funnier. The second hastily erected may-pole, to replace the magnificent one that was burned to ashes the night before, was obviously the electricity pylon that blew over – leaving the town without power for a whole day – in the April storms. And the May Queen (Kerry and Dan's sixteen year old daughter Katie who looked a little drunk, stoned or both by the end of the night before disappearing with a young farmer) had given a speech imploring the entire community to 'go fuck itself'. As usual for a Dourstone do the dancing had gone on well into the next morning and any complaints were dealt with by telling the residents, in no uncertain terms, they shouldn't have bought houses on the square: sometimes involving eggs.

Patrick was beginning to wish he had gone home with Polly – who left before everybody became incoherent. He had been having a good time, and she didn't mind. The guys from the Dad Club usually give him stick for always going home with her whenever she asks, and he wanted to prove he wasn't under the thumb. Instead he found himself still out at three in the morning laughing like a drain with a bunch of teenagers around the charred remains of the second maypole, dodging flaming ribbons.

Today, the day after, is the day, the first match with The Dads – who are showing no ill after-effects from last night's indulgence. Playing football, being on a team. It is like being back at uni. He hasn't done any regular sport since then. Polly is into more refined sports: fencing, archery, gymnastics – not his thing at all – and he hadn't felt the need to seek anything out in London; it held many more interesting leisure activities. It is only five a side, so the fact he is a lot more out of shape than he thought (and utterly broken by scrumpy) will not be a problem for a full ninety minutes. Nobody has told him how long it will be for though, apparently it depends.

'Ready Paddy?' Delia grins, lacing up her boots. Some gentleman long ago in her footballing career tried to explain this league was neither mixed nor ladies'. She had assured him she was no lady and it wouldn't be a problem by wedging her boot into his gentleman areas. Nobody questioned her right to be on the pitch after that, particularly as she had been the top scorer for an unbroken three year run before Graham knackered up their chances.

'Ready as I'll ever be,' Patrick says, jumping to his feet in a display of eagerness and doing that jogging on the spot thing he's seen proper athletes do.

It's only a friendly match, since the season is nearly over, and their losing a man as early as they did led to disqualification from this year's league.

'You'll be fine,' Clive says, grabbing his shoulder, 'the goal's tiny.'

Despite his best efforts to play up front, Patrick has been stuck with the job of goalie. Having also been metaphorically picked last, it feels like a replay of primary school, before the summer he reinvented himself: appearing at secondary school as the confident, sporty individual he had always seen himself as. Clearly the years between university and now have been something of a relapse.

'Come on,' Jack says, rallying the team as they run onto the pitch. Well, onto the hardwood floors of Hatherleigh community centre. The other side look big, and young, barely out of school.

Patrick suddenly remembers that being young is in their favour, not his. The home team point and laugh as they realise Delia is a woman.

'They're new,' Dan whispers in Patrick's ear, 'they've not met her before, they'll regret that.'

A nervous muttering breaks out in the meagre audience, who aren't new, have met Delia before, and are now expecting a show.

An hour later it is all over and Patrick is sweating like an inappropriate metaphor.

'Well done mate.' Dan slaps his naked sticky back on the way to the showers. 'You're definitely in. Next season we'll be unstoppable.'

'Thanks,' Patrick replies. 'Though I only saved that last one because I slipped over, I was heading the other way. More luck than judgement.'

'Modest as well,' Clive laughs. 'Don't care how you did it, we won mate. Four-two. That's a result in anyone's book. And anyway, I'd rather have a lucky team-mate than a judgemental one. First round's on me once we're back in Dourstone.' He envelopes Patrick in a sweaty back-slapping hug.

'You're on.' Delia laughs, appearing from her cubicle in a towel. Patrick is suddenly gripped with the thought that she might come into the showers with them. What is the etiquette for that? She's one of the boys, part of the team, but every inch a woman.

She sees the fear in his eyes, 'Don't worry, I'm not going in with you lot, there's a single shower in the ladies room. It wouldn't do to taunt you poor boys with all this.' She flashes the inside of her towel with a laugh and a wink. 'Well played though, good job.' And she goes.

'Don't mind her.' Jack chuckles. 'She gets a bit crazy with the wins, well, even more so than normal. And don't tell Wendy about the flashing either, she doesn't like it. Now be quick or she'll come back and whip you with that towel.'

'True,' Clive and Dan chorus.

'I've got the scars to prove it.' Jack bares his arse to reveal three red lines. 'Got those off her a minute ago for that shitty pass in the second half.'

Back home the pub is distinctly lacking in victorious atmosphere. Saturday's May Day celebration has left most of the town hungover and sedate. But the five-a-side team are celebrating. The landlord has booked a karaoke evening that, up until now, has been just the host – in blue-sequinned jacket and brothel creepers – going through his Tom Jones repertoire.

Jack and Dan are howling their way through 'Try A Little Tenderness,' and it is excruciating. Delia, Patrick and Clive are sitting at an old church pew directly opposite, cheering and laughing while adding the odd awkward harmony. The few other locals that have dragged themselves out are at the other end of the bar or outside in the smoking shelter – whether they smoke or not. Some things are best left unheard.

'Better than Graham,' Delia shouts in Patrick's ear.

'What, the singing?' Patrick replies, laughing as Dan completely misses a high note.

'No mate, you in goal. Much better, we'll get the cup next season, for sure.'

'Thanks mate.' A vision of cracked, white bone and broken sinew clouds Patrick's mind. 'Listen Dee, was Graham really a wife-beater? There's a lot of rumours flying about.'

'I couldn't see it myself. I mean, he drank a fair bit, we all do. But he was a friendly drunk, fun to be around, not an angry one. I suppose they do say you can never tell, but I never saw a mark on her, and they seemed pretty happy in public. On the other hand, as a card-carrying, man-hating lesbian, you're all the same, you're all the enemy, and yes, of course he hit her.' Delia gives a lop-sided smile.

'Yeah,' Clive joins in, ignoring Delia's last outburst. He's heard it all before. 'He seemed happy. Nothing wrong, well, the last week or two before he went he seemed worried about something. Always looking over his shoulder.'

'Really?' Patrick asks, intrigued now. 'Did he ever say what?'

'Not to me, but we weren't that close really. He was more Jack's mate, they're both outsiders, more in common.'

'Oh, are you a proper local then?' Patrick asks.

'Yep, generations of us back in that churchyard, apart from the bits that got left on the farm.' He waves his prosthetic hand.

'Me too, apart from the being from "that London" bit.' Patrick chuckles. He's finally conceded he isn't that local.

'Yep, that accent won't do you any favours.' Clive laughs, despite his being almost indistinguishable. 'Anyway Susan's in the WI with her, and Lady Mel told them all he did it. Battered her, told her what to do, where to go, what to wear, all of it. She won't talk about it to anybody else though. Well, you don't do you?'

Patrick nods. 'No I suppose if you were scared...'

'Exactly.' Delia nods back. 'Wendy says she was terrified, but broke down one night. Told Lady Melissa everything, don't know what she did, but he vanished pretty quick after. I don't blame him, that woman's fucking terrifying.'

'But no contact with any of you? No explanation? That's weird.'

'You'd best ask Lady Melissa what she said,' Clive says. 'She might have made it a condition. She's very persuasive.'

'Jesus, rather you than me,' Delia says. 'I'd sooner let it drop. Come on, we're up.'

She drags Clive and Patrick up behind the microphones to slaughter The Bee Gees' 'Stayin' Alive.'

11

Then...

That first Wisthound Weekend I donned purple velvet robe and wicker tinner's mask: we are all equal in the night, distinguishing features obscured by protective garments. We hoisted the hurdle upon our shoulders, struggling figure gagged and bound to it, sacking wrapped around him assuring his anonymity. I was still convinced all this was merely symbolic – half of me still held to the belief this was only a scarecrow or bag of corn. After all, demon dogs are figments of the imagination, if they really were frequenting the town I would surely have come across them in our endless wanderings over the moors.

   'Feed The Devil's dogs as the cold begins to bite,' we chanted as we marched to the altar stone atop the hill. 'The first snows of winter stained with blood in the night.' Sophia had shown me the stone earlier, stained a deep copper colour, I assumed, from the driving rains and red earth of the region. Eventually we reached it and set down our burden. Lord Elias led us in further chants, the wording of which I shall not record here. I have heard enough of it this night, and shall doubtless hear it again soon enough.

   We carefully tied the sacrifice to the stone, the bonfire of the earlier procession's end still burning over towards the road. The crowds of revellers that surrounded it had vanished. At a moment, a look was shared between all those out of doors, silence fell, and they left – mainly for the inns, but away from this place, off the streets, and away from our dreadful parade. More words of power were spoken, before a low growling marked our signal to leave. I was not quick enough, I saw the familiar faces of Lord Elias' hunting pack, twisted into unfamiliar grimaces as they appeared from the trees. Their usual eager-to-please faces hungry for blood, their eyes glowing a deep blue. Even now, years later, even after what has happened this very night, I maintain that all this cannot be real. They are just dogs.

The sound of their feeding spilled down the hill as we returned to the Manor for a night of feasting, having staved off The Devil for another year. It is a sound that will not leave me until the end of my days; it will be the last thing I ever hear. I cannot pretend it did not affect me, I confess, as we walked back I slipped from the company to pull up my mask and leave my evening repast against a tree.

Shortly after our return, the dogs arrived, their maws grizzled with blood and the lead dog carrying a grisly trophy. I hoped to find the poor man we left to their tender mercies at their head, grinning with the fun of having tricked the foolish city gentleman. In some ways he was, but it was merely his heart, gripped in the strong teeth of Lord Elias' favourite pup. I kept my demeanour, I did not faint, I did not cry out, I believe I did not disgrace the family name. Elias took his prize from the dog, grinning like a mad man.

'Another year of peace for us all! Dourstone retains its heart!' he cried, holding it aloft before disappearing into his cellars. A cheer went up and all drank to the town's health.

I stayed for the drink, the strong alcohol helping steady my shattered nerves. I was part of this. I had blood on my hands. In civilised society I would hang with the rest of them.

As the party split into smaller groups, I looked around for the Lord and Lady, but could see neither. They had spoken no words of comfort, nor explained the full extent of the ceremony before we set out. I imagine they assumed I had realised their story of dogs and devils was literal, and not the allegory I had supposed.

Now...

Lady Mel strides ahead of all, in full Miser Sue costume, leading a pantomime horse. Nobody can quite remember who Miser Sue is or why she heads the march, but the outfit looks like a cross between a witch and a French maid. Polly is at least ninety percent sure the horse won't make the full ten miles in costume. She isn't sure if she can last the course, after all, she is pregnant and the endless rain of the last few weeks has broken into uncharacteristic sunshine.

It was decided that the bounds would be beaten on the actual Whitsun weekend, since nobody wanted the traditional and sacrosanct cider-drowned antics of Oak Apple Day contaminated with a walk. Dourstone being one of the last places in the country still to celebrate it, the local employers grudgingly give their staff the day off, and those who commute are often mysteriously ill that day if refused annual leave. It is accepted by those who employ Dourstonians that they will not be in on the 29th of May.

The two had been combined once before, when Whitsun had fallen upon the glorious 29th, and nobody had been happy about it. This year May will be filled with local celebrations not even the weather can dampen. It has relented for today, at least, and most of the town have turned out to tramp over stiles and fences, through back gardens that weren't there centuries ago, and across the river where the bridge no longer is while being roasted alive in thick wellington boots.

The problem is all of those fences, stiles and other people's gardens they have to negotiate. Not to mention the thickening mud that threatens to suck everyone down to the centre of the earth. On top of this, an awful lot of people have brought dogs, and all these filthy dogs need lifting over the afore-mentioned fences, stiles and other people's gardens. Polly has been forewarned and decided against trying to drag Fenrir round. He had an early morning run over the moors in the mist, accompanied by an unexpected stag that appeared like a scene from a Disney movie. It watched them intently for five minutes before snorting twin jets of steam and sauntering away.

Cronus is at the front, leaping all obstacles without aid, and intimidating the pantomime horse by snapping at its heels. Polly doesn't think dogs should be able to laugh, but this one definitely gives a chuckle each time the back legs of the horse veer away from his jaws.

At the rear is the stick man, a traditional figure who bears a terrifying resemblance to Mr Punch (for Polly). Local folklore has it that he would chase stragglers and beat them with his stick, hence the name beating the bounds. Given how slowly everything is moving he is currently sitting in a hedge with his Mr Punch head in one hand and a clay pipe in the other. It has rendered him a little less scary. He gives Patrick a wave of recognition as he pulls a bottle of home-made scrumpy from the folds of his costume. Patrick waves back.

'I didn't know you knew the priest,' Polly says.

'Yeah, Father Hearne,' Patrick replies. 'I meet him out on the bike sometimes.'

'Look at you with all your secret friends,' she laughs. 'And a priest no less, how does that square with your atheism?'

'Takes all sorts to make a world, and I'm not sure how that massive dildo he's waving about squares with his Christianity,' he says. The traditional stick of the stick man has been carved into quite a lewd shape and painted a lurid shade of purple in case there was any ambiguity about the symbolism. 'I hadn't realised it was him inside that massive plastic head.'

'Is it not papier-mache?'

'Might be made out of clay for all I know Pol, nothing could surprise me today. This place is weirder than I remember.'

'You must have done this before?'

'I did, when I was eight, but I don't remember much about it. We were just running about everywhere, me and the local kids.'

'Thought you were local.'

'Well, yes, I realise you may have had a point about that. I've seen it from the other side now I actually live here.'

'My God, you've learned something!' Polly laughs.

'Well, most of the kids I knew then have left now, apart from Lynn. Some of their parents remember me, a bit, and a few old guys in the pub who remember everyone and everything that ever happened here. Nick's moved back, I knew him back in the day. We were the best of friends one summer, I thought. He barely remembers me. In fact I don't think he remembers me at all, you know that face people get when they're pretending they remember, just to get out of having to admit they don't?'

Polly nods. Polly knows it well.

'Yeah, I think it was that. I am a DFL.'

'Yep, the both of us are Down-From-Londoners baby, but at least this one will be local.' She pats her bump.

'Yeah, is that good though?' Patrick laughs, as they finally reach the head of the queue for the next stile.

'I don't know why we're doing this,' Patrick says three hours later. He's been trying to help his friends with their children all morning, but to no avail. They are all in full family unit mode. There's no space for the childless. He is in a hurry for this kid to arrive so he and Polly can have the same experience.

'It's fun, and it gets us in the community spirit. It's a good thing to be part of somewhere, don't you think?' Polly replies.

There are definite partitions in the entourage, from parents all eager to indoctrinate the next generation, to old folks enjoying this route they have tramped all their lives. Not to mention those who have brought enough alcohol with them to kill a (pantomime) horse. Patrick and Polly are feeling isolated.

'It would be if we were Pol,' he replies, 'but look at us. We're the only childless couple here not getting pissed.'

'You can get pissed if you like.' Polly sighs. 'You're not pregnant.'

'No, but I do need to keep up appearances Pol, I'm still Doctor Sumner to these people. We could knock off early and go home.'

'How is that keeping up appearances? And do you really want lumpy here...' She indicates her swelling midriff '...to be denied the joy of us telling them about the time we did it without them?'

'They will never need to know if we lie about it,' Patrick suggests. 'And if we leg it, then I can get pissed without fear of reproach.'

'Fine, but I'm staying. I want to do this Patrick. With or without you.'

'With then.' Patrick opens his backpack and pulls out a bottle of water. 'Here, have some of this, it's hot and you need to keep your fluids up.'

'Always the doctor.' Polly smiles, he has already topped up her suntan lotion five times today, and made her wear this ridiculous straw hat. 'It'll be fine, I'm sure we'll be out of these muddy bits in no time, on to open ground and moving properly.'

'This is Dartmoor Pol, it's all muddy bits.'

He walks off ahead, looking at the scenery and saying nothing.

'Are you two okay?' Polly jumps a mile as Mr Punch appears next to her waving a stick. His leering painted face and hooked nose has haunted her since she was very small. Punch sits at the heart of her darkest, unexplored fears.

'Christ on a bike, I nearly had the baby here.' She laughs.

'Sorry, sorry,' says Father Hearne, pulling his fake head off and letting it swing on its strap behind him. 'I'm not actually Christ – just on his payroll – and I'm not on my bike today. Didn't mean to scare you Mrs Doctor.'

'I'm neither a doctor, nor his Mrs,' Polly says. Patrick is still close enough to hear this. He carries on walking. 'I'm Polly, pleased to meet you Mr Punch. Sorry to scream, and for the blasphemy, but I've always been a bit scared of you.'

'Really?' Father Hearne asks.

'Yes, I put it down to the puppet on the top shelf of my grandfather's spare room. It used to keep me awake all night.'

'Did it talk? You know, "that's the way to do it," and all that?'

'No, it was just lit through a chink in the curtains by the street lights, used to freak me out with his unblinking eyes.' Polly shudders.

'Lucky you're a rational grown up now then, not jumping at shadows and stick men.' He laughs.

'Yes, isn't it.' Polly agrees, wishing it were true. 'What stick men?'

'Me. I'm the stick man don't you know,' he stage-whispers. 'Calling me Mr Punch is a bit like calling the place a village, don't let them hear you.'

'But you are dressed as Mr Punch,' Polly says, stumbling a little on the uneven moorland.

'I'm afraid not,' he laughs, taking her arm. 'The stick man of Dourstone does indeed closely resemble the famed Punchinella, but just as Lily Munster resembles Morticia Addams, they're separate entities and to confuse the two will enrage the faithful.'

'Fair enough, Mr stick man, but didn't I see you doing the Punch

WICKER DOGS

and Judy a few weeks ago?'

'You got me, fair and square, I'm Father Hearne, the closest thing you'll get to a local priest in this town.'

'I know, I came to your Easter service, it was... interesting.'

'I will take that as a compliment Polly, thank you very much.'

'How come you're participating in this very pagan ritual then father?' Polly asks. 'And waving that... thing?' She indicates his very phallic staff.

'Well for one thing I owe Lady Mel quite a lot of favours. I take it you know Mel?'

'Yes I do.' Polly doesn't need to pry, if Lady Melissa Dewer asks you to do something, it is impossible not to.

'And for another, there was a historical society talk a few weeks ago about the origins of the stick man, and his links to the Lord of Misrule – your friend Mr Punch – and some of the traditions associated with it rather put most people off the gig.'

'What traditions?'

'Oh, it's all linked to Green Man stuff, king for a day, given everything, spoiled rotten, and then you get your head cut off to ensure a good harvest. That kind of thing.'

'Oh, I can see how that might put people off.'

'I know, but it's the 21st century, it's all symbolic these days. Bit of fun, nice day out for the kids, hardly any ritual murder.'

They crest a hill, reaching familiar ground. The stone circle. Polly breathes a sigh of relief, it's almost over, she has nearly completed one more step on the road to being accepted. Being local.

Patrick is laid out on the ground in the centre, waiting for them. He is thinking of the cart he found here months previously, of the foot underneath. He shudders and gives a weak smile, sitting up as they approach. 'You're not going to like this Polly.'

'Hello Patrick, I know what you're going to say.' Father Hearne chuckles. 'We're going that way, I've done this a few times before.' He points across the circle to a path leading down through the woods, away from the town, away from their cottage, but at least out of the sun. 'Do you two want a go on this?' He offers a large plastic milk bottle of home-brewed cider.

'No, I'll stay on the water.' Polly smiles politely, sipping at her bottle.

'You know this isn't even half-way yet right?' He laughs.

'Give me that.' Polly has a long pull on the thick brown gloop to a disapproving stare from Patrick.

'Thought so.' The priest laughs, passing it to Patrick who follows Polly's example.

Neither of them enjoy it, but neither wants to back down.

Come the end of the walk the council have laid on free cider and pasties in the square for all who took part. You get the odd teenage chancer with a bit of mud rubbed onto their clothes trying to get in on it dishonestly, but nobody minds. Most Dourstonians admire that kind of initiative. Lynn has been here getting it ready all day.

'How does she seem to you?' Polly asks Patrick, looking across to the trestle table where she stands doling out free refreshments. 'Is she fixed now? Can we leave her to it?'

'What? Lynn?' Patrick asks back, between grateful swigs of rejuvenating, crisp, commercially-produced cider. Father Hearne's home brew had been drier than not drinking at all.

'Yeah, you know, without Graham. You were down there again the other night, checking she's okay.'

'Oh yeah, she'll be right. But it still doesn't make any sense Pol. I've been over it and over it, and I can't work out where he went, or why. Somebody somewhere's lying.' He hasn't told Polly the history between him and Lynn – or the recent misunderstanding – and at this point it would do more harm than good. Polly's hormones are turning her temper far quicker than he is used to. He'll tell her all about it once the baby is born.

'I don't know why you're so obsessed with Graham anyway, Pat,' Polly says. 'It's not healthy, you should be concentrating on me and the baby, not the whereabouts of a bloke you met once and a foot you imagined. It doesn't matter any more. Like you said, she's fine, people look out for each other round here, give it a rest for just one night please.'

'Okay, sorry, you're tired, it's been a long walk. I told you you shouldn't do it in your condition.'

'And don't fucking patronise me. I know what I can and can't do.'

'Sorry again. We can go home in a bit if you want, it's okay, I don't mind.'

'You go Patrick, I'm staying here. It's a nice evening, and most of the company is pretty good. I think I'll have my one permitted drink now. See you at home.'

'What about that scrumpy earlier?' he says.

'I had one fucking sip, and it was vile, doesn't count.'

And with that she walks off through the square, leaving Patrick bewildered. He finishes his drink and walks off up the hill towards home. He knows Polly well enough to know that if he carries on antagonising her she'll only get angrier and everything will be worse. He turns around to look on the square from the top and wishes he could stay. But he can't, he's tired – too tired to trust himself not to upset Polly. The day's sweat is starting to form an uncomfortable crust on his skin and he just wants a bath and a cup of tea. Then probably straight to bed. Polly's hormones can wait until tomorrow.

'You heading home as well?' Patrick is surprised to see Susan hurrying up the hill towards him with a gaggle of children. 'I'll walk back with you, we're on your way home.'

'Oh, okay. Is Clive not doing the babysitting tonight? I assumed he'd be taking all the kids, like usual,' Patrick replies.

'No, not tonight, he's taken the little ones back and I'm taking over in a bit. It's his turn – he'll bloody waste it though – we were going to get Dan and Kerry's Katie to do it, but now she's May Queen she thinks it's her duty to be out at all events, all year, all bloody night long. And she's the only one old enough to do it. I drew the short straw. You?'

'Oh, I'm just tired, don't want to say anything to aggravate Polly, and she's hell-bent on staying out, so I'm going home. She'll come back soon, she's pregnant after all.'

'Yeah, sure she will, you want to come in to ours for a drink on the way?' Susan takes his arm. Patrick doesn't think she's going to let him say no.

'On your own then?' Lady Mel, now out of costume, looking vibrant and ready to take on the world in a floor length patchwork coat, says to Polly. You wouldn't think she had just walked ten miles across rugged moorland and housing estate.

'Yes, I've sent him home. He's being an overprotective dick again.'

'Fair enough, are you dancing then?'

'I would if there was any music, is there anything?'

'Yes,' Mel states. 'We've got local legends The Artful Badgers coming over to play. They're always a good night out.'

'Excellent,' Polly says, 'can't wait.'

'You'll have to,' Mel explains. 'Susan was organising the music and she forgot to tell them we wanted them here early. They're turning up for a nine pm start, same as they always do.'

Polly looks at her watch. It is only seven o'clock.

'Should I go home and wait then?'

'Hell no, stay here, it'll be fun. There's food, drink, company, fun. I'm sure one of the locals will pull out a banjo or something soon.'

Polly decides to make a night of it. She isn't that pregnant yet; Patrick can sit at home and wait.

'White Russians!' Susan shrieks as she finishes messing about with bottles in the kitchen. 'You'll have one? Of course you'll have one.'

Patrick is discovering it is difficult to say no to Susan's relentless cheeriness. They are going to have a good time. Clive had been waiting for her to get back, his face serious about something as he left for the square. He had washed and put the little ones to bed, and the older children are slumped in front of a TV in one of the big upstairs bedrooms. Patrick can hear the theme tune through the ceiling:

We are better, when we work together, if we are apart then everything goes wrong,

If we are in harmony, we will get there faster, come on now and join our song.

It's annoyingly catchy and Patrick is worried it will never leave his brain. Clive is a great dad though, Patrick hopes he can be half as good.

'Of course.' He assents to that drink.

'Excellent, get this in you.' Susan comes back in, she has stripped down to an almost see-through T-shirt and tiny shorts.

'Thanks.' Patrick takes the glass and drinks. It is sublime. He has never really been one for cocktails. His parents only ever provided the entirely clear, entirely alcoholic options, and his university friends favoured pints, then shots, then pints, then shots, then pints, then shots. This is lovely, and all too quickly it is gone.

'Good man,' Susan splutters, having finished hers as well.

'Another?'

'Why not?' Patrick means this, Polly has made it clear she wants nothing to do with him tonight. He's got plenty of time before she gets back, why not get drunk. He's not spent much time with Susan, Susan knew Graham and Lynn far better than him. She might be able to help his investigations. And she seems nice, and fun, and he needs nice and fun. Things have been much too tense of late.

'You're not tired yet are you?' Mel says. The band are packing up, the bar is refusing to serve anybody else and the crowd are finally dissipating. Polly is surprised to find even after a ten mile walk and a night of dancing the tiny spark of life inside is no more tired than her.

'No, what's the plan?' she asks, red-faced and filled with adrenalin.

'Back to the Manor, after party. Everybody else seems to be bailing so you're my only hope of fun.'

'Well, if you put it like that,' Polly agrees and they set off downhill towards the Manor. It's quite a way out of town, but nothing compared to the walking they've already done today. They are there before they know it.

'Coffee? Water? Actually are you even allowed coffee?' Mel shouts across the vast kitchen.

'Since it's technically a new week now, I'm entitled to another real drink. I'll have a glass of white please, if you've got one.'

'Excellent idea, I'm not sure if I believe all this nonsense about not drinking when you're pregnant anyway. All things in moderation and the little tyke'll have to get used to it eventually,' Mel says, filling two ornately cut wine glasses from a very dusty bottle. 'May as well give her the good stuff.'

'Her?'

'Yes. I think you've got a girl in there. I say think, more know. It's a girl, take my word for it dearie.'

'Did the dogs tell you?' Polly laughs, taking a modest sip of her wine. It is exquisite, like nothing she has ever tasted before. Polly has never believed the myths associated with expensive vintage wine, and has argued at length with Patrick's father on this very subject. It is galling to have to admit he may actually be right.

'Dogs, no, not them,' Mel chuckles, as Cronus appears through an enormous flap in the kitchen door. 'She told me herself.'

'But she's little more than a bundle of nerve endings at the moment,' Polly says. 'She can't. Even if such a thing were possible. Which, let me be clear, it isn't.'

'Her potential exists though, in the air, in the trees, in the ground, in the very bones of the earth. The spirit that has been marked out to inhabit her is female, and wishes to remain so. She will be born a girl – unless something goes dreadfully wrong. Which it won't.'

'And what if something does? Say I have a miscarriage? Or a still-birth?'

'Well, then the spirit moves on, takes another, she might end up in a boy, she won't like it but she'll work through it. She won't die though, not unless...'

'Unless what?'

'I don't want to think about it, and I don't think you really want to know Polly.' Cronus has laid his enormous head in Mel's lap and she is gently tickling him between the eyes. 'It won't happen anyway, this baby is a blessing, whatever the circumstances of her conception. In doing a bad thing, your chap has created a good thing. Balance.'

'You still think he tricked me?'

'Have you asked him?'

'No! I trust Patrick, he wouldn't do that.'

'It's never the ones you think it'll be, you ask Lynn.'

'Why is everybody so obsessed with fucking Lynn?' Polly bursts.

'Why, who else is?' Mel asks, moving round the table to sit closer to Polly.

'Patrick won't stop trying to find out what happened to Graham, where he is. It's like he's trying to impress Lynn.'

'Like?' Mel's leg pushes up against Polly's.

'No, not like, he is.' Polly is thrown. Maybe Patrick does want Lynn. After all, Lynn is local. A proper ticket to Dourstone respectability: marry your way in. 'Although, it isn't like Lynn would be pleased to see the bastard back here again. This obsession isn't helping anyone, I don't know what's got into him.'

'Maybe the baby's scared him off?' Mel suggests. 'He wouldn't be the first to freak out and run away in the face of impending responsibility.'

'Run away?' Polly screws her face up. 'First you say he's tricking me into having a baby, then you say he's scared of that very thing and going to leave me. Which is it?'

'I never said any of it had to make sense.' Mel laughs. 'Men rarely do. He doesn't know what he wants, he thought he did, but now he's not sure and even he doesn't know what he's thinking.'

'So what can I do about it?'

'Same as women have done throughout the ages girl, get your head down, stop worrying about it and get on with your life. He'll make a decision sooner or later. Nothing you can do at this stage will make any difference.'

'How so?'

'Well, you try and be extra nice to him say, and he doesn't notice, then you'll end up resenting him and pushing him away. Or you try and have it out with him, stir it all up a bit, have the big argument, call him a spineless eel, all that, and he still leaves. There's no guaranteed way of getting the outcome you want, so balls to it I say. Either heave him out, or wait to see what he does. Those are your choices.'

'Bit bleak.'

'Very bleak, but trust me, I've been around the block a few times, I know of what I speak. Intervention makes things worse. He'll work it out before baby comes along – that's your priority. Don't you worry about anything, you're a Dourstone lady now, we'll help you no matter what.'

'No matter what?' Polly doesn't want to think about what no matter what entails.

'No matter what. Now come on, let's go in the drawing room, there's a fire in the grate.'

There was, further instilling Polly's belief that Lady Melissa Dewer has staff. Good staff to have kept a fire burning this long into a late spring night. They sit together on a large sofa, warming their bones from the sudden cold.

'You can stay over if you want,' Mel says, putting an arm around her. 'It's too late to be walking back up that hill.'

Polly makes vague noises of protest, but gives in. It makes sense.

'Do you want to phone your fella?'

Polly reaches for her phone, but it is in her bag, in the kitchen, and her head is heavy now. Nevertheless, she makes the effort. He may be an arse, but he'll worry himself to death if she isn't home. She staggers off to the kitchen and finds all evidence of her and Mel's recent occupation have vanished. Apart from her bag, neatly hung on the back of a chair.

She pulls her phone from the bag, only to find it dead, battery completely drained.

'Fuck it, let him sweat for the night. I'll call him in the morning,' she mutters to herself before going back to the sofa. Lying in Mel's arms she drifts off to a more peaceful sleep than she has had since she first realised she was pregnant. The warm embrace of her friend becomes all enveloping, and she finds she cannot see, or move. She struggles against it, and her bonds begin to wriggle, holding her tighter, there are more limbs than can possibly belong to one person. She pulls her head free from inside the cocoon that holds her, only to find she is being held inside a horse's carcass. It's entrails wrap around her, holding her tight inside. She screams for help, but quickly realises she is alone on a dark moor as the sun begins to kiss the horizon. She has been inside this rotting horse-flesh all night.

A hare hops up, brushing her face with its nose and speaks in Lady Melissa's voice. 'Don't struggle, it'll let go if you accept it.' Then it nuzzles her face and hops away. Polly slows her breathing, accepting the warmth of the dead animal that has almost certainly saved her from dying of exposure while trying to ignore its peculiar musk. The guts begin to recede and she pulls an arm free, then her torso, and finally her legs. She falls back onto scrubby grass, bloodied and aching, but alive. The hare hops back. 'Good, you're free, now come, follow me.'

Polly is surprised to find herself a hare as she hops away over the tors with the Melissa hare; then disappointed to find herself awake on the human Melissa's sofa. It is still dark outside, she huddles in closer to Mel's embrace and sinks away to lighter dreams.

'I don't think Clive is coming back,' Susan slurs as she pours out the last of the good whisky. 'Just me and a fucking house full of fucking babies.' She bangs her head on the table, threatening to wake those babies up.

'Not so bad,' Patrick says. 'Get the bed to yourself, nobody snoring and poking you in the eye all night.'

'Clive doesn't do that.' Susan grins. 'He's a perfect angel, sleeps silently on his side of the bed. I, apparently, am the problem.'

'Problem?' Patrick asks. 'Have you two got problems?'

'Not a big one, no, not a big one. I'm just way too much fun for him.' She laughs. 'We've got a plan to make it work though.'

'Really, what kind of plan is that?'

'Well, every now and then...' Susan takes a deep breath and a mouthful of whisky before continuing '...he's going to go out for the night and not come back.'

'And? I thought that's what you're upset about?'

'It depends on how you feel about the other half of the plan,' she says, staring him in the eye and placing a hand on his leg.

'Plan?' Patrick has a bad feeling about this.

'We have different sex drives. He's happy just being a dad now, can't keep up with my needs. So are you in? Can you fulfil my needs?'

'Do you mean?' Patrick can't quite bring himself to say it.

'Sex Patrick, yes, lots of it please. You can tell Polly, not tell Polly, whatever you want to do, all the same by me, but it's on the table – literally if you want.' She waves her arm over the dining table. 'Purely a business arrangement you understand, I love Clive, don't want anybody else. He understands, it's just sex I'm offering, no strings, no problems.'

Patrick is speechless. At no point in his life have women thrown themselves at him, he had to work hard to get Polly. This sudden promotion to sex-symbol is difficult to process.

'Well?' She crosses her arms and taps her foot – hardly seductive.

'It's not that I don't like you, not that I don't think you're attractive, it's just that...'

'Fine, you're not interested, that's okay. I thought you might be, another drink?' She smiles, straightens up in her chair and slides another bottle out of the sideboard.

'No, I can't, Polly will be home by now, she'll probably be wondering where I've got to.' Patrick could honestly do with a drink, but would like to be somewhere else now.

He sprints from the house and up the road to his and Polly's tumbledown cottage where he tip-toes inside, pours himself a stiff drink and takes it out to the garden. He doesn't want to wake Polly, she will ask him why he is so flustered and he really doesn't want to talk about this with her, or anyone, ever.

He stands in the shadow of the shed door, breathing heavily from his run up the hill, drinks his rum, much quicker than intended, and looks at the stars. It looks late, it is late, he confirms with a glance at his watch. Is he an idiot for turning down no-holds-barred, no-strings-attached sex with a gorgeous woman? He's kind of old-fashioned really, it genuinely has never occurred to him to have sex with anyone other than Polly since they met. He loves her. But he is a man, and feels he may have let the side down by once again not indulging in what sounded like the beginning of a letter from the pile of stiff old damp magazines he found in his father's garage.

Once he has calmed down he knows he did the right thing. Fenrir lopes out to watch him, head tilted to one side.

'I didn't do it you stupid dog,' he says, ruffling the fur on top of his head as he ushers him back into the house. He leaves the dog munching on a biscuit in the kitchen and tip-toes up the stairs to bed. The top step gives its signature tell-tale creak and he freezes where he stands. There is no angry moaning, he is safe. He carefully turns the handle and sneaks into the bedroom where he discovers he didn't need to tip-toe. Polly is not here. He turns the light on, throws his shoes down on the floor and screams.

12

Then...

That first Wisthound Night I left the party at the Manor, my thick coat and scarf giving small comfort as I set out into the freezing dark. I had no idea where I was heading, but seeing the fire still burning on the heights opposite, I resolved to head through the hollow where Dourstone nestled in night-time mists and return there. Maybe its horror would be reduced? Perhaps the man would be there, laughing at having fooled me with a pig's heart thrown to the dogs. But those screams had sounded so real, so terrified.

Despite the snow and cold, the square had refilled with revellers determined to make it through to sunrise falling in and out of taverns. A lone fiddler played reels to keep the night going and even Elias' hated priest was out, preaching abstinence and shaking his head at the wickedness all about – did he guess at just how wicked it was? Or did he already know? I rested there a while, smoking on my pipe and watching the merry-making. It calmed me to see some normality. How different it was from our macabre journey earlier, with streets empty and silent.

Eventually I steeled my heart, thanked the farmhand who shared his brandy and began my walk up the hill. The fire at the top made it appear a volcano, and my visit to Vesuvius on a tour of Europe a few years ago was recalled to my mind. Sparks leaped into the night, accompanied by an uproarious sound. I thought it to be the endless screaming of the poor man we condemned, but as I reached the top, it was revealed to be laughter, merriment. The youth of the town had gathered at the fire, there was warmth, they had brought strong drink and were playing dangerous games leaping across the flames from a makeshift scaffold. I could see no sign of my victim upon the altarstone, though the red stains sparkled in firelight, fresher than before.

It was there that I met Thomas Sumner, sitting upon a straw bale. He offered me cider, and I accepted. Like calls to like, if you know what I mean, and I had an inkling we shared a secret. His down to earth chatter was calming, after the night's ordeal, and we whiled away the hours towards daylight speaking of trivialities. His strong hands would stray to my own from time to time, leaving me little doubt as to his inclinations. I dared to speak of what had occurred that night, and he put his fingers to my lips, shushing me.

'We don't speak of it to outsiders,' he said.

'But, I am...' I could not find the right words. 'Not... I was involved, I am... part of the Lord Elias'...'

'I know full well what part you play,' Thomas said, staring into my eyes. 'A precarious one my friend. Be careful of the Dewers, they keep us safe. This...' He pointed to the altar stone hammering home his point. 'Keeps us safe. The Lord protects us all.' I had a feeling he did not mean the Lord God Almighty.

'So we are safe.' I nodded.

'We.' He indicated himself and the other assorted locals. 'We are safe. We are Dourstone. You, you're just a blowin, down from London. You may find you fall from grace.'

How right he turned out to be, if only I had listened.

'Perhaps.' I winked. 'Perhaps I am more a part of this place than you suspect.'

'I was behind you as you spewed all over your mask.' He laughed, clapping me on the shoulders. 'I've been part of this place, it's rituals, since I was born, and I've never lost my guts once.'

'Why didn't you come back to the Manor?' I asked, thinking myself the only member of the party to have left.

'I did, but not for long,' he explained. 'I've been coming to this fire my whole life on the Wisthound Weekend, I wasn't about to stop when I was elevated to bearer. No, I'm glad of the honour my Lord and Lady have given me, but here's my place. Besides, I prefer a jug of cider to the fancy wines his lordship serves.'

I nodded in agreement, he was quite right. This fire, with its unruly wild-eyed, drunken youths dancing across flames to some imagined orchestra, had a magic all its own.

Now…

June brings on a mighty heatwave the like of which has not been seen in the damp, misty wasteland of Devon since the British began complaining about weather. Polly starts to feel the child complain as the heat becomes unbearable. The extra weight is becoming a real problem and slowing down would be the sensible option. Fenrir has taken it, and spends his days lying in the pond with his legs in the air, when he isn't dashing back into the house to shake pond all over the walls.

But that would mean giving in to Patrick. He's become an incessant nag when he's around. Polly doesn't know what he's getting up to, but he's been out a lot. Mel's advice to not push it is hard to stick to, but she's trying. He's out again now. He was football training all Saturday, after a full week at work, then out with the team after. And he's got the nerve to leave on some secret errand as soon as the last mouthful of his bacon sandwich hit the bottom of his stomach.

Polly is increasingly starting to plan for a life without him. Well, not really plan, it's more idle day-dreaming. She is fairly sure if it came to the crunch she would fall apart, no plan, no idea. But the inkling of an idea is taking form in her mind. Before this she had never even considered the possibility of a life without him.

'So?' A voice on a phone.
'So I think he's on to it.'
'And where is he now?'
'He's here, in the library, asking for the newspaper archives.'
'Don't let him leave.'
The phone goes dead.
'Can I change the films over myself please?' Patrick asks from the other side of the room next to the ancient, clunking, orange microfilm reader.
'Of course, they're just in the case behind, chronological order, as long as they've been put back right,' Edwina answers, in her role of duty librarian.

Patrick was surprised to discover Dourstone still had a library until he found out it had been saved from government cuts by WI volunteers and a community whip-round. The building itself is a cluster of temporary structures jury-rigged together: prefab concrete and wooden panels propped up on piles to keep out the damp, with connecting passages fashioned from whatever lay to hand, plywood, MDF, tar and wrinkly tin all mingling together in an orgy of reclaimed materials. Inside, the dark wood bookcases and dewey-decimal file card system hark back to the glory days of the library service. Patrick breathes in the past, remembering his childhood of a million book fairs at similar institutions, left to the tender care of some lackey while his mother networked.

There is nothing in the archives about Graham's disappearance since there is nothing remarkable about it and it wasn't that long ago. He wouldn't have given it a second thought if it weren't for that foot, Father Hearne's insinuations and Lynn's insistence that all is not as it seems. As it is, it is all he can think about.

A bit of idle web-searching furnished him with a clue. Since it happened on Wish Weekend, and Father Hearne hinted at some kind of connection, Patrick started cross-referencing news stories from past Wish Weekends, checking for strange behaviour. After all, it came from an ancient dark tradition, and maybe that joke about killing Graham for saying village had a kernel of truth.

Things connected. There were other, real, unexplained disappearances that coincided with the festivities. The local paper was only online so far back, and Patrick was about to give up when Lynn reminded him of the microfilm archive at the library as he was changing the oil on her car – watched the whole time by an enormous pair of panting grey dogs.

He knows he should be at home, tending to his pregnant girlfriend, but there has been such an atmosphere recently. She is not due for ages yet and he has promised himself he will pull it together before the baby comes. They will be okay. He doesn't know if she knows about that night with Susan, what she knows, what Susan may have said, what Clive may have said. Polly's absence that night has hurt him as well. As if she doesn't need him, her and the baby, cutting themselves off and leaving him to fend for himself in answer for crimes left unsaid.

The unspoken pressure is no good for either of them and so he has come to the library for the microfilms nobody felt worth scanning to digital. He can see why, it is mostly farming news and craft show results. But it is paying off, there's something going on here.

As he scrolls down to another December and another missing person, a familiar surname catches his eye, Hooper, the same as Dan's. Could they be related? It's only from the '80s, Dan might remember that. This is a genuine lead. Patrick grabs his phone and fires off a text.

You got time for a quick word? Need your advice on something.

That seems vague enough.

Sure, meet you in the pub about six?

Patrick checks the time, almost five. No point going home, Polly will only nag him about being out all day and then leaving again. He's pretty confident he can still play the 'you stayed out all night without telling me where you were' card though. Morally he is in the right – unless she does have a half-truth picture of his night with Susan. He can't believe she would get herself pregnant just to trap him and then do everything in her power to piss him off so much he leaves.

He takes a picture of the article on the reader's screen then jumps as a wet slobbering face jams itself between his legs.

'Find what you want then?' Lady Melissa herself has taken over library duty. The best thing about it being run by volunteers for no salary is that they are happy to open on Sundays. The worst thing is that you can't complain about them, even if they let their stinking old dogs sniff your crotch.

'I think so,' Patrick replies, hastily turning off the microfilm reader. 'I'll get out of your way, let you lock up.'

'That's fine, I've got a bit more to do in here anyway,' she says, clicking her fingers at the malamute, who takes a long while before raising his head and sauntering back to her side as if he was going to do that all along. 'Any help you need, just let me know. Local history is my speciality, seeing as I am very nearly local history.'

'Thanks, I'm sure I'll need to pick your brain at some point.' Patrick smiles, keeping as much distance between the dog and himself as he can.

'That you will,' she grins, watching him all the way out of the door.

Once he has left she flicks the reader back to life and has a glance at the pages Patrick has left onscreen. She nods to herself, and smiles, before removing the film to put it back with its brothers and sisters. Cronus rears up to place his front paws on the window sill, then gives a strangled howl to tell his mistress Patrick has just gone through the door of the Drop of Dew.

Patrick sits in the beer garden drinking a glass of elderflower lemonade filled with ice. Cigarette smoke wafts from the next table, and while Patrick wants to complain, he remembers being told, 'you non-smoking bastards wanted the inside so much, you can fucking have it mate. This bit's ours now,' the last time he tried. Looking over at the corrugated plastic and scaffold-pole monstrosity that has been constructed as shelter against the collapsing old cob walls he can't blame them.

'What the fuck is that?' Dan laughs as he strides into the garden carrying two pints of lager. 'Pete the barman told me you were on soft drinks but I thought he was joking. Here, I got you a real one.' He puts the drinks on the brittle, leaf-mould stained table and takes a long swig from one as he sits carefully down. He has seen too many people go straight through these picnic tables to ever trust one completely.

'Thanks,' Patrick says, he doesn't really mean it. He's grown out of the urge to drink competitively but is unable to tell other men he doesn't want to.

'So, what did you want?'

'It's a bit awkward really Dan,' Patrick begins, realising he and Dan barely know each other. 'But I wanted to ask you about Jim Hooper.'

'My dad?' Dan's face changes its jolly Sunday afternoon drink glow for a paler, more serious expression.

'He was your dad? Oh, sorry, but I've been working on a kind of local history project,' Patrick lies, hoping the flimsy cover story he has constructed will hold up. 'His disappearance has come up in one of the threads.'

'Dad didn't disappear,' Dan scoffs. 'He ran off with some tart from up country. Just after I was born, never met him, never want to.'

'So you haven't seen this?' Patrick pushes his phone across, the screen taken up with the newspaper story about his dad and a full page photo of his dour expression.

'No.' His face drops even further at the vision of a father he doesn't remember. 'I haven't seen that. But it was a long time ago, I'll try and ask Mum about it next time I visit.' He looks serious, worried even.

'I don't want to intrude, really,' Patrick says. 'But I feel like there's something going on around here I can't quite put my finger on. I don't know if your dad's part of it or not, but I'd like to know what your mum has to say please?'

'Okay Paddy, we're friends. I don't have no deep, dark family secrets. Mum told me Dad was kind of a dick and couldn't cope. He ran off with the first girl that smiled at him rather than having to live with a screaming baby. I never questioned it.'

'Thanks.'

'But don't hold your breath waiting for answers,' Dan adds. 'Mum's got early onset. She's up at the home already, only 64, it's heartbreaking. Some days she don't even know who I am.' His eyes begin to look watery, Patrick wishes he hadn't started this. There are better ways.

'I'm sorry,' Patrick says. 'Don't feel you have to. I can look into other avenues. I'm probably just being paranoid.'

'Maybe, but I don't mind mate. I'll have a word.'

'Thanks, want another?'

'Go on then, it is the day of rest after all.' Dan looks happier already as he settles himself in for a sunny afternoon's drinking away from his own fatherly responsibilities.

Patrick heads in to the bar to refill their glasses.

Polly sighs, sits down at the table and eats her roast dinner alone. She leaves Patrick's plate in the oven awaiting his return. It tastes dreadful, hot meat and vegetables making her hotter and more angry in this endless heatwave. She knows Patrick loves a proper roast on a Sunday, and this was an attempt to make amends for their near-constant fighting. She can't help niggling at him over the smallest things, whether they matter or not – usually not. She doesn't know if it's hormones or something fundamentally wrong. Lady Mel assures her on their regular walks that Patrick should be bending over backwards to make sure her life is easier, continually emphasising that in her state she can do no wrong. Polly thinks this might be quite an outdated view – hence this backfired peace offering.

She rings his mobile again.

He spots all the unnoticed missed calls as he answers.

'Sorry Pol, I'm at the pub, no signal here.'

'The pub.'

'Yeah, Dan needed to talk some stuff through.' Patrick mouths sorry at Dan for throwing him under the bus.

'Well, your dinner's in the oven. Not Fenrir, yet.'

'Sorry, won't be long, love you...'

Polly hangs up, and throws her phone into Fenrir's padded bed with a primal grunt of frustration.

13

Then...

As the sun rose, we staggered home together and I discovered my hunch about Thomas Sumner was right. Leaning hard upon his strong shoulder, pining for the gaslights of London town, I mentioned some of the clubs I frequent, and somehow, even here, he knew what their names signified. When I stumbled into the ditch next the path, he followed me down where we made the beast together. The illicit, deadly beast that would have both of us hung in polite society; but here, upon the first real morning of winter on a lonely roadside, felt as good and righteous as any other act. We neither of us feared prying eyes or repercussions.

I had missed genuine male company. This was not entirely infidelious to my beloved Lord Elias, who treated me so callously in the face of the night's horror. Manly as he seems, he is, alas, incomplete in certain areas. I do not complain, I am not unsatisfied with our lives, but this. This is different, release, he cannot understand my nature. It could never happen again though (or so I thought) for if the Lord and Lady found out they would deem it the insult to their hospitality that was never intended.

Upon my return I found the Manor still in full swing, the town's women and men of influence in various states of undress and debauchery, now lolling on the furniture as the sun began to peer through the windows. I realised I need not worry about the monogamous nature of my strange new family, both Lord and Lady were engaged in amorous pursuits. I did not tell them of my own dalliance, but resolved not to feel any guilt or to rule out any repeat performance. I went to my bed and dreamed of Thomas.

Now...

'Are you sure you don't want to go home?' Patrick asks.

'Very, I am having a good time,' Polly says. She is sitting in a camping chair, drinking nothing more exciting than fruit juice and has only been up to dance twice. This pregnancy is driving her insane. Patrick's fussing about it is arguably worse than his ever-growing spawn draining her energy and crushing her bladder to the size of an acorn.

'Okay, but let me know when you've had enough yeah?'

What would have been a fête in days gone by has been re-branded a festival. The usual jigs and reels and folk music have been substituted for two stages of bands. This was supposed to ensure seamless changeovers between acts, but, owing to the nature of entertainers, egos are taking over. Acts are setting up on the wrong stage, then having to move to the other – nobody wants to be on the small one – and as a result it is taking twice as long as it should with an awful lot of long, silent, gaps. As usual in Dourstone the whole thing is an excuse to fill the square with drunken revelry. By calling it a festival (or more properly, an arts festival) the locals have realised they can stretch it over four days.

The town has been celebrating its local (they have taken a very wide interpretation of local – much to the chagrin of a few people in town) artists, musicians, actors, and writers since Thursday and shows no sign of flagging this Saturday night. Polly has been fully participating in everything – apart from the drinking – and Patrick has been unrelenting in his criticism: disguised as concern. The heatwave of June has given way to a humid and drizzly July, so the central portion of the square is covered with an improvised marquee: scaffold poles draped in stitched together old tents, anoraks, tarpaulins, and hope. The people are mostly dry, but there are still a few maniacs dancing barefoot out in the rain.

'I'll be fine, go back to your friends,' Polly hisses. She is happy sitting here, listening to a ska band and watching a tent-full of people unused to dancing try to keep their limbs in some kind of order.

Clive spoke to her earlier. He showed her pictures of Patrick, quite clearly and definitively Patrick, leaving Clive and Susan's house at some ungodly time in the morning. The date and time stamps confirm it as the night Polly stayed at Mel's. The night Patrick went home because he was 'tired'. She doesn't quite know how to confront him.

Clive says Susan has form for this sort of behaviour. He has forgiven her more affairs than he can remember, but felt it his duty to tell Polly. He doesn't know whether it was perfectly innocent or not, doesn't care. He loves Susan unconditionally and would rather not know details. His face implied there were definitely details. Polly will not be doing any forgiving, that's for sure, but she needs to get her plan of attack clear. Careful, considered, planned, that's how she works. She'll talk it through with him tomorrow. Not now, they're on a knife-edge as it is and even if it turns out to be nothing, it'll be a massive something. It could break them up, and she is about to be mother to a child she doesn't think she wants. She needs him.

A grizzled form approaches from the swirl of mizzle-drenched dancers outside. Melissa's beaming face comes into focus through rivulets of silver hair, indistinguishable from rain in the streetlights. 'Hey, Polly, join us, I can tell you want to.' She would like to join these barefoot maniacs, but is aware Patrick will freak out if she does.

'I can't, baby.' She points to her bump in explanation.

'Baby will be fine, it'll help the girl. If she's going to live here she'll need to learn to dance, especially in the rain.'

'What the hell, go on then.' Polly kicks her sandals off, hurdles the low wall separating wet road from dry square and lets rip. Dancing brings sweet release and the gentle patter of rain on her face is blissful after months of endless heat.

'Are you coming to my after party?' Mel asks, whirling past Polly as the tempo increases.

'Baby.' Polly shakes her head.

'She's invited too.' Mel caresses the swell of Polly's belly. 'I'd just have her if I could, but I see you're quite attached.'

'Patrick won't like it.'

'He doesn't have to come if he doesn't want to.'

'You know what I mean.'

'I do,' Mel says, 'but I don't care, he can't tell you what to do. You're your own woman, grow a pair of ovaries and get on with it.'

'Polly! Get out of the rain!' Patrick shouts, running from the pub where he has been getting drinks. 'You can't afford to get a cold!'

'It's 23 degrees, I'm dancing, it's perfectly warm. I am not going to catch anything. Stop fussing,' she placates, rubbing his arm.

'But you won't be, it'll get cold. You can't do this in your condition Pol, come inside with me.'

'No. I'm having a good time, stop being an old woman Pat,' she insists, spinning away to rejoin the dance.

'Fuck's sake Pol. I'm just looking out for you, this is my baby too.'

'Don't I know it, I feel like a fucking incubator; just a vessel for your precious bloody heir.'

'You're not an incubator Polly. But you do need to take care of yourself.'

'I do thanks.'

'Are you a doctor?'

'What?'

'Sorry, but I know what's best for you, I've got bits of paper to prove it.'

'Me too, my birth certificate. I'm going to go back to Mel's tonight. We'll talk about this tomorrow.'

'Polly...'

'No, what's best for me tonight is to be somewhere you're not. Without the stress of your mother-henning. I need a good time, I promise not to drink, smoke or shoot up heroin while I'm gone.'

'Please...'

'Tomorrow, go back to your friends. Or go and fuck Susan again. Whatever.' Polly didn't mean to say this. She didn't want to bring it up. Not like this, not yet.

'Fuck Susan? What are you talking about?' Patrick's face turns white.

'I've seen photos Paddy, I don't want to talk about it. Don't want to be near you right now, leave me alone.'

'But Polly, I didn't... we were just talking... it was... complicated. I should have told you, you'll laugh when I do, really you will.'

'I don't think so, fuck off.' Polly spins on the balls of her feet and dances back into the crowd. She is tired, she wants to sit down, but she doesn't want Patrick to see.

Patrick gives up and goes back to the pub. He knows when not to push it and he doesn't much like ska music, his dad does though and all this nostalgia is becoming too much.

'Fuck it, let's get pissed,' he says to Jack at the bar.

'I would,' Jack replies, 'but kids.' He points out of the window at Edwina struggling to control their children.

'Fair enough.'

'Enjoy it while you can chap, not long now.' He slaps him on the back.

'Anyone?' Patrick turns to the others in the pub, hiding from their families, Wendy is there, grinning maniacally through the window where she can see Delia desperate to hand the kid over.

'I would,' she says, 'but I think I'm going to have to take over in a minute, Delia means well, but she's not great at this bit.'

'Which bit?' Patrick asks.

'The tiny baby end, she'll be fucking great once he's big enough to kick a ball around though. I'll send her in, she can have the rest of the night with you lot. You look like you need it.' Wendy grins. 'She's good for that too, sympathetic ear, boring advice. Kid'll be glad of that one day.'

'Thanks Wendy.'

'I've got a pass,' Dan says. 'Kerry's agreed to hold on to the kids all weekend.'

'Lucky dog,' Jack says. 'How did you swing that?'

'She went on a hen weekend to Brighton last month. She owes me. There were some incidents.' Dan's face darkens for a second. 'But it's worked out brilliantly. Five tequilas please barlord!' He pulls out a wad of cash.

'Excellent.' Patrick drains off the pint in his hand, eager to get to the little drinks. He hasn't spoken to Clive about that night. He wanted to forget it, it was embarrassing. He doesn't know how it's got back to Polly, or what he's going to say. He hopes the truth will be believable enough when she calms down.

'Five?' Jack says. 'I told you, kids!'

'One's not going to hurt you big girl,' Dan insists, passing one over.

'He wishes he could drink like a girl,' Delia quips, running in and throwing the baby to Wendy.

'Come on, I'll take you back,' Mel says, taking Polly's arm.

'But the band haven't finished,' Polly replies, determined not to let anybody else tell her what to do.

'It's okay, I'm not him.' Mel takes Polly's other arm, steadying her escape and holding her gaze.

'I know, but you're acting the same, I know what's good for me. I want all of you to stop ordering me around.'

'I'm not ordering you dear. But you're only dancing out of sheer bloody-mindedness now. He's inside, he can't see you. He'll never know that you're tired and just want to go home and lie down.'

Polly does want to go home and lie down, but doesn't want to admit it – not even to Mel.

'What about your after-party?'

'It was only ever going to be me and you,' Mel admits with a laugh. 'The days of my famous Manor parties are long gone. Though I am tempted to resurrect the tradition.'

'How about tonight?'

'How about when this little girl can come in person?' Mel rubs Polly's bump.

Polly knows she's right. But she doesn't want her to be. She can see a new mum across the square, all smiles and happiness, baby wrapped across her chest in a psychedelic sling. She can't understand this, you spend nine months waiting for the bloody thing to get out so you can stop carrying it everywhere, then you strap it straight back on again, like trying to force the pus back inside a popped pimple. Life is not going to be the same, not ever again.

'It's a deal, you're hosting the christening.' Polly hopes by that time she will have had the life-changing thing you're supposed to. That she will love this joy-sucking parasite with all her heart.

'Lose the Christ bit and you're on. Now let's go.'

Polly admits defeat and they sneak out of the square towards the Manor.

'Oh, forgot to ask you,' Patrick slurs. The doors are locked, the curtains are closed, and the bar is lined with hardcore drinkers. Patrick has not been this drunk in a long time. 'Did you speak to your mum?'

'Yeah, I tried, but...' Dan stops to let out an enormous belch. 'She's not well. She's only called me Dan once in the last few weeks.'

'Sorry man, didn't mean to put you on the spot.'

'S'okay, last week she chucked a shoe at me, thought I was my dad,' Dan laughs. 'I tried to get some information out of her, but you know, nothing. She just kept on shouting until the nurses made me leave.'

'Don't worry about it, it doesn't matter anyway,' Patrick says. 'She's at the home on the end of that council estate right?'

'Yeah, it's shit, but it's all we can afford.'

'It's not that bad, a lot of my patients are there, I visit. Don't feel bad.'

'Thanks, whisky?'

'Yes, my turn – barlord, we will have two Laphroaigs please, and make them double.'

'Good choice. How much trouble are you in Patrick?'

'I don't know yet, not exactly. How do you and Kerry manage it? With two kids, still so happy?'

'We're not happy Patrick, nobody is. We just know enough to keep out of each other's way once in a while. Equal work, equal funtime, and know when to keep your mouth shut.'

'Really?'

'I don't know, I don't have the answers, you've had a fight, get used to it mate, you'll have a lot more once that bun's out of the oven. For now, there's nothing you can do about it, so get that down you and let's try and have a good time.'

'Okay, sorry.' Patrick gets the drink inside him and tries to have a good time. He can't stop thinking about Polly though, she is changing. It's as if she resents him for the baby curtailing her life. As if he has forced her to do something they both wanted. 'You know Clive and Susan pretty well right?'

'Yeah,' Dan replies.

'Has she ever... you know... tried anything with you?' Patrick asks.

'Susan? Try anything? You're joking right? What happened?'

'Well, I went back with her for a drink after the bound beating. Me and Polly had fallen out, again, and she... well, she made some suggestions and I left. She said she and Clive had "an arrangement", he was just leaving when I got there.'

'An "arrangement"?' Dan asks. 'What kind of "arrangement"?'

'Well, I could have done anything I liked, apparently, no questions, no strings, no guilt. That's what she said. I didn't know what to do, so I made my apologies and left.'

'Fucking hell mate. You're sure Clive knew?'

'I had no reason to think she'd be lying, he saw me come in with her, didn't question it or anything.'

'I'd have done it, she's hot.' Dan laughs. 'Are you gay or something?'

'No, I love Polly. Won't cheat on her. Never occurred to me to.'

'That's sweet, wish I could say the same. I mean, I love Kerry. But we've been together so very very long, I wouldn't mind a change, if you know what I mean.'

'Yes Dan, I do know what you mean. But you've never had the chance with Susan? You don't know anything about it?'

'No mate, first I've heard of it. Why?'

'Because I've been keeping it secret out of respect for Clive and Susan, but somehow somebody's given Polly photos of me.'

'What? I thought you said you didn't do it?'

'I didn't, I don't know what these photos are, she just said photos. And she thinks I've fucked Susan. Which I haven't. And I don't know who's behind it.'

'Well, it's not me mate, but you should probably talk to Clive. On your own, check he did know. She's fucking clever, fucking devious too, make sure he knows you didn't do nothing. You don't want to get thrown to the wolves.'

Patrick hasn't considered that. He might just be a pawn in some marital game.

'Get this inside you girl.' Lady Melissa appears on the verandah where Polly sits at a much repainted cast-iron table. Even in the moonlight you can see how much work goes into this garden and once again Polly wonders why you never see the staff.

'I'm not drinking, I told you that.'

'This isn't alcohol,' Mel says, putting two glasses on the table. 'Herbs, mostly, good for you, good for baby, good for everyone. Don't touch the one on the left.'

'What's wrong with the one on the left?'

'Nothing at all, except it's mine and it's mostly gin.' Mel smiles, lifting the glass in question to her lips.

'Thanks.' Polly laughs, taking the drink. It tastes warming. 'What am I going to do Mel? How do we fix this?'

'Fix what?' Mel replies.

'My relationship with Patrick obviously, what else would I be talking about?'

'Oh, I don't know. Not sure if it matters.'

'Doesn't matter?' Polly shrieks. 'We're having a baby together. Of course it matters.'

'You don't need a man to have a baby – other than the obvious.'

'I can't bring it up on my own.'

'Don't call her it, she's a person, not a thing.' Melissa sits up a little straighter.

'Fine, I can't bring her up on my own then, does that help?'

'No, but I will. I have considerable resources and I care about you. If it comes to it, and it might, you can come here. We'll help you with the child.' A small group of malamutes appear as if from nowhere thanks to the optical illusion of the ha ha. It is an artificial steep cliff at the end of the garden intended to work as an invisible border and stop livestock walking all over the lawns. Due to the singular nature of the pack it has been used as deep cover to sneak up, leap over the top and sprint towards Melissa before stopping abruptly, pretending not to have noticed her, having a sniff of some bushes, sauntering up to the verandah and finally jostling for prime stroking position. 'What have you buggers been doing? Out hunting Jack Sharpnails again?'

'Jack who?' Polly asks.

'Or whatever you call them these days, little spiky things, curl up when they're scared?'

'Hedgehogs?'

'Yes, them things, Jack Sharpnails, that's what we called them when I was a girl. The dogs are mad for them, never managed to catch one, but never stopped trying. Idiots.'

Cronus pads out through the French doors and lies down at Polly's feet, waving a paw to ensure she rubs his belly while he checks his pack have pulled off their manoeuvres. Polly feels safe with this enormous dog and his pack. She thinks of Fenrir, worried this is like cheating on him. It might be possible to carry on without Patrick, Mel will help, lovely, helpful, supportive Mel. She will always be there for her.

'Shall we go in? I've quite cooled off now.'

Polly nods, the evening has turned cold and the damp sweat in her clothes is threatening to prove Patrick right, despite the warming nature of that delicious drink.

'Where should I sleep?' Polly asks, the day's exertions starting to tell.

'I'm afraid my room's the only one made up in the house. Ridiculous I know, big old place like this and just me rattling around, I should give it to the National Trust. But I don't want to, and I don't need to. You can take my bed, I'll have the sofa.'

'Don't be silly, I don't mind sharing, if it's a big enough bed.'

'It is a very big bed, do you want heads together or top and tail?' Mel grins.

'Your bed, your choice.' Polly laughs.

The bedroom fits with the rest of the house. Vertigo-inducing ceilings frame tall, thin banks of leaded windows looking out over a battlemented porch to the front lawns. Heavy brocade curtains hang opposite a series of portraits: the ancient line of the Dewers, Polly assumes. Pride of place is given to a Victorian gentleman in a top hat, sat atop a hay bale and laughing in what looks to be Dourstone square. It is a beautiful picture of a beautiful man. She can see something of Patrick in him, but then she always sees something of Patrick in everyone.

A second herbal drink has quite cheered Polly up and she all but forgets her worries as she peels off sweaty clothes with no care for propriety.

'Sorry, but it's so hot,' she says, throwing herself down on the four poster bed in just her pants.

'Don't worry about it, I don't stand on ceremony, as long as you don't?' Lady Mel follows suit, pulling off her clothes down to the last stitch. Polly feels a pang of jealousy that Mel's body looks better than hers. She doesn't know how old this intriguing lady is, but in this light, and out of her clothes Polly would put them at the same age, however impossible that sounds. She is glad of the lack of niceties as even her pants are making her too hot. She extricates the suddenly vast expanse of beige underwear from underneath her hated bump and flings it across to join her other clothes on a red velvet-upholstered regency chair.

'Who is that?' Polly asks, pointing to the laughing man in the top hat. 'One of your ancestors?'

'Old Nathaniel? No, no, not family, none of these pictures are family,' Mel says.

'Really?'

'Really, I prefer the rather more scandalous part of the Dewer history, Nathaniel Harker there is a shining example.'

'Who is he then?'

'He was a friend of the illustrious Lord Elias Dewer, came down to see the Oak Apple Day celebrations and didn't leave for years.'

'Any particular reason?'

'Well, the local gossip had it that he and Lord Elias were a little closer than friends, and rumours of sodomy ran through the town. Especially after Nathaniel got caught out with the barrel-maker one night. He left shortly after. Never came back. They say my dear old ancestor was never the same. That losing Nathaniel fair broke his heart.'

'That's sad, different times though. Maybe if Elias lived now they could have been together?' Polly looks into the painted eyes where the sadness behind Nathaniel Harker's laughter hides in thick oil paint. 'Maybe they could have been happy?'

'Maybe they could at that. But not wearing all those bloody layers in this heat.' Mel lies back on the bed, her smooth, elastic face close to Polly's, and laughs. 'It's much too hot for clothes.'

Polly agrees, nodding, 'I feel like a whale already, and there's still ages to go.'

'You look fantastic though, glowing with life, vitality. You will never be more beautiful than you are now,' Melissa tells her, wriggling herself comfortable on cool sheets.

'Don't be ridiculous, I am fat, swollen and awful.'

'You're not, don't let anyone tell you otherwise.'

'Easy for you to say, look at you? What's your secret?'

'I am possessed of certain spirits that keep me this way,' Mel replies, sitting up and taking a drink.

'Is that it then?' Polly says. 'Gin?'

'Not just the gin, it's probably the lighting, it's very forgiving in here.'

'Must be for you to keep saying I look good. If I look so beautiful then why hasn't Patrick so much as touched me since I started to show?' Polly says.

'Because he's an idiot,' Mel counters. 'If that's true, is it true?'

'It is. I think he's scared it'll damage the baby if we do, you know, anything fun.' At least she had been, before Clive showed her that photo.

'A girl shouldn't be denied her rightful pleasure because she's full of baby.'

'It's not just that any more either, I... I saw something today,' Polly states, mind made up to confide her fears. Why shouldn't she tell this woman everything? She has offered her so much, been so kind, she is a true friend. Polly takes another slurp on the herbal drink, it really is comforting.

'What is it?' Mel shifts position, propping her head on her arm.

'Clive showed me a picture. Patrick leaving Susan's house the last time I stayed here. Really late.'

'And what did you think?'

'I don't know.' Polly's head is pleasantly spinning, the warm feeling becoming something other.

'What has he said?'

'I haven't really asked him yet, don't know how to. I wanted to plan it out first, but I just blurted it out and cut him loose. And now I don't know what to think.'

'I think you do. I think you're trying to deny it. Men always think with their dicks; always let you down.' Mel tuts, giving a dark look.

'Patrick doesn't though. He isn't like that. It might be perfectly innocent.' Polly leaps to his defence.

'He's already lied to you.'

'He hasn't lied, he just omitted to mention it.'

'Same thing, if he'd no reason to feel guilty he'd have told you. What else has he "omitted to mention"?'

'Oh Christ Mel, he's a doctor. It might have been work – confidentiality – I never even thought of that!' Polly suddenly has a terrible inkling she may be grasping at the wrong end of the straw.

'Bullshit girl, this is not work.' Mel reaches across to touch Polly's arm. 'Susan's well known for this kind of thing. That's why Clive moved her back here, to get away from all the men she'd had affairs with. New start, fix their marriage in a new place. Fewer problems, fewer ghosts. It looks like she's making new ones, and you're the collateral damage. Sorry.'

'I don't believe it, Patrick isn't like that, but... but why wouldn't he tell me?'

Mel looks deep in her eyes without saying a word.

Polly starts to cry.

'Oh god he is... isn't he?' Polly sniffs. 'I'm this big fat baby-making machine he can't bear to touch so he's got himself something prettier to play with.'

'I'd like to say no, but...' Mel says, opening her arms. Polly accepts the hug and they cling to each other in the heat of the night, sweat and tears mingling together in the crook of Mel's neck.

'Thank you,' Polly whispers as her tears start to subside. 'You're a good friend.'

'Well, I've been around a while, I know how these things work.' Mel smiles, stroking a finger down the length of Polly's spine that sends a warm shiver through her and the baby.

'How old are you anyway? If it's not too personal a question,' Polly says.

'That is pretty personal,' Mel says, as her finger continues to work its magic up and down her back. 'A lady never tells her age, you'll learn that once you turn thirty. As for me I'm old enough to know what I'm doing.'

'And what exactly are you doing?' Polly says, very aware she is enmeshed with this woman in a hot, naked, sweaty mess. The glorious feeling of smooth, soft skin against her own brings an unexpected arousal.

'I think you know. There's a long queer streak in my family and I'm going to help you get what you need.' Before Polly has time to ask what she means Mel kisses her on the mouth, removing any misunderstanding.

Polly cannot believe what she is doing. She has never done anything like this. Patrick has been her one and only lover. She isn't sure if she is doing this in revenge, from idle curiosity or just to feel sexy again; whichever it is, it feels right. Her night is spent rapt in previously unknown pleasures until she passes out in their mingled sweat. Consumed, happy and Patrick quite forgotten.

The night is dark, rain hammers across empty moorland. Lightning illuminates the valley where Dourstone should be, but Polly sees only a handful of scattered huts by the river. It is not a night to be abroad, but somebody is. A dark hooded figure on horseback crests a tor, surrounded by a steaming mass of black hounds, their eyes glowing a ghostly blue. His black stallion rears up with a whinny as another flash of lightning silhouettes them against the sky.

Polly realises she has not moved in space, she is atop the opposite hill, where the Manor should be, but isn't. The pack stream downhill towards the settlement, raising such an unholy din the inhabitants are roused. There is nothing they can do to stop the hounds destroying their crops and slaughtering the livestock penned outside their homes. But still they try to call them off.

The figure on the horse throws back its head and laughs. A deep, terrifying laugh that chills Polly to the bone. His face is familiar – illuminated by a flame he has conjured from nowhere – but she cannot place where she knows it from. He kindles a fire from one of the larger huts, despite the driving rain. The settlers are on their knees, begging with their would-be destroyer for mercy. He responds by spreading the fire further and sending the dogs to take care of the remaining food. A light appears next to Polly, and coalesces into human form. Shining blue and phasing in and out of real-time it seems unstable, but very much there. It moves unseen, in the shadows of bushes and homes, following the dogs.

The settlers continue to wallow in the mud, pulling at the rider's robes, sure now that all is lost. Until the ethereal figure returns, not hidden this time, but determined. It sweeps across to the settlers, pushing them back from the horseman. The rider lunges towards the newcomer, only to find his way blocked by the pack, returned from pillaging and stood in orderly ranks between dark rider and shining light. There is an altercation, the wording of which Polly cannot make out from her vantage point. Then the dark stranger leaves.

Dogs, settlers and glowing spirit watch his departure before returning to the shelter of the huts. Those who have lost theirs are taken in by their neighbours. There is a discussion, voices are raised in thanks, and eventually a woman steps forth. The light of their saviour passes into her.

She leaves the people and makes her way towards the hilltop where Polly still stands, a purposeful look on her face as the huge black dogs stream behind.

Muffled screaming wakes Polly. She looks to see Mel's coffin-nail ring in her hand. She must have pulled it off in her sleep. Next to her is a frightened old woman – hair splayed around wrinkled folds of leathery flesh, unrecognisable from the devilish beauty she fell asleep with – clawing at the sheets as if trying to dig her way through the bed to freedom.

'Help me, let me go, please!' Mel screams in a voice Polly has never heard before, her face the face of a terrified child, usual flashing silver eyes now dulled to a matte grey. 'No more, I don't like it, make her go, make it go away!'

Polly remembers Mel telling her about the fits the ring was given her to cure. She had thought it an old wives tale, some kind of psychosomatic thing, but maybe there's something in it. She grabs her by the wrist, trying to get to her ring finger. Mel starts to slap at her, punch her, kicking against her legs. Polly is scared for the baby, what if Mel kicks that? She doubles down, grabbing her and pulling her close enough to render the kicking impotent.

'NO! NO! PLEASE! DON'T LET HER TAKE ME AGAIN!' Mel screams, Polly rolls her over, holds her arms down and sits across her liver-spotted chest. With a final burst of extra strength she forces ring back onto finger. As it slots into place behind the knuckle Mel's body gives a final electric jerk. She calms down and that familiar silver glint returns to her eyes.

'Thank you dear,' she says, the years vanishing from her body and returning to her wry expression as Polly looks on. She puts it down to being half-asleep, then falls back into bed, and tries to deal with the other half. Unfortunately the third person in the bed has decided to start kicking.

14

Then…

The next spring we made plans, Elias was concerned the encroaching railways and romance of the moors were attracting too many outsiders, they would ask questions when they saw the red altar stone. They would not understand the rituals. I admit, I still did not, though the Dewers had taken time over the winter to explain. I'm afraid their tall tales of warring earth spirits still sound like madness, though they, and the people of Dourstone, are quite convinced.

From what I can tell, what happened to that man on Wisthound night was no worse than the hanging the fellow deserved. Victims are not chosen by random chance, the ceremonies form a kind of justice. They pick the worst, the thieves, the murderers, the rapists, the faithless husbands. The altar stone's dark hue is begat from the blood of centuries of Dourstone men, almost always men – in answer to the suffering of certain local women at the hands of witchfinders. Both Lord and Lady took a great deal of time explaining the injustice the fairer sex has endured. That the ancient sport of witch-hunting went back centuries further than Matthew Hopkins' Army's attempt to industrialise the process; how they are taking great pains to remove this institutional prejudice here. The feminine rule of the town may not be explicitly known, but it is implicitly understood. I have never known a place so respectful of its womenfolk and where so many hold local office. Father would hate it.

Elias, in response to the growing problem of outsiders, such as myself, intruding into Dourstone business, resolved to raise a stone circle, like the many others that litter the high moors, and encircle the place of the altar stone. He would remove the stone itself – years of blood now unmistakeable despite my best attempts to convince myself it be just mud – and place it inside a cart, which could return it to the top of the hill when needed.

The day we raised the circle the priest brought his photographic apparatus along, and made a picture of myself with Lord and Lady Dewer stood next to the altar stone. This strengthened my Lord's resolve to hide its true purpose. He could not have this image distributed, there would be talk, there would be investigations. He took it away, ensuring no copies could be made and hid it deep within the Manor, further souring relations between him and the priest. I would that I had that image now.

Now...

'I think you'll be fine, it's just indigestion,' Patrick says, getting up from a high-backed chair with special plastic foot extensions.

'Well, if you say so, but I still think it's bowel cancer,' the old man he has been examining insists from what he has decided is his death bed: a high, narrow single, that could easily prove to be true if he were to roll out in the night, covered with an old fashioned purple crocheted blanket.

'I've got your blood, I'll let you know when I get the results back, but like I say, have a couple of Rennies and see how you go.'

The man grumbles his assent as Patrick leaves.

'Thank you for coming out doctor,' says the carer once they are in the corridor, lined with identical white safety-glass-windowed and pass-code-security-locked doors. Doors with small, smudged from overuse, whiteboards bearing the occupant's name. 'We can't be too careful these days, all you get on the news is neglect from care homes. Sorry to waste your time.'

'That's fine,' Patrick answers. 'Anybody else need anything while I'm here?'

'No, you can get on, thanks Doc.' She smiles and tips him a wink as they head for the main door. The reception area has the air of a mid-twentieth century dentist's waiting room, itchy brown chairs surround a coffee table covered in out of date lifestyle magazines where uneasy relatives can sit and wait for someone to accompany them through the labyrinth. Staff sit in a walled-off space next to the dark mahogany doors, hidden behind more security glass with an intercom system for communication.

There is a communal dayroom at the end of the corridor but it too has a security lock, and you need to be shown in. Patrick would rather not, it is difficult to tell whether the residents are still alive once they've been parked in front of the blaring television.

Suddenly there is a moan and a crashing noise from down the hall. 'Sorry, I've got to get this, see yourself out?'

'No problem, see you again.'

As he heads towards the exit, Patrick notices a familiar name on a self-closing door that hasn't quite finished closing. Hooper, it's Dan's mother. It wouldn't hurt to nip in and have a quiet word would it? Dan wouldn't mind. Dan wouldn't know. He could just go in there, ask a few questions, see what she has to say and if she isn't coherent it won't matter. He jams his foot in the gap before it clicks shut.

'Hello, I'm Doctor Sumner, just wanted to pop in and check you're okay.' He enters a room identical to the previous one, aside from different faces peering out from familiar frames. He recognises Dan, Kerry, Katie and her still-a-baby-in-this-picture brother Alfie grinning from a Poundland photoframe in pride of place next to the bed.

'Yes, hello Doctor, I'm quite well thank you.'

'Good, I have a few questions if you don't mind answering them – to do with another patient. Obviously, I don't mind if you can't.'

'No, that's fine. I don't mind.'

'I gather your husband disappeared, a long time ago. Can you remember where he went.'

'What husband? Are you flirting with me?'

'No Mrs Hooper, I'm not, sorry.'

'Well good, you're too old for me anyway, my father would have you run out of town. And I'm not Mrs Hooper, she lives on the next farm up, got all them kids. Nasty old bag.'

'Sorry, names aren't important, can we get back to the subject, I realise this is difficult for you...' Patrick continues, he's dealt with enough alzheimers patients before to know not to upset them with where and when they really are. She goes quiet, her eyes glaze over as she gazes through the window – with its uninspiring view of the car park. If she were to stand up she would just about be able to see over the low wall to make out some trees in the distance. Patrick waits for her to come back, prepared for disappointment.

'It wasn't my idea,' she blurts out, returning to lucidity. 'They said it was for the best. Needed one for the dogs, Wish Weekend. There has to be blood see, otherwise it all ends.'

'What wasn't your idea?'

'Told my boy he'd left, ran away with another woman.'

'I know that, but why the investigation? The missing person's report?'

'I didn't know. They told me the truth later, it was all for the best, but I didn't know at first, got sent this letter.' She reaches into a draw and pulls out a damp, yellowing piece of paper. 'Kept it for proof. In case I needed it.'

She hands it to Patrick who reads a letter signed by her husband that claims he had been living in Doncaster and was not coming back.

'Is this real?' he asks.

'No, they wrote it for me, before they told me the truth. Better that way. I showed the police, ended the investigation. All better. He wasn't a good man, cheated on me, with my friends. They told me, showed me photos, told me things they couldn't have known otherwise. He denied everything, said they were out to get him. Paranoid. Lady Melissa never lied to us. We keep the secrets.'

'What secrets?'

'We keep the secrets.' She begins to rock in her chair, muttering under her breath.

'What secrets Mrs Hooper? Please, who keeps them?'

'Dourstone, proper Dourstone Nymet, the people who love this place – the women's institute, the council, the big farmers. We look after it, feed the dogs. If we don't feed the dogs everything ends you see. We keep the secrets, so everybody lives. We keep the secrets. We keep the secrets.'

'Thank you, I'll leave you in peace now.'

'They killed him, left him to die, killed him, all the same, fed the dogs. Told me I was better off without him, they were right, didn't see it at first, but they were right. Better off without him. Saved the town, kept the secrets. We keep the secrets. We keep the secrets.'

Patrick slips out of the room with a brief goodbye. As he walks to his car he hears her screaming 'WE KEEP THE SECRETS! WE KEEP THE SECRETS!' and the clattering of carers rushing in.

He's tried to put the Graham thing behind him, but since he and Polly had that big bust up last month it's been a useful distraction. August has been no better. Polly seems to have put an invisible barrier between them, he feels there is some big important thing she isn't telling him. He can't tell her about his investigations, the smallest thing sets her against him now. It feels as if the weight of their own secrets may come crashing down to destroy them.

When Polly finally came home the day after the festival they sat down for an important conversation. He explained himself, told her everything, expected her to laugh at Clive and Susan's weird, swinging relationship. She would have laughed about it in London.

She did not laugh here. She told him it was Clive who showed her the photos, that he was angry, sad and definitely not okay with it.

Patrick told her he had done nothing, that he never would. He told her how difficult it was to say no to Susan insisting on his coming in for a drink, how he didn't want to offend their new friends by refusing, how she kept on pouring more drinks and how he finally figured out how to say no once she suggested something he really wasn't comfortable with. If he hadn't been there, he wouldn't believe what he told her. He sounds guilty, it feels like a lie, especially when he tries to justify his not telling Polly earlier. Claiming he didn't want to expose Susan and Clive to ridicule, that he respected their privacy and didn't want to cause a scandal.

It sounds as if he cares more about these people he barely knows than the mother of his unborn child. Loyalty is an important thing to both of them, and he is not displaying his best side. He knows now he should have told her straight away, but that's not a lot of help at this point.

Since that one conversation the subject of their relationship is being roundly ignored. Every time he decides to try and have the big talk, she disappears out to a WI meeting, or Lady Melissa turns up so they can't talk. It is becoming impossible, and this new information that the WI are part of whatever is going on doesn't help.

As he reaches the car, a familiar sit-up-and-beg bike rolls into the car park.

'Ah, Patrick! How are things? Are you keeping well?' Father Hearne trundles to a halt, just before his bike crunches into the bumper of Patrick's Landrover. 'Not cycling today?'

'No, working, need the doctor's bag,' Patrick explains, opening the boot to stow said item away.

'You could fit that in a basket you know, better for you, better for the planet. You're only a few minutes ride from here aren't you?'

Patrick has to admit the priest has a point, but doesn't want to get into the ins and outs of riding up and down these hills for home visits in summer heat. He isn't sure his patients would take him quite as seriously in full Lycra.

'How about you father, what are you up to?'

'Visiting the sick, elderly and dying. It's quite a big part of the job these days.' His face takes on a serious hue as he leans on his handlebars to light his pipe.

'Listen, you warned me about this place, people vanishing. What do you know about the WI?'

'Women's Institute? It's all chutney and cherubs as far as I know, I try to keep them very much at arm's length.'

'Nothing sinister then?' Patrick presses.

'Well, Lady Melissa is fairly sinister all by herself, and she chairs it. They run the town, pretty much. Without them nothing would get done.' Father Hearne muses, as he puffs his pipe to a fierce red glow. 'They've got the organisation, the skills, they could do it, if there is an it to be doing.'

'You said it was a conspiracy!' Patrick splutters.

'Well, I was just thinking out loud you know, it's allowed.'

'Okay, okay. I think I'm starting to over think this.' Patrick rubs his head.

'I am as worried as anyone about Graham's whereabouts,' the priest says. 'But you need to worry about yourself.' He puts his hand on Patrick's shoulder. 'Get some rest, look after that lovely not-wife of yours.'

'Yeah, maybe I will, good thinking.' Patrick gets into the car and drives off with a friendly wave. He's not sure what to think any more.

15

Then...

Relations between the Dewers and me cooled shortly after we moved the stone and raised the circle. I believe they had somehow discovered my ongoing relationship with Thomas Sumner. The Lord and Lady frequented my bed still, but our lovemaking became more perfunctory, functional. I began to feel I was now merely a means to an end. Given the debauched parties I had been witness to I had no idea it would be an issue. I realise now that there is a line, a line between loving relationship and mere sexual pleasure.

A line I crossed.

I must confess I became ever more enamoured of Thomas, spending as much time as I could in his embrace. I did not love Elias and Sophia any less for that; had I been brave enough to make us into a foursome I believe all would have been well. But Thomas has a wife, a reputation, and a public profile in the town. For all the secrets this place harbours, it is no more tolerant of sodomites than anywhere else. His business would collapse, and the two of us would not survive. I could not betray him. For all the Dewers' depravities, they maintain a perfect public appearance. They have respect, and none suspect the sapphic nature of their relationship.

My second Wish Weekend in Dourstone brought two counts of great joy for Lord Elias. Firstly it became known through the town that the priest was conducting unholy relations with his choirboys, ensuring an easy choice for the dogs' meal that year. Secondly, he discovered he was carrying my child. We began preparations for the ongoing story. Sophia had padding made up in various stages, and cover stories were concocted for the inevitable absence from public life Lord Elias would have to endure. Our deceptions would become ever more difficult to uphold.

That weekend my previous reservations were quite quieted, my constitution stronger than before. I joined in with gusto, securing the hated priest hidden inside the stick man's costume atop the cart, pushing it to the rise of the hill, then leaving it for the dogs – never entertaining for a moment that I would find myself in his position. I tried, and failed, to recognise Thomas under his dark velvet robes and tinner's mask as we processed, and could not find him at the Manor reception. I suspected he had not bothered to complete the return journey. As soon as I deemed it polite, I made my excuses and left the growing mound of pulsing flesh in the evening room to return to the hilltop in search of goodwill and good people. It did not disappoint, and I spent another wondrous evening in company of Thomas and his family. He introduced me to his wife, she gave me a look. I think she knew. I think she understood, and did not mind – there was an echo of that first morning on the moors with Sophia. If only the world were filled with such women. Our conversation touched on their lack of children, and I was again reminded of my relationship with the Dewers. I would not be able to help these good people in the same way, I do not think Mrs Sumner would be so amenable, or that I would be able to perform.

Once we had discovered Elias' condition, our nights of passion ceased and conversations over dinner became less intimate, more mundane. The looks we exchanged became less loving, more suspicious. I was overjoyed at my impending fatherhood, excited to be a part of this story. We should be a glimpse of the future, a family with two fathers and one mother (or vice versa, biologically speaking). Maybe one day when the world is less judgemental this will be normal, everyday, unremarkable. Alas, not even we three were capable.

I thought to return to London, forget Dourstone, forget the Dewers, forget Thomas. See my father, cap in hand, with plans to re-energise his business, regain control from those who have now utterly taken it from us. Or resume my medical studies, ignore my father and hope he never hear of my return. But I could not, I loved these people, I loved this place – love this place still – and I love you. I could not leave. I felt sure that Lord Elias and Lady Sophia would revert to their old jovial selves just as soon as things returned to something closer to normal.

In hindsight I suppose there may have been a degree of jealousy in their own relations, the Lady Dewer being desirous of a child of her own, and denied it by her husband's need. Perhaps the *imbalance of humours necessitated by his child-bearing state made him even more difficult than usual. Whatever the reason for their neglect of me I did not resent it, allowing them the time they needed, dividing my time between Thomas, wandering alone on the moors and making merry in the taverns. A little too merry most nights, for the hurt in our little family disturbed me greatly and there is wondrous redemption to be found at the bottom of a glass.*

Now…

'We give our thanks for the fruits of the land,' a familiar voice chants from behind a hare mask. Polly shudders with a memory of clinging horse entrails.

'We ha' the neck, we ha' the neck,' a reply goes up across the square from a crowd waving sheaves of corn high above their heads.

'Toiled by oxen, horse, foot and hand.'

'We ha' the neck, we ha' the neck.'

'We offer the surplus to feed the poor.'

'We ha' the neck, we ha' the neck.'

'Keeping us bountiful for ever more.'

'We ha' the neck, we ha' the neck.'

'Home of our hearts, that we love without limit.'

'We ha' the neck, we ha' the neck.'

'This blessed land, this Dourstone Nymet!'

'We ha' the neck, we ha' the neck.' The crowd descend into incoherent cheers, waving their corn and drinking to the harvest. Father Hearne removes his mask, replaces his homburg and strides through the crowd to grateful back slaps and hand shakes.

Another stage has been set and the local musicians are having an informal session with banjos, fiddles, squeeze-boxes and all. Dan and Kerry's former May Queen daughter, Katie, is dressed as Long Meg, all brown autumnal colours and straw crown. The lampposts that surround the low walls of the square are bedecked with straw dollies, straw wreathes, straw dogs. A theme that continues all around, hanging from porchways, door-knockers and trees alike. The first wicker sculptures of the season have been erected around the edges. Fierce-looking hounds as tall as Patrick guard entrances and exits – their smaller straw-built cousins looking up at them from flower beds. It won't be long now until the town is filled with them – dogs guarding every corner when the cold begins to bite.

The end of summer has brought a plague of hayfever, colds and hypochondriasis of biblical proportions, leaving Patrick working every hour under the sun, and there are a lot of them before the autumnal equinox. Pair this with a tired, hormonal partner who cannot do any of the things she used to and you have a recipe for shouting matches – the boiling undercurrent of the Susan thing they are not talking about ever present.

The anniversary of Graham's disappearance is fast coming up, and if Patrick is right, somebody else will vanish. Another disembodied foot for Fenrir to stumble across.

'You're part of the WI right?' he asks Lynn, who is working the barbecue.

'Yes, I am, why?'

'I think they might have something to do with Graham's disappearance. I spoke to someone from a long time ago, she had a similar problem, they told her in the end, but... she didn't get the answers she wanted.'

'You're still looking into that then?' Her eyes light up.

'Yeah, sorry, I thought you might want to know where he'd gone. I can stop?'

'No, don't stop. Thank you. I'm not sure I like the idea of there being answers I don't want, but thank you for trying to find them. I thought, after what happened...'

'No, no, just a misunderstanding. We're friends, you were in a bad place, I want to help you out. I think there's something more to this, something deeper. I'll keep you posted.'

'If there was a WI hand in it I think you can guess which one it was.' She looks daggers across the square to where Lady Melissa has her hand on Polly's back, whispering in her ear.

'Polly? But we only moved in that day,' Patrick blurts out.

'Don't be stupid, Lady Muck over there. She's behind everything round here, don't you know that yet.'

Patrick does know that. But he doesn't want to believe it. She is fast becoming Polly's best friend and the last thing he needs is to stir things up.

'You're sure you don't need anything else?' Mel asks, caressing Polly's neck.

'I'm fine, thank you,' Polly replies. There has been no repeat performance of that night. Nor any regrets. Quite the opposite. But Polly is not the cheating kind, and, however rocky their relationship, she feels indebted to Patrick. She must at least try to keep them together: for the baby, for her own self-respect, and for the memory of all their years together. He says nothing happened with Susan, and she believes him. She has to. He had reasons for not telling her, not good ones, but reasons, and she doesn't want to throw everything up in the air for what could be nothing. So she is carefully avoiding the subject. And not telling him about her own infidelity.

Mel is not pushing for anything more either. She carelessly described it as a night of fun they both deserved.

'Not everything has to be significant dear,' she explained the next day over coffee. 'Stop taking things so seriously. Sex doesn't have to mean marriage.' She left the offer of a good time on the table for whenever Polly wants it, but didn't force the issue.

Polly is surprised at the depth of feeling she has for Melissa. She doesn't think she's gay – she has not found herself lusting after any other women – but she is a little in love with this enigmatic creature. She has a special magic all her own, an aura that entrances and hypnotises everyone around her to which Polly is very happy to surrender. But her moral compass won't let her be involved with two people at once, and she is still wracked with guilt at having let herself slip even once. Not enough to stop spending time with Mel, if anything she is seeing more of her than she did before. She makes everything so easy, dismissing worries with a flick of her wrist, while Patrick, well, Patrick worries. All the time. About everything. He can make picking a sandwich into an endless quest, so watching him make baby decisions and plan their family's future reminds her of a fat bluebottle butting its head up against an open window.

'Well, I'm going to the bar anyway, shout if you change your mind,' Mel says, her flowing yellow skirts sliding through gaps in the crowd like liquid sunshine as the last rays of the real one strike the Church tower.

'I will,' Polly mumbles, watching the crowd part in front of Cronus. She reaches down and strokes Fenrir's neck, glad of his unswerving loyalty.

'You alright there?' Lynn wanders over, having a break from selling burned meat.

'Yes, fine, you?' Polly replies.

'I'm getting there now, yes. Thanks to your man, he's very helpful isn't he?' Lynn smiles.

'He means well, yes.'

'I hope it's not taking him away from you too much, his trying to find Graham, I don't know how he's going to succeed where the CSA have failed, but I'm so glad he's trying.'

'Well, he's like a dog with a bone, if there's anything to find, he'll find it.'

'Not that I want him back, but I could do with his money, you know?' Lynn explains.

Polly nods and gives Fenrir's ears a rub.

'As long as you're alright with it,' Lynn continues. 'With him doing stuff for me, given the history.'

'What history?'

'Goodness, didn't he ever tell you? I was his first... you know? Back when we were kids.'

Polly is stunned. She feels utterly stupid and betrayed.

'You mean?'

'Yeah, drunken teenage fumble, that was all. It meant nothing, I would have thought he'd told you. It's a funny story.'

'Funny, yeah. Maybe he did, might have slipped my mind,' Polly bluffs.

'Hope I haven't caused any trouble, all ancient history now, be seeing you.' Lynn heads back to the barbecue.

Polly strokes Fenrir's head a little harder than he might like. Why has Patrick never told her this? And he's spending so much time helping Lynn out, Polly even asked him to. They're going to have to have another little talk later.

'I need to talk to you Lady Dewer,' Patrick says, finding her at the bar.

'It's Mel, Patrick, why've you suddenly gone all formal on me?' she replies as Cronus lets out a low growl Patrick feels through the floorboards.

'Well, it's quite a formal business. I need to talk to you about local history, to do with the WI, local clubs and associations over the years. I gather your family have been at the heart of this community for as long as anybody can remember.' From what he's found out, she's been at the heart of this community for as long as anybody can remember.

'Well, I'm sure I can give you a few minutes tomorrow if you nip over to the Manor,' she sighs. 'But right now it's a party, which may or may not be historic, but this is no time to be going into all its origins – sex, death, rebirth and all the usual pagan filth if you're really interested. How are you holding up anyway?'

'Oh, I'm fine, how's my girlfriend?'

'What do you mean?'

'Well, Polly spends more time with you than me these days.'

'Didn't know it was a problem, I'm just trying to help out, what with you being so busy and all.'

'Sorry, yes, thank you for all your help,' Patrick seethes, remaining polite.

'It's okay, still not proposed though have you?' She winks. 'Well done, don't let her trick you into anything you don't want to do.'

'It's not that, Polly doesn't want to get married either. At least she never did before – what has she said to you?'

'Oh nothing, I just get this feeling you know, you do when you've been around for a while, like I have. I think she might have changed her mind. It might help? You never know.' Mel wanders off, Cronus parting the queue who nod deferentially as she passes.

'Saw your young man in there,' Mel says as she returns to Polly. 'Think he might have had a few too many again.'

'Really?'

'Yes, kept on about you being his girlfriend, as if you're his property or something, like he wants me to back off, spend less time with you. Blokes get funny after a few drinks don't they? Brings out the misogyny.'

'Patrick doesn't, he's practically a girl,' Polly says. 'You didn't tell him about... you know?' How would he react if Mel did tell him? Would he be upset, angry, hurt – or horny? Some guys love the idea of their girlfriend with another woman, though probably not a pensionable one, and not when they're this pregnant. No, he'd be hurt, especially after everything she has accused him of.

'Oh no dear, don't worry about that. Your secret's safe with me. No, but he's got some funny ideas in his head. Getting very possessive. They all do Polly, no man is without his essential manness at the end of the day.'

'If you say so,' Polly mutters, she doesn't want to discuss Lynn with Mel. Mel probably knew already, all these locals know everything about each other, even the incomers and the holidaymakers. She's probably the last to know. She turns her attention back to the band who have just struck up 'The Wild Rover'. At least some of them have, a tall, splendidly-moustachioed old gentleman seems to be playing the opening bars of 'The Entertainer' on a banjolele while a wild-eyed old woman sitting on a stool has begun 'All Things Bright and Beautiful' on the accordion.

16

Then…

When there was no chance of further public deception both husband and wife entered confinement and, for appearance's sake, the town were told Lord Elias had gone away on business. Lady Sophia was glad to be kept from public view, as the layers of padding she wore to convince well-wishers she was with child were not pleasant in summer heat. Lord Elias was not best pleased when she conveyed her relief, pointing out he could do no such thing, and had been wearing as much on top of having an actual baby.

To ensure no accidental discovery, Elias had to vacate the master bedroom and was hidden away in a tiny room at the top of the west tower. A spiral staircase winds its way through the old servants' quarters – vacant now for years since the refurbishment of the east wing attics – eventually reaching this room, musty and damp-smelling when first we began to make it homely. It has a window that looks out over the town, so Elias might keep watch over his domain, and once we had a cheery fire burning in the small grate it felt more comfortable. However, my lord was unused to such meagre quarters and the bad mood brought on by his condition worsened. There was only one thing that could bring him relief and return him to his former self.

Finally, on a humid night that teetered from the edge of summer to break into thunderstorm, there came cries from the tower room. Lord Elias' ordeal had begun. When Lady Sophia ushered me in to meet my progeny next morning I wept for joy. The sun cast its rays through the tiny window that had been Lord Elias' only connection to the town he so loves; but the view that customarily held me spellbound for minutes upon entering held no appeal. Not in the face of this beautiful, fragile, tiny creature.

A son, an heir to the Dewer name, a boy at last, the curse broken.

So I thought, but my Lord's face said otherwise. I have never seen him look more his true sex than that day, laid in bed, the child crying from a cradle the other side of the room while a maid fussed over. Elias' face was flushed from his exertions. His hair unkempt, thrown carelessly back over the pillows and more dull grey than it's usual flashing steel. Without his usual hirsute accoutrements he looked every part the lady he truly is. Burning silver eyes stared dispassionately at me from a woman's face; all his usual assumed masculinity thrown aside in this, most feminine of all occupations, motherhood. I loved the man, not this woman who had no time for my child.

That is unfair, I love the person Elias is. Still. I was not used to seeing him vulnerable, and in that moment, he was, supremely vulnerable. He had spent a long night in that most dangerous activity from which so many do not return; my own mother included – Father still blames me for her demise, has never even tried to pretend he doesn't. Seeing those we admire, father and mother figures, in their vulnerability is never comfortable and I fear I did not carry myself well. Elias did not make it easy though, and, even when fear left him and strength returned, he was no more parental.

I asked him of the babe, and he shrugged, remarking that we would have to get back to trying. When I suggested this was the heir the family had sought for so long he told me I understood nothing, then lost his temper and sent me away in a rage.

I wept all the way to my own chambers.

Now...

'Wait in here, I won't be long, can I get you a drink?' Lady Melissa says. Patrick has turned up at the Manor, on schedule, leaving Polly with just Fenrir for company again. He's got his phone, he's ready to jump in the car and drive in case the baby comes. There's a bag in his car ready, there's a bag in her car ready, and a spare in the house just in case.

He had opted for near-complete honesty when Polly confronted him about Lynn. He told her everything – apart from Lynn's recent pass at him – how they would always be friends because of their shared experience, how he wanted to help her to make up for vanishing. That he would have told Polly but for their agreement years ago never to talk about past sexual encounters after a particularly dirty story from his rugby playing days had provoked a fit of jealousy. Polly wasn't happy, but she accepted it.

'Cup of tea would be nice,' Patrick replies, putting his doctor's bag down.

'Coming up, just need to feed the dogs, you understand, won't be long.' She smiles and disappears down an imposing wood-panelled corridor.

Patrick looks down the seemingly endless oak shelves, the lines of leather-bound volumes speak of a long history. An ancient family seat, its store of knowledge built up generation after generation, shelf by shelf, spanning the length and breadth of this enormous room. From faded brown copies of the Pepys diaries in the darkest corner to an Ikea unit filled with trashy paperbacks by a comfy leather sofa. He can imagine Regency gentlemen arguing the worth of Romantic poetry in this room, then their Victorian counterparts denouncing Dickens before being overtaken by turn of the century Bloomsbury types, down for the weekend swooning over Virginia Woolf.

He selects an impressive looking copy of *Gray's Anatomy* and flicks idly through the pages. He is surprised to find it is a first edition. It must be worth a small fortune. He looks about himself, realising how much money is locked in these books and wondering if the strange old woman he is waiting for knows. She must know, leaving them carelessly scattered about this enormous dusty old library is a conspicuous display of wealth.

Some pages flutter down from the book in his hand, and he is gripped with a terrible fear he has halved its value. He snaps it shut, puts it down and crouches to pick up the evidence. He is relieved to find they are handwritten, not printed, and he has not damaged the precious tome.

He unfolds the yellowing paper and sees an old-fashioned flowing hand. His curiosity is piqued as he reads:

I awoke at the centre of the stone circle Lord Elias and I raised in happier time. Moonlit figures, disguised by velvet robes, checked I could not escape....

'You know, I think you might have been right,' Melissa says, boots thumping up the stairs. Patrick reflexively stuffs the papers in his bag.

'Right about what?' Patrick asks.

'Us being related, I've been digging about a bit in the family history,' Mel replies. 'There was a bastard around the same time as your great-grandfather turns up, at least, there's some kind of scandal in Lord Elias Dewer's diaries involving a maid. It's probably that. Of course there's no proof, most of that kind of thing got buried.'

'Well, maybe we could have a bit of a dig?' Patrick is thinking of the inheritance. Polly keeps telling him how Mel has no living relatives, she feels sorry for her. That's why she spends so much time here. Patrick is happy to encourage it if they get a cut of the Manor.

'Maybe we could. There's plenty of records about the place. Us gentry don't have much better to do than record our life stories, however dull they are. A bit of self-important scribbling goes a long way to feeding the ego.'

'Was there ever a Lord Dewer?' Patrick asks. 'I mean, for you, not this Lord Elias, if that's not a bit personal.'

'Not at all, no, and yes. There was someone, all too briefly, a long time ago.' Melissa's misty-eyed stare moves to a picture on the wall. 'But he died, and left me here, alone and childless.'

'Oh, I'm sorry,' Patrick says. 'I didn't mean to bring up bad memories.'

'Oh no, not his fault, entirely my own, and I'm happy enough. I've made my bed, and for a great many years I've had a very good time in it.'

He follows Melissa's gaze to a sepia-toned photograph of the stone circle. Two men and a woman stand proudly against one of the uprights. The equipment strewn around them shows it is still in the process of being constructed. He notices a large flat stone in the middle of the circle that is no longer there, it triggers something in his memory, but he can't put his finger on what. 'Who's that?'

'That, my dear boy, is our very-probably-common ancestor. Lord Elias Dewer, with his wife Sophia and business partner Nathaniel Harker erecting the stone circle to add a little magic to our world.' Her eyes soften.

'What happened to that big one in the middle?' Patrick asks.

'What big one?' Mel squints at the picture. 'Oh yes, never noticed that before, no idea. Probably got nicked by some farmer to build a wall, happened all the time back then. Now what did you want to ask me about?'

'It's to do with the Wish Weekend, and a pattern of mysterious disappearances,' Patrick continues.

'Disappearances?' She laughs. 'I think someone's been on the scrumpy...'

'We keep the secrets,' he says. 'Does that mean anything to you?'

'Have you been talking to that batty old Mrs Hooper? She always says that when she's having one of her turns. Thinks she's living in a Hammer Horror film, deadly conspiracies all about.'

'Oh.' Patrick deflates. 'But I've looked back through all the parish records, somebody vanishes every Wish Weekend. They never come back, sometimes there's a thin explanation, but never any trace of them after they leave Dourstone. I don't suppose you've any records here that might explain any of it?'

'What do you mean, explain?' Mel asks. 'Are you accusing me of something?' She leaves the room.

'No, not at all,' he shouts. 'It's just that the Manor has been the heart of this town forever, I thought you might have some old books in here or something. Something useful.'

'Plenty of old books here, you're welcome to have a look,' she says, coming back in with two steaming mugs of what might be tea. 'But I don't know what you'll find. Surely you don't think the legend of The Devil and his dogs is real!'

'It must have come from somewhere.' Patrick shrugs. 'Local customs tend to grow out of grisly pagan rituals and most myths are based in fact.'

'Not round here, most myths are based in mist, rain, snow and not being able to go anywhere for half the bloody year because of them. People got bored. They told stories.'

'Maybe.'

'Definitely. And even if there was some ghastly ceremony going on in the neolithic it's just another excuse for a party these days. Now how's that girl of yours doing?'

'Oh Polly's great,' Patrick lies, 'excited about the baby.'

'Good, well she would be wouldn't she? Gives a relationship a bit of stability. More chance of...'

'You're going to say marriage again aren't you?' Patrick sighs.

'I can only relay what I know, what I pick up. I see a lot of her, you could do a lot worse than make her an honest woman.'

Patrick drinks his tea, it is not tea.

'This is... interesting, what is it?' he asks.

'Herbs, nettles... things, old family recipe. It's calming. Good for the soul. You seem stressed, thought you needed it.'

'Well, yes, thanks. Am I alright to have a poke about in here now?' he asks.

'I don't think that would be the best idea, it's getting a bit late, and Polly's not getting any less pregnant is she?'

Patrick looks at his watch. He has been here for over two hours. How has that happened?

'Sorry, yes, you're right. I'll be off, thanks, I'll come back another time. Thanks for the drink.' He does not mean this last bit, but he's a polite young man from a good family. Wouldn't do to let the side down.

'Quite alright, and stop all this displacement activity,' Mel says. 'Concentrate on your girl and your imminent family, not mad old women and made up horror stories.'

'Yes, sorry, will do,' Patrick mutters as he leaves.

Once she is quite sure his car has cleared the end of the driveway, Mel picks up her phone and sends a single text message.

Do it tonight.

17

Then…

Over the next few days I asked again and again to see you, and was rebuked every time. Lord Elias returned to normal duties – back in his usual suit, telling the townspeople the foreign air had quite helped him lose the extra weight – and left Lady Sophia and the extra staff hired before your arrival to look after you. I was kept away. Elias told me not to get too attached. He said you were sick and may not last, before cutting your attendants one by one. Had you been the daughter he wanted I know things would have been entirely different.

I snuck in one night, you were all alone in the huge nursery Elias and Sophia spent so long making perfect for the expected heir. You cried to yourself with no answer, so far from the inhabited parts of the Manor that none heard, your lungs not yet powerful enough to rouse others. I hugged you to my breast and you quieted. I have heard other newborns make more than enough noise to wake the very dead, and, fearing your quiet sobs indicated some more serious condition, I used my medical training to make a decent examination. There was, and is, nothing wrong with you. I began to fear what my lord had planned, the Wish Weekend was nearly upon us. Could Elias use his own flesh to quiet the hounds for another year? Would it help his cause to have such a significant sacrifice? I would not put it past him. I wanted a confidant, but I could not tell anyone of the Lord's true nature. I had promised, my word is my word, and despite all I love him.

Now...

'He'll be back soon,' Polly says to the huge brown eyes staring mournfully from her lap, 'and he better have remembered your dinner.'

Fenrir whimpers before getting up and walking to his empty bowl. Polly is sorry to be torturing him with the smell of cooking. She doesn't think it would be any consolation to know her own dinner will now be thoroughly overcooked from waiting for Patrick – again. She toys with the idea of hitting the panic buttons by telling him her waters have broken early but doesn't. Instead she settles for an old-fashioned *where the hell are you?* text message.

'Right here! Sorry I was so long, that friend of yours can't half talk,' Patrick explains, bursting through the door, phone in hand.

'Why were you at the Manor?' Polly asks, disappointed she doesn't have to ask which friend.

'Research, work thing, I heard she's got some really good old books up there – it was not a lie.'

'Good for you, I hope you remembered to pick up dog food?'

'Shit, sorry, no. I forgot, I'll go now shall I?'

'No, he'll be fine, he doesn't like food.'

'Okay, I'm sorry, I'll just be a minute.' Patrick runs out of the door, grabbing his car keys from the hook they have only just alighted on.

While he is gone she silently fumes. This is all his fault. She does not want this baby. The more she thinks about it, the more she believes she doesn't want children at all. She has come across fictional families that make her long for that kind of connection, but now dismisses that as good story telling. Her mother was barely there for most of her childhood, always working. The closest thing to a parenting role-model she has is her grandad. A drunken rogue who spends most of his time propping up the bar at the Beaver Inn, where her mum works at the weekends, the setting for her happiest childhood memories. Grandad is nice, but his tall stories and don't-ask-where-I-got-it-from-know-what-I-mean gifts are no template for raising a child.

Patrick's upbringing was little better, his parents lavished money, things, an expensive boarding school education and foreign holidays on their only child in place of love. He wants this though, the chance to have a proper family. He's bought stacks of parenting books that she shuffles around their unread pile by the bed every few days in the hope he thinks she's reading them.

She sits down in Fenrir's bed, hugging his neck to her face, the hopelessness of her situation overwhelming her. She is having this baby whether she wants to or not. Patrick will use it to cement them together forever. And then they may as well get married. And then she may as well take his name. Because double-barrelling is all very well but where does it end? Two more generations down you've got eight surnames all hyphened together. Becoming a Sumner will be easier for the children. Because he won't stop at one. There will be more and then all that will remain of Polly – fun, ambitious, clever, brilliant, dragged herself up by her wedge-heeled sandal straps Polly – will be somebody's fucking mother.

Her phone bleeps, it's an email from Susan.

Hello Polly, I'm sorry to have to tell you this, but I can't live with the guilt any more, and my therapist says I need to apologise to the people I have hurt. I slept with Patrick, months ago. It meant nothing to either of us, it was just a thing. A drunken stupid mistake. Clive told me he has spoken to you about it, so I assume you know. I hope you and Patrick have already talked this through and are able to move past this. Please accept my apology, and I hope we can still be friends. I understand if we cannot.

Sorry, and please don't blame him, the fault is all mine,
Susan.

'Got it,' Patrick says, bouncing back through the door. 'Here you go, you great brute.' He tips a can of meaty chunks into the huge metal dish by the back door. Fenrir doesn't move, just stays cuddled into Polly's side.

'What are you two doing down there?' he says. 'Come on, get up, I didn't drive all the way to the shop and back for you to not eat that stinking crap.'

'He'll eat it, give him a minute,' Polly says, still stunned by the words she has read, unable to believe it; although on some level she has always known it was true. How could she be so stupid? Wanting things to be okay, wanting Patrick to be the faithful lapdog she had always pictured. All lies, again. Did he lie about Lynn as well? Is he carrying on with the whole town behind her back? Is everyone laughing at her?

'Talking of stinking crap,' Patrick continues, 'what is that in the oven?'

'It was salmon roasted in three colour pepper, before you fucked off out again. Now it's anti-sushi.' She has no idea how to begin the argument they need to have.

'Anti-sushi?'

'Yeah, fish that is as cooked as much as it possibly can be before becoming charcoal.'

'Sorry, but...'

'But what Patrick? But now you've got me knocked up and locked up I'm the last thing on your to do list?' Right after doing Susan, she thinks, maybe that's where he's been? Maybe he wasn't even at the Manor? Maybe he stopped off for a quick one with Lynn as well?

'No, is that what you think?'

'No, I'm just tired; fat, tired and pissed off with everything.' She doesn't want to do this, maybe if she ignores it it will end.

'I'm sorry.'

'Well, it's your fucking fault, so you better be.'

'How is this "my fault"?'

'You're the one always going on about having a family, I didn't want this, you did. You made it happen.' In trying to avoid the real problem, Polly's subconscious has dragged up another, equally divisive, subject.

'How could I make it happen? I'm not a fucking miracle worker, it was an accident, a good one, but an accident. Unless it wasn't?'

'What do you mean, unless it wasn't?' Polly shouts, pushing Fenrir to one side and standing up. 'You think I did this deliberately?'

'Women like you don't get pregnant by mistake Pol.'

'Women like me? And what, pray tell, are women like me?' Not like Susan, she thinks. Not sexy, exotic, willing women. She knows her restraint will break soon, she will spew her rage at this betrayal for all the universe to hear, but she wants him to admit it of his own free will. Give him enough rope. Say nothing.

'Organised, sensible, clever, educated.'

'Fuck off you snob, you think just because I've been to university I'm not going to get up the duff? That it only happens to kids on council estates using clingfilm for condoms? Have you forgotten where I'm from? Do you know how fucking patronising that is?'

'That's not what I meant.'

'Doesn't matter, you think I did this deliberately.' She pulls up her shirt, waving her bump at him.

'I don't know what I think Polly, what do you want? Do you want to get married? Is that it?'

'Marry you?' She stares him in the eyes. 'What makes you think I want to marry you?'

Fenrir looks up from his bowl and gives a growl.

'You're a manipulative little man. You dragged me down to this weird town where you could feel big and clever and better than everybody else, then switched my pills and got me pregnant so I can't get away from you, and wandered off to fuck everybody in town but me!' The dam has broken. It is out there.

'Enough!' Patrick shouts, his temper breaking. 'Who have I been fucking? What are you talking about?'

'Susan has told me everything.' She folds her arms over the bump. Having finally said it, she thought she would feel better. Instead she is flooded by panic, this is real, not some intellectual exercise in how to approach the subject. Accusations have been made, and they have to play this out. 'I know.'

'Know what? I told you the truth, I was stupid, but I left before anything happened.'

'Then why would she say otherwise? What possible reason could she have to make this up Pat?' She thrusts her phone at him. His face falls.

'I don't know why she'd say this. Maybe she's an attention seeker?'

'Bollocks Pat, just admit it. I don't think I care about the shagging any more, just the lies. I take it you've been fucking that Lynn since before we even moved here. Is she why we moved here? Is she?'

'I'm not lying! Lynn is ancient history, I told you!'

'Don't you shout at me, don't you dare shout at me.' Polly runs at him, slapping at his arms. 'Fucking liar, lying cunt, fuck you, fuck you!'

He sees himself from across the room, out of body, almost out of mind. He can't stop himself from doing what comes next. His inner monster is in control and it knows the only way to stop this. His hand comes up and slaps her, hard across the cheek. She reels back, shock on her face. He has never hit her before. Not so much as raised his voice.

She reaches behind to the kitchen counter, steadying herself where she has landed. A knife, in her hand where she grips. Hysteria takes hold, and she lunges – pure hatred in her eyes. Unknown strength drives her arm towards his neck. He grabs her, bends her wrist back. Hits her again and again until her fingers finally release the knife into his. She falls to the floor and he breathes deeply, trying to regain control from the snarling beast inside. He hasn't bargained on the one outside, Fenrir leaps up, all teeth and claws, pushes Patrick down to the kitchen floor and goes straight for his throat.

Patrick swings his arm round instinctively to fend off the dog, hot blood flows over his arm and the dog leaps away screaming.

He didn't know dogs could scream.

He looks to his hand, sees the knife still there. He didn't know, hadn't realised.

Across from him sits his pregnant girlfriend, terrified, screaming, and knelt over Fenrir's body, her blood mingling with his as it pours out over the floor.

'Christ, I'm sorry, he was going to kill me, you were going to kill me, I can't, I didn't...'

He gets to his feet, and gently moves her aside.

'I can patch this, then I'm taking him to the vet. He'll be okay, I'll make this better.'

He rummages in his doctor's bag for supplies, shoving the papers from the Manor down. He cleans the wound, ties a tourniquet, then picks up the dog.

'Wait for me, I'm sorry. We'll talk when I get back.'

She looks at him, red hate behind her eyes. She has never looked at him like that before. He is not sure he ever can make this better.

Patrick falls back through the door, grabs rum bottle and glass and collapses on the sofa. It is the middle of the night and he doesn't want to wake Polly. He cannot believe what he has done, what happened in such a short moment. He takes a big swig from the bottle before pouring a large measure. He knows he has a temper, losing it scares him so much he has worked hard to keep a lid on it his entire life. Since he has been with Polly it's been easy. Until now. These last few months it has been getting steadily harder and harder to stay calm, and now this. He isn't fit to be a father and he doesn't deserve Polly.

He doesn't blame Polly for believing Susan, it looks pretty suspicious. But why is she accusing him of things he has not done? Why frame him? Is she trying to split him and Polly up? It looks like she's managed it but he can't for the life of him think why.

Fenrir is in a bad way. Patrick doesn't begrudge him the small fortune in vet bills this will cost. He was protecting his mistress, and if he's this fearless, he is worth keeping around to look after Polly and the baby if Patrick isn't. Patrick stayed at the vets all through the operation, helping where he could. Once the dog was stabilised he wanted to bring him home but Edwina assured him he needs to stay in for observation. He couldn't tell her what happened, so came up with a far-fetched story about an accident while out walking in the dark. Edwina's face held little trace she believed him, but he hopes she keeps it to herself. Not for his own sake, but he is worried what might happen if anyone finds out the dog attacked him. He knows the worst he would get for damn near killing a dog is a fine, but Fenrir could end up dead for an entirely justified act of aggression.

He tip-toes up the stairs, so as not to wake Polly, and carefully opens the door, wincing as the top step gives its signature creak.

Once again the effort is wasted.

She is not there.

This time he does not blame her.

Polly doesn't think she will ever sleep again. She doesn't know what to think. Patrick has been sleeping with another woman – maybe two other women. Patrick, shy, difficult Patrick. The boy who took months to build up enough courage to even smile at her.

Patrick hit her. Patrick has killed her dog. She can't go back, not ever. She doesn't recognise the man she has run from. He bears no resemblance to the good natured bumbler she has loved so long. As soon as he left she grabbed the baby bag from the porch, threw some extra clothes in and made straight for the Manor.

Mel seemed to know what had happened already. She was standing next to the doric columns of the Manor's imposing entrance as Polly came into the yard.

'You can stay,' she said, holding the door open.

'Thank you,' Polly replied, not meeting her eyes.

Those are all the words that have passed between them in the last hour. Polly sits on a big deep green leather sofa in the evening room, wishing she could have a real drink but not giving in. The baby is so close now she is surprised all this stress hasn't brought it out. She is nursing another of Mel's herbal drinks. It doesn't seem to be relaxing her, but there's only so much good unfermented plants can do for your mood. The dogs seem to know, a wave of grey fur spreads across the floor to Polly's legs, anxious to know about their fallen friend.

'I just didn't see it coming.' Polly breaks the silence.

'Nobody ever does.'

'I don't know what I'm going to do. I didn't want this baby, I don't want this baby. He does, but I can't let him have it. I can't kill it now, it's too close.'

'You'll stay here. I'll look after her. You'll feel differently when she's out. I'll help you every step of the way.'

'Thank you.'

18

Then...

I raised questions. All shut down. Lord Elias more unresponsive than ever. He began to come to my rooms again at night, but it felt more assault than act of love, his eyes now evoking a terrible sadness. Lady Sophia no longer accompanied him, it was just the two of us. More intimate, more personal, it should have been everything I wanted, but... he was so stoic, so perfunctory. We made love, properly, nicely, without the urgent, heated lust of before. The fantasy was stripped away and it felt like man and woman, rather than man and man. Night time Elias seemed to be fading more and more into his true self, a strong, formidable woman. But I am not attracted to women, however strong they may be. I took myself away when I could, seeking solace in Thomas at the barrel-works.

Word reached us the Church would send another priest to meddle in the town's affairs and Elias spoke at length in the square of the sins of the previous father. The townspeople rallied to his cause and were riled to action, burning the church to an empty ruin one terrible, sacrilegious night.

On that night I stayed with Thomas, fearing for my very life with the Lord in such a rage. Both our nervous systems had been tested to their very limits by the evening's violence. I slept, soft in his arms, watching moon and stars through the window, woken periodically by the crash of falling beams from the church roof as it burned. The last crash was not the church, but Thomas's bedroom door being broken in. The men and women of the council came and dragged me away. Thomas did not try to protect me, just smiled, and took his thirty pieces of silver. They congratulated him on a job well done. I had been entrapped, so I thought. Betrayal, from the only person I still trusted. I should have left, gone home, forgotten this place, these people. You.

Now...

This enormous room has been Polly's home for the weeks since she left Patrick. Her grand surroundings make her feel like the heroine of a gothic novel. Isolated from the world for her own good. Patrick hasn't been in touch. She expected him to turn up at the door all apologetic, cap in hand to offer the world on a plate. But nothing. Polly understands now, as she feels another contraction rip through her. It's all her fault.

She attacked him, then set her dog on him, why would he want to speak to her? She has been getting it all the wrong way round, she is the one at fault. He only acted in self-defence. She would like the chance to speak to him, maybe Susan was lying, maybe she wasn't, either way, she hasn't heard Patrick's side, there might be reasons to forgive him for the one betrayal she hasn't yet reconciled. She hasn't left this house since that night, can't bear to see anybody. Mel has been wonderful, catering to her every whim, hugging her in the night when she wakes up screaming. The nightmares began that first night, and have not stopped: Patrick morphing into a werewolf before tearing at her flesh, always the same, never any less terrifying.

The fight with Patrick, followed by her mad dash to the safety of the Manor took it out of her. There was a chance she might have damaged the baby, so the furthest she has strayed from the master bedroom is onto the battlements outside her window, for a touch of calming Autumn sunshine that turns cold too soon. What has she got to go out for after all? A town full of gossips laughing behind her back? She doesn't even have a dog of her own to walk any longer.

She lies back and pulls her legs as close to her body as she can while another wave of pain rushes over, it can't be long now. Nathaniel Harker's painted smile is losing its comforting charm. She is less warmly inclined to him than she was, but still concentrating on his picture over the other, more austere, faces that watch over her.

'Mel! Mel! Call an ambulance!' she screams. 'I can't do this.' She very much wants to be somewhere with clean, almost-white walls, beeping machines and reassuring staff in scrubs. Not a four-poster bed from a period drama where the baby is presented to the household with the grim-faced news of its mother's demise. She has a feeling she is in what is known as a confinement, and she is tired of being confined. However, there is a baby coming, a red weather warning for travel and Lady Melissa's old Landrover has packed up. The chances of getting to a hospital tonight are slim to none.

'You'll be fine,' Melissa replies, appearing at the door with another bundle of towels. 'We can do this, it's not my first barn dance you know.'

'Really? You've done this before?' Polly is intrigued. 'When?'

'Long time ago, when I was a girl we could never get to the hospital, and the doctors wanted too much money. Had to do it ourselves.' Mel busies herself moving pillows, wiping Polly down with a wet towel, grabbing flesh and looking at her watch, giving the impression of someone who knows what they're doing.

Polly once again finds herself wondering exactly how old this woman is. And what she means by do it ourselves. She has a vision of a younger Mel, pulling a baby from beneath her skirts while she scrubs her dogs, without missing a beat, then throwing the baby to them.

'Have you never had any children of your own?'

'None that survived, no,' Mel says glibly. 'And stop worrying, this might all be a false alarm anyway. How far apart are you?'

'Fucking thing's still inside me isn't it?' Polly snarls. This baby is a parasite, she'll be glad to get it out.

'Nearly there boy.' Patrick smiles as Fenrir limps the last few steps to the top of the hill. His shaven fur is starting to grow back where Edwina saved his life. They stop at the stone circle where Patrick sits on one of the lower rocks, stroking the dog's head. They have settled their differences. The effort he has put in to nursing the dog back to health has made them firm friends.

He has made endless polite requests to visit Polly at the Manor, all turned down. The impolite ones have not fared any better, the threat of Melissa's dogs being enough to send him back up the drive and home again every time. He knows that's where she is, everybody knows that's where she is. He doesn't want to hear the town-wide rumours, but in his job, he has no choice. Many of his patients haven't connected him to 'that woman living with Lady Dewer' but plenty have. He can see it in their sympathetic eyes.

He knows he has gone too far to ever get her back, hurting Fenrir like that. Hurting Polly like that. He doesn't blame her for not wanting to see him; not believing he didn't sleep with Susan. He knows he didn't, but what right has he to expect her to believe him? He'd still like the chance to explain, but has had no opportunity. At least she knows her dog is alright, she must have glanced at his barrage of messages, even if she hasn't replied to any. Fenrir can go and live with her and the baby once he's fully recovered. She'll need him for protection, even if she doesn't need Patrick.

The last of the Autumn sun disappears behind ominous black clouds spreading across the sky like Kahlua through cream, and Patrick starts to think this might not be the best place to be. The weather forecast was unambiguous this evening, there is a storm on the way. The met office have called it Storm Melissa. He can't help but laugh at the unstoppable force of nature preventing him getting what he wants having the same name as the oncoming tempest he can taste on the wind.

He no longer cares about the suspicious disappearances. It doesn't matter. The only thing he can concentrate on is trying to become a better person, someone who deserves Polly. Someone who can be a decent father and role-model to their child. The sort of person who strips down to their underwear and gets into freezing Dartmoor pools to do hydrotherapy sessions with a wounded Irish wolfhound. He has barely given a passing thought to the thing that had gripped and obsessed him since he saw that foot in the face of more pressing problems. A leopard may not be able to change its spots, but it can put on a striped onesie and vow never to show them.

'Ready boy?' he shouts to the dog who ignores him to sniff at the base of a stone column. 'Fenrir,' he adds, more sternly.

Fenrir gives a short bark then rolls on his back in argument, he has been doing a lot of rolling recently, the large cone-shaped collar surrounding his head prevents him licking his itches.

'Come on, your stitches will be out in a couple of days and you'll be back to running about in no time, you can see her again soon.' He walks over and reattaches the lead to his collar, receiving a friendly lick that leaves a dark mark on his hand. There is an unmistakeable odour of fox-shit. He doesn't shout, not even when scrubbing it from his fur later on with his bare, freezing cold hands. This dog can do no wrong.

Polly's waters break at the same time as Storm Melissa.

Lightning flashes outside as rain batters the turrets and parapets of the Manor's ancient roof. Gutters become flowing rivers. Downpipes shake with unaccustomed traffic. Gargoyles spew the darkened filth of rotting leaves over deep-pooled flowerbeds. Polly screams as the contractions become more urgent. This baby is in a hurry, and her worry it might actually be an alien sent to kill her is not helped by the melodramatic weather.

'Okay, show's beginning then,' Melissa grins, coming back in with a bucket of hot water. 'Let's meet this girl.'

Polly has read plenty of books where they deliver babies with nothing but hot water and towels; but they were all fiction, most over a century old and very few of the mothers survived. She wishes she had read the pile of childbirth books left abandoned by her and Patrick's bed, but there had been plenty of time for that later. The baby has been an abstract concept up until this point. She is fairly sure that these days the actual delivery should involve sterilised things and very strong drugs. There are no drugs here apart from Mel's weird herbal drinks, and they aren't any good for actual, physical pain. At least not this kind, it hasn't stopped Mel forcing them down her though. She is terrified these Victorian conditions will have her emulating one of Dickens' trademark absent mothers.

The indoor lights go out as the outdoor light show begins. Power cut. Fenrir whimpers in the dark, unhappy about the storm thrashing all around. Patrick shrugs. He has no candles, just the torch on his phone and that won't last long. He is the embodiment of his mother's claim that this generation are completely unprepared for anything that can't be solved with an app. But Patrick has found there is usually somebody to help in a jam. He has always believed in the goodness of other people; it's been stretched of late, he admits, but somebody in this forgotten town will remember proper power cuts and know how to cope. He has a fair idea of where that will be, but opts for second choice.

'Pub?' Patrick suggests to Fenrir, who tilts his head. They'll be prepared for a power outage down there. They've got candles, cask ale and company. 'It'll be worth a few minutes in the rain boy, promise, and at least your head will stay dry.' He points at the lamp-shade shaped collar still round the dog's neck.

Fenrir gets up and limps to the door with a hearty bark of agreement, Patrick puts both their coats on and opens the door. They are immediately engulfed by rain, vision almost entirely obscured by the sheer force of water until the sky is split by a crackling blue strip of lightning. The town appears through the storm, laid out stark and clear in blinding blue light. As it vanishes again Fenrir rushes to the only sign of life, the familiar warm glow of the Drop of Dew. Patrick doesn't bother holding him back and runs behind, primal fear of the storm reawakened deep in his being.

It is open, it is full. When the weather gets tough, the tough go to the pub. It seems the entire town are huddled in here by fire and candle light, enjoying those drinks that do not require electricity to pour.

'Evenin' Doctor,' Pete the barman smiles through his bushy beard, 'and you Mr Fenrir, how goes the limp.'

Fenrir barks an abrupt reply as Patrick removes his saturated dog coat, hanging it next to his own on an overflowing clothes horse placed precariously close to the roaring fire.

'Lovely night for it,' Patrick grins. 'Pint and a small bowl of Ruby please.'

Once he's got his drink, and settled Fenrir down by the fire with his bowl, Patrick searches the room for a friendly face. Over by the window he sees the Dad Club and their families staring out into the storm: including Clive and Susan. In no mood for a fight, he resolves not to bring up Susan's lies unless they do. It would be nice to have friends again, and he will not win anyone round to his side by throwing accusations about, certainly not in front of all these children.

The way they are looking at him, they know. Even those glancing up disinterestedly from phone screens, newspapers and books. Of course they know, in a small town like this everybody will know he battered his girlfriend and stabbed her dog.

He knew everyone knew, it is obvious from the way his patients look at him when they come in. The way people only come in if there is actually something wrong, rather than the usual stream of borderline hypochondriacs just wanting a chat. He had hoped for it all to have blown over by now, this is his first foray into the pub since it happened.

'Long time no see,' Jack says. 'How are you holding up?'

Everyone has brought their big child-entertaining bags.

'Not too bad mate,' Patrick replies, sitting in the spare seat offered. 'Been better.'

'I bet you have,' Kerry says, fiddling with her phone and not meeting his eye.

'How's Doug?' Dan asks.

'Doug? Who's Doug?' Patrick replies.

'It's the accent,' Edwina explains, her eyes flashing with a look of kindness and sympathy reminding him of their shared secret. 'It took me a while to figure it out when we moved down, he means how is the dog?'

'Wouldn't have been so bad, but the first bloke in on her first day at the vets was old Tony over there, he said Doug was done for and asked if she could finish him off,' Jack explains. 'She nearly shat herself.'

'Yes, thank you for bringing that up.' Edwina shifts uncomfortably in her seat.

Dan rolls his eyes and, if anything, the dirty looks Patrick's been getting increase. This was a bad idea.

'Anyhow, as to the dog,' Patrick enunciates. 'Fenrir's getting better, yes. He'll be back to normal soon, won't you boy?' The dog gives a short bark of agreement from his place on the hot flagstones by the fire.

'That's good,' Lynn says frostily. Patrick hadn't noticed her in the darkest corner, flanked by two sleeping children. Candlelight plays tricks on your mind.

'Can I get you all a drink?' he asks, standing up and fiddling with the buttons of his shirt. 'I know you all think very badly of me, and I don't blame you. I did an awful thing and I can't forgive myself, I don't expect any of you to forgive me, or forget, and I'm not asking you to. This is just a gesture of thanks for your former friendships.'

The table grunt their assent and he squeezes between them to the bar.

'I don't know what any of you have heard, but you can ask me anything you like. I'll try to clarify,' he suggests, passing drinks across.

Their eyes meet, an unspoken conversation as they make a decision. The silence holds a while, shadows flicker behind faces, the pub strangely quiet with the jukebox out of action and background conversations reduced to a low murmur in unconscious acknowledgement.

'No,' Delia speaks for all. 'In the past now. We appreciate the honesty.'

Smiles all round the table, a glint of white teeth behind shadowed skin. Drinks are taken in hand, incomprehensible words of kindness muttered. Patrick's eyes meet Susan's and she puts her finger to her lips and winks, Clive nods and raises his glass. That's a situation to unravel another time. For now he needs a support network. These are the people he is going to have to trust.

The loudest roll of thunder yet peals out – drowning out a tiny cry of life newly begun in the master bedroom of Dourstone Manor – accompanied by an instantaneous flash of blue light illuminating the now dog-effigy filled square outside. They all raise their glasses in silent toast. Patrick is a father.

'Told you she'd be a girl,' Melissa coos, red-faced and smiling, as she wipes the necessary filth of birth from the baby. 'Strong one too, that'll be good.' She flinches back from the child's loud, forthright cries.

'Can I hold her?' Polly asks, feeling completely destroyed, yet interested – only interested, not desperate, she notes – to see this thing she has been carrying inside her all these months.

'In a minute,' Mel replies, wrapping it in an ancient blanket to keep the chill of the old damp house away. There is a fire in the grate, now down to a small heap of glowing coals, which, combined with the body heat coming from Polly and Melissa, has done a fairly good job of heating the room. But now the main event is over the house's natural cold is returning.

Eventually Mel passes the tiny scrap of humanity over. Polly isn't sure what she's supposed to feel, but suspects it should be more than this vague indifference. Her overwhelming feeling is one of gratitude this thing is finally out – almost an ecstatic joy she is no longer an incubator – and a hope she might be able to get out and about again. Not just yet though, right now she doesn't think she'll ever get out of this bed. Nathaniel Harker smiles down at her once more, his unmoving painted face returning to its warm, supportive smile.

She holds the baby tight to her chest – more from a vague intellectual interest in whether physical closeness will make her feel some connection than any need – looking down at its wrinkled walnut face. She hopes it doesn't look like her. She can't see Patrick in it either, only walnuts – maybe her grandfather. It wriggles around in her arms, and she loosens her grip, unsure of what to do. It shifts position to lock its mouth round her nipple and commence feeding, without so much as a please. Polly gives a little gasp of surprise at this unfamiliar feeling. This might be the relief dairy cows feel when the milking pumps are attached.

'Is this normal?' she asks.

Mel snaps round, checking nothing is wrong.

'Yes, yes, that's good. Healthy appetite; you're basically a feeding trough now. Get used to it.'

Polly nods, accepting her new role, looking down at this shrivelled, pathetic thing leeching away her last reserves of energy, sapping her will to live. Sentencing her to life – as a parent.

What could be mistaken for tears of joy flow down her face.

19

Then...

As I was manhandled up the hill the realisation that what I am was revealed to all hit me with a fear I have never before known. I was left in no doubt I would ever leave this place, never stroll aimlessly across Hampstead Heath, gaze into the depths of Mother Thames, or lean on a corner and watch the lamplighters illumine that jewel of cities. At least I would not swing at Tyburn in view of my friends and family. The people of Dourstone deal with their deviants in a different way. Even then, I knew my end – though I could never have predicted this brief reprieve, or that I would give it away for a vain hope.

Now…

Autumn has lost its fuzzy late summer feeling as the dark takes back control. It's the point of the year where people argue whether it's winter or not in pubs across the land. The paltry light spat out by the dying battery of Patrick's mobile phone is all he has to see by, and the hounds carved on the granite posts of Dourstone Manor's long driveway suddenly seem less comical. They almost seem to move, turning their faces to watch his progress.

On one hand Patrick is very happy to learn he has a daughter, healthy, nameless and happy. He has dreamed for years of his and Polly's first child, hope for the future, a tiny life created from the best parts of them both. He imagined himself and Polly, breathless with joy in the delivery room, deciding on names, ringing friends and family with the news, arranging visits. A Facebook post that necessitates turning off notifications from the deluge of likes, and 'Congratulations – you'll never sleep again' comments. All the usual stuff.

On the other, he found out from a note, pushed through his letterbox, on notepaper headed *Lady Melissa Dewer, Dourstone Manor*, and signed the same. No word from Polly. He fears she may never speak to him again. He has not told his family, has no photo to post on Facebook, and no hope of helping decide a name. He is helpless, cut out, cut off and beholden to this woman who has taken Polly away.

That's unfair, he thinks. He drove Polly away. Melissa is protecting her from a man they both see as a monster – and not without good reason. Knowing it is his own fault doesn't help his frustration. At the bottom of his well of self-loathing, there is now a tiny spark of joy and hope (both good names, he thinks) in the shape of a child. A link between him and the woman he loves. A reason to try and be a better person.

That's why he set out in hopes of visiting his daughter. Fenrir is at home, Patrick doesn't want to risk him tearing his stitches out playing with the pack. The dog is getting stronger every day, and Patrick thinks he might be forgiven. (For Fenrir's injuries, he probably hates him for driving his beloved mistress away.) But he has spent enough time around dogs to realise they aren't good at knowing their limits – he remembers a childhood labrador who insisted on running everywhere in a heatwave and consequently died – and the only way to ensure Fenrir doesn't harm his recovery playing with his friends is to keep him away from them until it is safe.

He does not know what to say to his new child, or her mother. He has no words to make up for what he has done. He doesn't even expect Polly to see him, but he hopes Melissa will intervene and allow him to at least see his child. For all her eccentricities she's a decent person at heart, and must argue for the child to see its father. He tried to phone ahead, but as usual nobody answered. He can't just sit at home waiting for an invite, and so here he is – again.

The only guiding light is thrown out through gaps in the curtains in those few inhabited rooms. He can see light from an upstairs window and hopes to see Polly's face peering out, maybe a smile at his arrival. But no. Nothing. He finishes the long trudge to the door where another hound firmly grips a knocker in its teeth. Patrick decides against disturbing it, and pulls a chain to the side instead.

CLANG! The old fashioned bell pull appears to ring an actual bell. Patrick reels at the sound.

'Hello?' A small wire-covered flap opens in the portal and an elderly voice sounds from behind.

'Hello, Lady Melissa? It's Patrick, can I come in?' He tries to keep the pleading from his voice. He can't help but think of a catholic confessional and expects instant judgement. Five hail Marys then fuck off and die.

'You again? I won't disturb Polly, she doesn't want to be disturbed.'

'I understand, just please let me see my baby?'

The flap smacks closed, bolts are drawn back, door pulled open with a textbook ominous creak. Patrick enters the dark hall. Lady Melissa stands before him, formidable in burgundy Edwardian dressing gown and fluffy slippers. Her face may have more lines than usual, but the expression remains implacable.

'I'll see what she says.' Melissa vanishes up the stair case. 'Wait there, unless you want to play with the dogs.'

Patrick worries this might not involve any squeaky bones that aren't inside his skin: he's bright enough to recognise a threat when he hears it. The oak panelled hall is an actual hall, not just a coat-filled bit of house where the stairs and doorways are, walls festooned with ancient weaponry: pikes, maces, swords, longbows, spears. They look functional, and very sharp. Tapestries hang from the walls, stopping short of the enormous fireplace, and the magnificent carved staircase leads to what could be described as a minstrel gallery, but should probably be referred to as a landing. This is not just any old house. It has history, it has a soul.

After what feels an eternity, Melissa reappears cradling a tiny bundle of life.

'Polly doesn't want to speak to you, but she will let you meet this one, here is your daughter,' she explains, descending the stairs.

'I get it, fair enough,' Patrick shrugs as he takes his child in his arms. 'Hello you,' he says. He can see Polly's eyes, his mum's ears, a slight look of Polly's grandad's nose – that's worrying – and the rest of his life in this face. 'I'm your daddy, I'm going to make sure nothing bad ever happens to you, that's a promise.'

'Let's hope she doesn't end up with a man like you then.' Melissa gives him a hard stare.

'It was a mistake,' he says. 'It will never, ever happen again. That's another promise.'

'I certainly hope you're right.' Mel's eyes flick towards the racks of sharpened steel about the walls, and she smiles. Not a friendly smile.

He notices a strange bracelet of entwined metal around the child's wrist. 'What's this?'

'Family heirloom, thought I'd pass it down to her. Given your story about your great-grandfather she might actually be the last of the Dewers – I've nobody else to give it to. Looks good doesn't it?'

Patrick is unsure whether he agrees, but doesn't want to antagonise.

'Yeah, lovely, has Polly picked a name yet?' he asks.

'No, she can't make her mind up.'

'Can I suggest Elizabeth? After my gran, not the queen. Let her know will you?'

'I will, and now that you've met her. I think you can probably be on your way.' Mel holds her arms out and gives a look which precludes argument.

Patrick hands his whole world over to this possible cousin yet virtual stranger and, with a kiss on the forehead, leaves the baby in her charge.

Her short life has ended. She is trapped in a shallow grave at an unmarked crossroads. A brief moment ago she was hanging from an oaken beam, circumstance having driven her to desperate measures. Her lover had turned out to have no intention of sticking by her. Had snubbed her once she was with child. Told the whole county of her lack of virtue, ruined what little reputation she had. She expected more from the lord's eldest son, but received much less. There was nothing more for her in this life, so she had finished it and was now trapped underground; condemned to this unconsecrated, inhospitable grave she can never escape. Her breathing becomes more laboured as she realises the air will run out soon. Why she needs air when she is dead and buried is more of a conundrum.

Reality drags Polly back with a lurch. Her eyes open to see an empty crib. She knows she should panic, that's what parents say. If you don't know where the baby is you can't rest until you know. It's an urgent, unending nightmare. Polly shrugs it off, assuming Lady Mel has her. She's been great, just like she said she would be. Polly hardly need do anything for the child but feed it, and she feels confident that if her equipment worked, Mel would do that too. But breast is best, and Polly is a never-ending decaf-latte dispenser. Intellectually she knows she is supposed to want to do it all herself, put the baby above everything. But, however guilty it makes her feel, her overwhelming reaction is relief that somebody else is doing the hard work so she doesn't have to.

'Good sleep?' Melissa says, entering the room with the baby in her arms.

'No, dreams again, bad ones,' Polly replies. 'Though at least it wasn't the Patrick werewolf dream. A change is as good as a rest. Did I hear voices downstairs?'

'Just a man come about some work on the estate. I sent him packing, I've got enough staff.' She lays the baby back in the crib, delicately supporting its head all the way down, a look of delight on both their faces. Polly would like to look at her daughter like that, but still sees nothing more than an imposition.

'Oh.' She looks put out. 'I hoped maybe Patrick cared enough to visit.'

'Of course he doesn't. Stop pining after him, after everything he did to you,' Mel replies.

'It's not for me, it's for her.' Polly points to the baby.

'If he cared about either of you he wouldn't have done what he did.'

'I've given him no chance, he might...'

'Might what.' Mel's eyes flash. 'Might give a shit about you? I didn't want to show you this, but...' She pulls out her phone, flicking through pictures.

'Show me what?' Polly asks.

'This, it's from the security cameras behind the Doctor's surgery.' Mel plays her a short video clip of Lynn and Patrick engaged in a kiss.'He's been at it with the whole town, doesn't care for you one bit. Now put him out of your mind.'

'But...'

'And whatever you think, there's been no word from him still – despite all your messages,' Mel insists, planting a kiss on the baby's head on her way out. 'Now get some sleep. I can mix you up a special drink for dreamless sleep if you'd like?'

'Not yet, but I'll let you know, thanks,' Polly murmurs, defeated.

Polly has sent texts, left voicemails, written emails, letters and every form of communication short of semaphore to tell Patrick he has a child now and needs to do something about it. But all to nothing. Clearly his assertion he wanted to 'talk about it all later' was bullshit.

Obviously she doesn't want him back, doesn't want anything to do with him after what he did, after he killed Fenrir. She would, however, very much like the chance to say this to his face. She did worry something might have happened to him, but Melissa assures her he's been seen in town, doing his doctorly works, even out and about with Susan and Lynn, at the same time. This video is just the icing on the cake, final concrete proof that it's all over.

She doesn't care about him, or this baby. He can have Lynn and Susan, break up a perfectly happy marriage and leave three children in broken homes that should have two happy, healthy loving parents. Live in some polyamorous world with his new harem. He has abandoned her to bring up his spawn – that he tricked her into having – all alone. She just wants to be able to leave this room, go out, leave the parasite behind. See real people again. Mel insists she needs to convalesce a while longer from the toll the baby has taken on her body and nerves. She is right, Polly grudgingly admits as she rolls over to go back to sleep.

20

Then…

I was taken to the cellars of the Manor, where none can hear you scream. Left in a tiny storeroom to rot, bread and water once a day to prevent starvation, no ventilation so what little tobacco I had would cause my eyes to water and my nose and throat to burn. No company, no comfort, no word of you. I lay on the hard floor in solitude and awaited my short, miserable end.

And then they came.

I was dragged to the cart, tied to the stone.

I knew what it meant.

Even though I had known it was coming, I have never known such fear, such guilt.

What if all those others were as blameless as I? Have I been complicit in murder of innocents? An innocent man of God even? I do not know, this troubled me more than my own imminent trial. I did not struggle. I lay back inside the stick man costume – another subterfuge I had aided Lord Elias in concocting – resigned to the inevitable.

I do not blame my Lord Elias. It is the Lady Melissa he was born into that wants this petty revenge.

Now…

'I'll take you to the people that need you most tomorrow,' Patrick says, removing the collar and lead from Fenrir, who jumps up – stitches out, fur grown back and at least twice the dog he was – then rolls on his back in front of the fire. Patrick doesn't really want to part from this dog, but he knows Polly and the baby need him more – even if they haven't told him.

He realises, with a sigh, that it has been a year since they moved into this house. This weekend is Wish Weekend, and he would be able to fully enjoy the festivities were it not for the gap in his heart where love used to live. He is not sure what to do, he has a child and a woman he loves but does not deserve. Should he leave? Go back to London, let them get on without him and send money? Let her grow up without a father? It might be best, he decides. After all, his temper could explode again, and he would never forgive himself if he did anything to hurt that tiny, perfect creature he has held only once.

There is still no word from Polly and his now six-week-old child. Only second hand news delivered via Lady Melissa's headed paper. Rumours abound that her and Polly are engaged in a full time loving relationship. The Lady is well known for her enormous and diverse sexual appetites, and Polly was the subject of considerable speculation even before she moved in. Nobody had the heart to tell Patrick before now and it was with great reluctance that Dan took him to one side and explained. He felt it better Patrick heard it from a friend than an overheard whisper in his waiting room. As long as Polly is happy, he doesn't care what she does. He would like to hear from her though, even if she just tells him where to go.

He understands, she believes he slept with Susan, everybody believes he slept with Susan. He can't understand why she is lying. Anytime he tries to explain to his friends it didn't happen they respond with a look, equal parts damning and sympathetic, before being told it doesn't matter and to drop the subject. He walked away, he knows he walked away, but he now feels as guilty as had he actually done the deed. Polly is forging a new sexual identity away from him, she can revenge herself by taking a lover. Even a pensionable old lady lover he has lost the right to have an opinion about.

He feels a headache coming on, so he goes to his doctor's bag, hoping to find some of the good painkillers he keeps there for medical emergencies – one of the perks of the job. There aren't any in the usual pocket, so he rummages down further where his hand closes on a sheaf of forgotten papers – shoved to the bottom of the bag in haste to help an injured dog. He pulls it out and reads: *I awoke at the centre of the stone circle Lord Elias and I raised in happier time. Moonlit figures, disguised by velvet robes, checked I could not escape....*

It feels a lifetime since his discovery in the Manor's library, he never got round to looking at the papers – forgotten in the events that happened afterwards. He makes up for that now, after finding the right pills, he knocks a couple back with a large glass of decent single malt – a calculated risk that usually results in a good night's sleep – and settles down by the fire to read.

He is not far in when he gets the feeling he may never have a good night's sleep again.

Next morning the urgency has increased. The pills and booze eventually did their work, and Patrick wakes to find himself fully dressed, slumped in the armchair next to the dying embers of his fire with all the attendant cramps and pains such a night entails. He is still in a state of disbelief. This can't be real, it has to be some manuscript for an unpublished story. Except, it fits all the facts, everything he was trying to explain when he was looking into the disappearances. He and Polly have been manipulated and he wants no more of it.

He picks up the phone and dials two nines before hanging up. What would he say? 'Excuse me officer, but I believe my girlfriend, who I recently assaulted, is being held against her will by a vampire.' Even he doesn't believe it. Nobody would think he was anything more than a jealous ex concocting a ludicrous tale to try and separate her from her new lover. But he is certain.

He puts Fenrir in the boot of the car – because he is scared to leave anything he loves alone – and drives off to the Manor, no visits, no ifs, no buts. He is taking his family home, they're not safe with that... that... he doesn't know what Lady Melissa is, but she cannot be human.

'Stay here boy, I'll be back when I know she's safe,' Patrick says, pulling up behind the stables where the car can't be seen, and crunching across the gravel. He rings the doorbell, jarred by its unpleasant timbre before shaking off his earlier fear, grabbing the brass hound's knocker and pounding it against the brass-studded door.

'Give me back my family, I know what you are,' he says, before Melissa has had a chance to say hello.

'Oh I don't think you do.' She smiles, not the least bit perturbed by his outburst. 'Come in, we'll compare notes.'

'Oh, okay.' Patrick is thrown. He looks over his shoulder to the stable block that hides car and dog before Melissa leads him up the stairs to the library and bids him take a seat. He finds himself complying.

'So,' she begins, 'what do you think you know?'

'I know you're at least a century and a half old,' he says, 'so I don't think you can be human. What are you?'

'Well, for one thing, I'm your great-great-grandmother, so you should show me some respect boy.' She smiles.

'You're what?'

'You heard me, don't look so surprised, why do you think you and Polly came here?'

'We wanted to... errr... a quieter life... we...' Now he thinks about it, it was an odd decision to make. He knew the place of old, but didn't really feel any strong ties. He's pretty sure his father only hangs on to the house to annoy the locals – they haven't been here once since Patrick and Polly moved in. For some reason he had been insistent on moving here, rather than up to the north coast, where Polly's mum and grandad still live full time. He doesn't even have anything against Polly's family, he likes them more than his most of the time. The look on this strange woman's face suggests she weaved some strange magick (it feels old enough to warrant the k) to entice them here.

'You came here because I wanted you to. I need an heir, a new vessel, this one can't keep going much longer,' she says.

'I don't understand.'

'And there you were saying you did, not five minutes ago, let me get you a drink.' She leaves the room, and Patrick finds himself feeling unusually content, the fires of his anger quite extinguished. His surprise was ridiculous, of course this is his great-great grandmother, it is obvious.

'Drink this,' Mel says, placing a mug of something hot and steaming next to him.

Patrick complies, sitting back in his chair. 'Thank you.'

'Right then, what do you know?'

Patrick summarises the story he read in the manuscript. Happy to be of help, quite comfortable, just a boy and his great-great-grandmother having a catch up.

'So that's what he meant.' Melissa chuckles. 'He said the world would know what I was, that my time was ended, and all he'd done was write a little story and hide it in a book nobody would ever think to look in. And you were the one to find it. How fortuitous – it's brought you here right on time. Saved us a great deal of work.

'Now, let me fill in some of the blanks. Your great-grandfather was my son, and I have no need of sons, that's why I sent him away – over sentimental of me to put him in the hands of the Sumners but dear Nathaniel had a far greater hold on me than he knew. It turned out to be a shrewd move once I realised the brat had broken poor Melissa's tubes on his way out. Keeping him in town meant I could keep watch on the family line until your uppity father decided to move to London. You were half on the right track when you suggested it was some dirty old Dewer that sired your line, but it shows how little you know of our family history.

'The Dewers of Dourstone have been descended down the female line since time immemorial. For centuries I have dressed as men, presented as men, called myselves Lord, hid our true nature. This body, this Melissa Dewer – was the first, the first Lady to claim the title in our own flesh, and that was after a very long time continuing the family tradition.'

Patrick nods. 'You're possessed.'

'A very ugly word. The Dewer women have provided me with a nice living these last – oh I forget how many – centuries. I don't ask much, and without my guardianship of this town, you have no idea what hell would rain down. I am, how do I put this, very much the lesser of two evils.'

'Lesser?'

'Lesser. You would not like to meet the other. He is... not kind.

He does not love this place as it deserves. The legends of Devil and wisthounds are entirely fictitious obviously, but based in fact – just as you said, clever boy.'

Patrick tries to raise an arm to scratch his nose and finds himself incapable. He doesn't mind, he is so comfortable, and Great-Great-Grandmama is so kind. She'll take care of him.

'My use of these bodies gives them extended life. But never quite long enough. This one has served me well, in all its guises, but it is time for it to sleep. I'm going to need you to do a little something to help. You don't mind a little sacrifice for the town do you?'

Patrick shakes his head as Great-Great-Grandmama picks something up from the table and walks towards him, smiling sweetly.

'Hello Doctor,' says Father Hearne, raising his homburg.

'Don't talk to him please Arthur, just get his legs,' Melissa says.

21

Then...

As the cart made its way from Manor to stone circle my mind dwelt on the sounds that had made me so sick two years ago and the screaming that followed for longer than I thought possible. Previous victims had been stronger, braver, more manly than I. How would I cope? To feel my flesh rent by sharp, filthy teeth as those powerful muzzles push insistently in, casting my tender skin aside like pie crust to feast on my organs. To see my intestines unravel and the hounds fight over the juiciest parts of my liver? How long would I retain the ability to watch? The imagined pain was already too much to bear. I began to panic, then passed out from fear, and what occurred afterwards I have already documented.

Now…

The road is long, and oh so familiar. She has travelled it in this hated coach, fashioned from the bones of her four dead husbands, for as long as she can remember. The dog leads her on, always ahead of the relentless rattling, a huge, black hound from the depths of hell, making sure she does not shirk her duty. Each night they make their way from her home back in Tavistock, across the high moors, to Okehampton Castle where the dog will pluck a single blade of grass before they make their way back.

The coach comes to rest in front of the house she so hated in life, where she is doomed to forever return. The dog looks up, an evil glint in its eye, and lays its blade of grass upon the granite there. She knows they must keep this up until all the grass of Okehampton Castle is gone from the mound.

The hopelessness of it all brings her to her knees, and Polly begins to sob. The dog joins her in an ever louder whimper that brings her back to the waking world. The sounds of merriment from town have finally died away. Polly is sad not to be able to attend the Wish Weekend revels, but Mel assures her she'll be back to full strength soon. She'd be livid to know Polly hasn't drunk her herbal drinks today. She's so sick of them she's been tipping them into the aspidistra by the bed.

And there was that one dream, that dream that seemed to happen here, long before the Manor was built. She desperately wants to get back to it. There's something there, a truth she can't quite grasp, but feels if she did, something would click. She would ask Mel about it, but Mel insists on the dreamless drinks – though all they bring are different dreams, wrong dreams that place Polly in unfamiliar bodies. Mel has been so good to her, so helpful with the baby. It would seem spoiled to ask her to stop, would almost certainly hurt her feelings. So the aspidistra has been getting all the benefits, if aspidistras dream.

Polly is beginning to feel more her old, active self again. This is the first time she's felt truly awake in a long time. She might venture out in the morning, go for a real walk. Take in the town, see what she's missed while she's been cooped up.

Another whimper from outside surprises her, the sound from her dream. It's not the mournful howl of malamutes in full voice, it sounds like Fenrir, but it can't be. She hops out of bed, surprised at how strong she feels, like she hasn't since the baby was born. It's been six weeks, she really must give it a name, but she has barely seen it. Melissa takes care of it day to day and she has been too weak and apathetic to argue. After all, she never wanted it, so why worry? It's one less complication in a life already too complicated.

Once this recovery ends it will bring all new dilemmas: where to live? Who to live with? Alone? With family? With friends? Stay in Devon? Maybe nearer her family? Go back to London? What of Patrick?

Well, what of him? He's made it very clear by his absence how much he thinks of her and the parasite. Melissa wants her to stay here, and there are definite advantages.

But it is time. Beginning with a little investigation of night-time noises. Then worry about the big stuff later.

After a difficult hunt around for her clothes she is dressed for the outdoors. Polly tiptoes through dark corridors, past rows of ancient weapons glinting in the moonlight, stern faced ancestry and fading tapestries to let herself out. She hears the howl again, accompanied by a faint scrabbling. It does sound like Fenrir. A cloud passes, and the moon illuminates the courtyard where all this began, pure white snow shining in the darkness. Polly sets off at a trot, rounds the corner, and finds Patrick's car behind the stable block, a familiar face silhouetted by moonlight in the window. The timbre of Fenrir's howl moves seamlessly from misery to unfettered joy.

Stopped in her tracks, unable to believe the evidence of her eyes, she rubs them, once, twice, three times before she accepts she isn't hallucinating. How can this be? She saw him, bleeding out on the kitchen floor. How could Patrick not have let her know he was alright? She fumbles in her coat pocket, yes they are there, her keys, including the spare for Patrick's car.

Quickly she unlocks the door, and it is him. Her Fenrir. He jumps at her, knocking her down to the frozen gravel of the drive. She doesn't care, it is so good to feel something, anything, again. He smothers her with licks and affection until she cries for joy.

Once the reunion is over he sniffs at the ground and races around to the house, giving a sharp bark. He jumps through the door ahead of her, and for the first time since she woke up, Polly notices the lack of malamutes prowling. She turns her head every which way, listening for them, a trance-like state. You can sense if they are there, even when you can't hear or see them. They have a presence all their own that weighs on your soul. Polly can no longer feel it. A sharp bark from behind reminds her there is a more important dog to attend.

She follows Fenrir through the house, where he runs past embers smouldering in the great hall's fireplace and up to the library. They enter and he runs madly around in circles, looking for something, careful not to knock the free-standing shelves over. Polly finds herself looking at a photograph of two Victorian gentlemen and a lady standing at the stone circle. One of the men looks familiar. It is, yes, Nathaniel Harker, from the painting upstairs. The other looks like Lady Melissa, but with a beard, she squints closer, clearly he is her ancestor, probably the Lord Elias she spoke of, but the resemblance is uncanny.

Fenrir stops, barks and points his head at an antique writing desk topped with an ornate ormolu hunting hound. There is nothing on it but the fanciful ornament. Fenrir does not move, but emits another short, sharp bark, pawing at the desk. Polly shrugs, then bends to fumble with the draw in search of whatever has spooked him, and finds her phone inside.

It can't be her phone though, she has that, it's in her pocket. She pulls it out, this is an exact copy, right down to the custom made case with the selfie of her, Patrick and Fenrir on Crooklets beach. How can this be? Why would this be? What is the point of going to all this effort to replicate a relatively cheap phone that still has six months of payments left? She flicks the screen and unlocks it with her passcode, her birth year. A flood of notifications greets her eye, text messages, voicemails, emails, all the channels of communication she has checked relentlessly every day. All from Patrick.

She falls back into a chair and begins to listen and to read. She sees now how Fenrir has been nursed back to health, brought here to look after her and the baby, how sorry Patrick is, all the work he has done to be a better person, anger management, meditation, mindfulness, everything. He doesn't expect her to believe him over Susan, but he did not do what he is accused of, and will not admit to a thing he hasn't done. He wants to help Polly, without expectation, he only wants what's best for her. Hundreds and hundreds of messages reinforce this.

But why has she got a different phone? Without any of this? She compares the two and finds her number has been changed on the new one. Only by one digit, along with Patrick's. A little deeper investigation reveals an app filtering system, diverting messages from all her other contacts to her new phone, but not his. It's a very impressive bit of coding, and she is briefly lost in it, admiring the elegance and simplicity with which it works. But then who could have done this, and why?

The who is obvious.

The why is not as simple.

'Come on boy, let's find Patrick,' Polly says, pocketing both phones.

Once outside she makes for the car, but Fenrir shies away, pawing the ground and whining. He has shown her the right way so far. She decides to carry on trusting him. He peels off under the dark, tree-canopied driveway and barks for her to follow. Polly wishes she had time to do some stretches before running after him.

The night procession has reached the snow-capped hilltop unseen this year. The cart stops in the
stone circle. Hooded figures chant their dreadful chant and remove the sides to reveal the altarstone, an effigy of the Dourstone stick man tied securely to manacles about its edge. It is pushed back and forth until it meets the exact centre of the circle. They bow their heads and hum low and loud for a whole minute, then repeat their prayer, check the stick man's bonds and process away down the hill, chanting all the way.

A soft rustling in the woods behind the stone announces their arrival. Saliva drips from teeth, eyes shine bright in moonlight. The pack have waited behind the trees for this, their yearly price, but the wait is over.

Cronus stalks through the stones, heading the pack who follow behind, awaiting command. Serried ranks of grey and white fur surround the clown-like doll on the rock, their leader turning his grizzled face from side to side to inspect his army. He raises his head – mismatched eyes now both a piercing blue – and lets cry the first sound. They follow his lead, turning their faces moonwards to howl their mournful song in unison.

Fenrir dashes up the hill, stopping here and there to reorient himself with a sniff. They pass through the square, strewn with discarded plastic cups that confuse him with their overpowering scent of spilled cider. His unswerving sense of smell carries them onward though, and they run, sliding on icy straw from bales ripped apart by gleeful children, until the line of houses gives way to countryside. Everybody knows the Wish Weekend party goes on all night, it's why everyone comes back. So where is everybody?

Fenrir stops at the gate to the cottage. The cottage she and Patrick moved into a year ago today with such high hopes. Before everything happened. They can go back, they can get past this. Patrick will love their child even if she can't, they can make a life – and a family – in this cottage. This cottage they still haven't painted, this cottage with the worrying looking crack running up the front and the not-quite-rotting thatch; filled with unpacked boxes of unused things they cannot bring themselves to part with.

Susan and Clive, and the pictures she saw, must be part of whatever is happening. They are part of Mel's inner circle and Mel pulls the strings round here. The good Lady Melissa Dewer clearly needed to drive a wedge between them, and she has played right into her hands – Patrick's history with Lynn must have been a gift. It is time to regroup, remember what side she is on. He must be inside, that's why Fenrir has brought her, to reunite the people he loves. There are no lights on, he must be asleep, she will go in and surprise him.

Fenrir barks twice, and sets off again, heading further up hill. Polly stops hunting for her keys, and with a lingering look up at the window (she can see frost forming inside, Patrick has not been keeping it warm enough to stop all that condensation, damp and awful that makes anything left in the fitted wardrobe stink) and follows, wondering where he could be taking her.

As they near the crest of the hill, the stone circle appears, silhouetted at the summit in bright moonlight. The cart stands at the centre, the fires of the evening have burned down to a faint orange glow and Polly is reminded of Patrick's supposed gruesome find last year. She had assured him he imagined it, but now she is not so sure. A dread fear grips her heart and she forgets to breathe: there is something on the cart.

She edges towards it, unwilling to see, but unable not to look. A cloud blows across the moon, faint foggy dimness smothering the light to leave them in darkness. Fenrir holds back outside the stones, near the glowing ashes of the fire, something has spooked him and he will not enter. It is Mr Punch, no, the Dourstone stick man, lying awkwardly over a stone that forms the base of the cart. Of course, she remembers seeing the scarecrow pass the window last year. The fright she got, how Patrick reassured her it was nothing to worry about.

She reaches down to touch it, it is warm, damp. The cloud moves aside, moonlight making it clear this is no scarecrow. The stuffing is flesh, the damp is blood, she is gripped with worry for the priest, what could have happened to poor Father Hearne? What is he doing out here? Was he really the Lord of Misrule, King for a Day? She pulls at the oversized head, its leering painted smile mocking her attempts to remove it.

'Polly, I'm sorry.' It finally gives.

She cannot believe her eyes. It is not Father Hearne, but Patrick, inside the stick man. And he is alive – despite the gore spread across the cart.

'No, Patrick, it's not your fault, she... she played us, every step of the way,' she says, untying him from iron rings set into the stone.

'You can stop it Polly, you have to.' He coughs, blood spraying from his mouth. 'She's going to possess her, take her soul, please. I love you.'

The terror in Patrick's eyes wakes something in Polly. Her indifference to her child coalesces around re-awakened love for Patrick and becomes something real; something good; something pure. The wedge driven between them has affected her judgement, clouded her mind, she has not been herself, but now the way forwards is clear.

'I will find her, and I will keep her safe. I love you too and I'm getting you out of here,' she replies, cradling his head and kissing him despite the deep cuts in his face. 'How did you end up like this? Who? Why?'

'The pack, her fucking dogs,' he wheezes. 'The bastards tied me to this rock, dragged me up here just like Nathaniel Harker, then the dogs came. Only they're not really dogs, or they are, maybe. But not normal dogs. And not really hers. Everybody's part of it, you can't trust anyone Polly.'

'Nathaniel Harker? From the painting? What about him? How do you even know about him?' Those friendly eyes from the bedroom wall come to mind, that sense of sadness urging her on.

'I found his...'

'Shit, this isn't going to work,' Polly interrupts. Beneath the ropes Patrick's limbs are held fast to the iron rings by thick, plastic cable ties. 'Hang on, I'll have to go and find something to cut these.'

Polly searches the hilltop without success. Not so much as a broken bottle or sharp-edged can left out. For some reason the debris of a weekend of debauchery has all been contained in compostable plastic glasses that will not sustain a cutting edge.

'I'm sorry Paddy, I'm going to have to leave you, I won't be long, but we need something sharp.'

'Fuck, please. Don't go. Don't leave me on my own.' Patrick's eyes are wide in terror.

'But... we can't all just sit here and wait. Look around you, there's no cavalry coming, it's only me and Fenrir and we can't get through this.' She pulls uselessly at the plastic encasing his wrists. 'He'll guard you, won't you boy?' She beckons to the dog who drags himself through the stones to sit next to Patrick.

'Thanks, I wish you wouldn't go.'

'I won't be long, promise. Don't go anywhere.' She kisses him goodbye and runs off down the hill.

'I love you!' he shouts after her.

'I know!' she replies.

Watching her disappear into the darkness Patrick is gripped with an idea. What if he is just bait? What if it is Polly the dogs really want? He has sent her off into the dark, all alone and covered in blood.

'Go with her boy,' Patrick mutters to the dog. 'Keep her away from here, she needs you much more than I do.'

Fenrir wavers between the two, not wanting his friends to be split up again, before running after Polly. Patrick turns his head at a rustling from the trees.

Minutes later, Polly has found the secateurs she asked Patrick to put away, on a hot summer's day that feels a million years ago, frozen onto a plant pot by the cottage gate.

'Why are you here? You're supposed to be guarding him!' she shouts at Fenrir as he rounds the corner. 'Come on, we need to get back before...' she doesn't want to finish that sentence.

They make it back, and Polly lets out a sigh of relief to find Patrick right where they left him. Alone. Polly sprints the last few yards.

'Got them, hold on, I'll just cut you...' She stops in her tracks. Something has happened, he has shifted on the rock, and things she is sure should be inside him are not.

A bark from Fenrir distracts her attention, he thrusts his head urgently into her armpit and paws at her. She pushes him away, Patrick is in more need than the dog.

'They came back Pol,' Patrick groans, still alive, just. 'But good news, they wanted me, not you.'

'Oh god,' she screams, straining at thick cable ties with rusting secateurs. 'What do you mean, who came back?'

Fenrir barks again, nearly overbalancing her as he pushes in.

Turning around she realises the gaps between stones are filled with glowing blue eyes, a suggestion of sharp teeth and a familiar carpet of grey fur. The pack have returned, silent as ever, though changed. They have not seemed this menacing since that first meeting at the Manor, where she mistook them for wolves. Their demeanour of lovable eccentric idiots is gone. This is a pack of dangerous creatures, mournful eyes now given a deadly glint. Polly doesn't think she will be able to distract them with a biscuit.

'I'm getting you out of here.' She lifts Patrick from the rock, dead weight in her arms, trying not to spill what remains of his insides.

'Don't bother...' he splutters.

'I'm not leaving you.' She hasn't come this far to leave him now, he can be saved, he will live.

Cronus pads out of the wall of dogs, growling low. He holds Polly's eyes in his, now burning with that unearthly blue light. This is the same dog who has sat by her side these last months, a friendly protector, his giant soft head lolling on her lap as he begs for crisps. It is difficult to equate that loving pet with this snarling predator, as if he is being worn by something else, something more dangerous. Polly doesn't like to think of something more dangerous than Cronus – she's seen him tear the legs from a deer without breaking his stride – but she has never been so wary of this monster.

He sits in front of her, in caricature of his familiar good boy pose. Polly is not fooled, but lowers Patrick and moves towards Cronus. She reaches for his face, palm up in gesture of supplication. The dog nods, giving a harrumph of approval and she comes closer, the silent act of negotiating respect one she is used to. His eyes are not on her, they are focused solely on Patrick, still laid out on the rock behind. Plenty of other dogs have eyes on her though, she is not going to fool him. She walks away from the dog, towards the stones, and a gap appears for her to walk through, dogs parting in deference as Fenrir bows his head to Cronus before loping to her side. She walks back to Patrick and the gap closes, short growls coming from the wall of animals, Cronus utters a sound of disapproval.

That makes things clear.

'I'm taking you with me,' she says to Patrick. 'Get ready.'

'No, don't... kill you too.' He knows his situation, it's only a matter of time, the jigsaw of his digestive system cannot be put back together now, not by the most skilled of surgeons.

'I can't leave you here to be...' She can't say eaten. She doesn't want to say eaten.

'Eaten?' Patrick grins. 'Already had most of the good bits.' He spits out another large gobbet of blood. 'Good eco-friendly way to die, circle of life and shit.'

'Hakuna Matata,' Polly laughs, despite everything. 'I'm giving it a go.' She reaches down, gets a decent grip on Patrick and lifts him from the rock.

'Hakuna Matata,' Patrick echoes, head hanging over Polly's shoulder as his viscera slide gently out of the large hole in his abdomen. He knew they would.

She loses her grip, letting out a scream as his organs slide over her, they fall together into the snow, and she holds him, refusing to let go. Fenrir whines next to them, tugging at Polly's sleeve.

'Now run,' Patrick says, eyes burning with life that explodes before leaving him forever.

Polly stares into those eyes, the only eyes she has ever loved – now glazed and dead. She doesn't want to leave him, but there is no good reason to keep his remains and no sense in both of them dying. He's not in that pile of offal melting the snow, he is gone. Fenrir nuzzles against her side, making urgent whimpers. She stands up, and they walk towards the wall of snarling teeth. The roadside exit remains blocked by malamutes so they circle the edge, Cronus watching them all the way round until they are under the trees where he nods and makes a gutteral sound. The pack make space, and woman and dog step through bloodstained muzzles, steaming pelts and those changed, terrible, blue eyes. They hit the treeline and make a run for it. From behind comes a single howl followed by the sound of feeding animals. Polly's eyes blur with tears as she negotiates the deep, dark woods.

Fenrir gives a warning bark and a thundering sound makes her turn, they are being pursued. Cronus, alone, he has left the pack to finish Patrick and intends to stop Polly. She stumbles on through dark trees and swelling blizzard. Branches grab at her hair; scrub and bramble trip her feet and the freezing cold burns her skin; but she cannot, must not, stop to rest.

A stray root catches her foot and she blunders to the ground. Fenrir continues on, oblivious to her plight. Her breath has caught in the fall and she is unable to shout. She can only make an urgent unheard cry for help that dies in the wind. Cronus hoves into view, leaping silently over obstacles, in his element now the snows have settled. He leers over her, blood and spit dripping from his maw as he pins her down with mighty front paws. Polly closes her eyes and tries not to choke on his foetid breath. She waits. There is nowhere left to run. She hopes Melissa's plans for her child are benevolent and prays to a god she has lost all hope in that the girl, Elizabeth – that's a good name – will live, and live well. She wishes she had been able to tell somebody her name is Elizabeth. Surely the final strike must come soon? She feels the cold ground seep through her thick coat, providing a counterpoint to the damp warmth of her underwear. Her bladder, still not fully recovered from the baby a month and a half later, has finally given up its tenuous grip.

A rush of air, a growl, then a yelp and a weight is lifted. She opens her eyes to see Fenrir's return, spilling Cronus from his perch. The two dogs circle each other: keeping to the edges of the clearing. Fog spills over the ground as the blizzard subsides. She looks to her saviour for guidance, the dog breaks from his ritual to nudge her into action with his head, he licks his friend's hand and gives a short good boy bark. She understands.

The dogs launch themselves as Polly jumps to her feet and runs. She doesn't know where to, but the from feels more important. She can't see how Fenrir can triumph, the rest of the pack can't be far behind, so even if, by some miracle, he bests Cronus he can't take out the rest. He has done this for her, to help her get away with no hope of his own survival. Polly cries freely as she crashes through a hedge, slipping on the icy road and grabbing hold of a bramble to steady herself. Hot blood warms frozen fingers as it spills from pierced skin.

Finally, a stroke of luck. She is opposite the cottage and this time she is firm, she will go in. She can rally here, prepare for what comes next. Her hands close on the keys that are blessedly still in her pocket. Once inside she locks the door and runs upstairs to Patrick's office. She knows he's got fishing knives in there, the secateurs wouldn't be up to the job even if she hadn't left them up at the stones. She doesn't intend to be a victim again tonight. She wipes yet more tears from her eyes, thoughts of Patrick, Fenrir and those wolves becoming too much.

There is a pile of paper on Patrick's desk, it looks old. Intrigued, Polly takes a look: *I awoke at the centre of the stone circle Lord Elias and I raised in happier time. Moonlit figures, disguised by velvet robes, checked I could not escape...*

There are pages of notes strewn about in Patrick's impossible doctor's cursive. She sits down, this is important. This is the key. This is what he wanted to tell her and didn't have time for. This is why he looked so scared their baby might be at the Manor. She reads on, this is impossible. This can't be.

She remembers the kindly eyes of Nathaniel watching over her during what she now realises was her imprisonment. His words now reach across centuries, helping, letting her know what she is up against. Reading his story, how he too was taken in, used and tossed aside by this creature – Polly has difficulty seeing Lady Melissa as a person any more – Polly wants revenge, not just for her, Patrick and Fenrir, but for Nathaniel as well. His face from the picture, his words from the page, his end, so like Patrick's. It feels fresh despite being over a century ago. They are the same, they are kin, he is, she realises from Patrick's notes, Elizabeth's great-great-great-grandfather. She can't wait to see Elizabeth and name her, tell her the full family story restored after all these years.

The parental instinct starts to burn. This cannot go on. Elizabeth is at the Manor, held by this thing that seduced and betrayed her. She has to go there, even if she has to rip her way bare-handed through every single mangy dog that woman has she will get her baby back.

She will make this right. Inspiration strikes and she rummages in Patrick's doctor's bag.

She looks up from her search to see a mirror and jumps out of her skin. She does not recognise herself, she has changed so much during her incarceration. She has not paid any attention to her appearance and her hair has grown out to its natural frizzy halo, made even more angelic by sleek blonde tips hanging from the black curls, making her unmade-up face seem darker than before.

Ten minutes later she comes down the stairs having cleaned herself off and thrown together an all black assassin's outfit. She sees her grandfather's sword hung over the fireplace for luck. How very lucky, she thinks, expertly flipping it down and tying it round her waist.

22

Then...

They have interred me in the library, I assume it is only temporary and they will throw me back to the dogs soon. I will not escape again. I threw myself upon Lord Elias' mercy earlier, not for myself, but for you. I hope he listens, and, for the sake of what we once had, lets you live. He said my seed was tainted. He needs a girl. I don't pretend to understand the things he told me. He tells a good tale, but must suffer from some kind of brain sickness. Spending his life presenting as a sex other than he truly is must have led to a degradation of mental capability, and, due to his power, influence, good health and long life, he has persuaded many others of his own delusions. I have encountered others more hermaphrodite than he, but they do not live in such fantastical deception. I am certain none of his rambling can be true, my death will serve no other purpose than to feed his dogs.

One thing is certain, he hates me for my infidelities, and assured me Thomas was acting under his orders. He spoke to me of the great difference between sex for sport and sex for love. The erotic parties he and Lady Sophia host are merely for sport, they hold no affection for the various partners attending.

Elias asserts that in his long life and many bodies (he claims he was here before Brute the Trojan first set foot in Devon) he has never once wanted anything to last. His usual – always female, he only uses men to breed – partners, remain faithful to him til death. I thought that was a beautiful touching thing, but Elias assures me he gets bored waiting for them to die so he can move on. He insists he added the ritualistic orgy to the end of the Wish Weekend ceremonies centuries ago to keep that boredom at bay. He cried when he came to see me tonight, told me I was different, that I had broken his heart and he would miss me forever. I told him he didn't need to, that time heals all wounds and we could repair our relationship, but he assured me it doesn't, and we can't.

He pulled a box from inside one of the Library's many cupboards and pulled out a brand new copy of Gray's Anatomy. *I had expressed an interest in returning to medicine, since the Dewers had taken over Father's business, I wished to be useful again and had thought to perhaps become a rural doctor, remaining here in Dourstone. Elias fully supported my ambition. He paid for this book, before everything went wrong, it was a gift, it cost him a lot to ship from America and I felt ashamed as he flung it at me. Truly, I do love this creature and should not have let my lusts wander. Time cannot be turned back though, and Elias has made it clear I am no longer welcome. At least I shall not have to live with my regrets for long.*

Now...

In the cellars of Dourstone Manor is a room, a room used for one thing only. Older than any other part of the building, the only light comes from a torch in Lady Melissa's hand. There is a lightwell high in the ceiling but the moon is behind clouds. We are below the earth, in the unspoken heart of Dourstone Nymet, a special place.

Lady Melissa Dewer places the baby on a peculiar-looking chair atop a raised dais. She walks steadily around it, lighting a perimeter of candles. The ground down here is nothing but earth, packed hard a long time ago. The walls contain hidden alcoves, decorated with bright, primary-coloured flaking paint and containing jars of gruesome-looking objects; figurines of ancient provenance and the accumulated occult detritus of centuries. The misshapen yellowing chair atop the dais faces a tall wooden altar, decorated in gilt and scarlet and unimaginably old with many well-used drawers and nooks.

She has left orders not to be disturbed.

'There wasn't a baby last year, after, you know,' Edwina says to Susan in the hall. 'We just did the procession, left him... in the circle... and then drinks back here. This is all a bit serious.'

'I've never seen this part before either,' Susan says. 'The rituals aren't always annual, there are differences every year. This is the first baby though.'

'I've heard...' Edwina stutters. 'I've heard things, rumours, from the old ladies when they bring their cats in. About Lady Dewer, things they heard from their grandparents, ancient secrets. I thought they were all crazy, making things up, now I'm not so sure.'

'If you want to be Dourstone.' Susan sighs. 'Then you have to learn not to question things so much. You need to keep your mouth shut and do what the Lady says. We keep the secrets, remember?'

'Sorry, I know. It's just, this is only my second Wish Weekend since I was initiated. I'm used to knowing what's happening and why, this is difficult, blindly following orders.'

'You'll know one day, they'll let you in on all of it when you're ready. You have to prove yourself first,' Susan explains, hand on

Edwina's arm.

'When did they tell you?'

'They haven't yet. I'm still a risk, owing to my big mouth.' Susan grins. 'It's a fair assessment.'

Edwina looks surprised, but reasons it will take longer for either of them to earn full disclosure, being incomers. 'You're not wrong,' she replies.

'I'm just nipping out to check on Wendy,' Susan says. 'She must be bloody freezing.'

She opens the front door and steps out into the mist and snow where Wendy stands watching the driveway, a long black velvet hooded cape over the top of her purple ceremonial robes.

'Are the dogs back yet?' Susan asks.

'No, no sign of them. They should be, I don't know what's keeping them.'

'They could have run round the place for the last hour, and be back sleeping in their kennels for all I know,' Susan jokes. 'I wouldn't have heard them. They're so quiet, they give me the creeps. Why can't she keep normal dogs?'

'She likes the malamutes,' Wendy says. 'They're an interesting breed, they're adaptable, not easily spooked. It's a useful trait.'

'Well, we all have to put up with her ladyship's impositions don't we?'

'We do, but it's worth it.'

'She doesn't ask that much of you,' Susan begins.

'You know nothing of what she asks of me,' Wendy says. 'You don't know enough about anything. And it seems to me she doesn't ask you to do anything you wouldn't do anyway.'

'What's that supposed to mean?'

'Whatever you like, you're pretty good at splitting people up, I hear you had practice before you ever came to this town.'

'That's not true, it was a rumour we needed, to make it believable. I love Clive, only Clive.'

'You didn't seem too upset when you had to go and sleep with that dishy doctor though,' Wendy snipes, making a playground kissy-face.

'I've told you, I didn't really. She wanted me to, but he wouldn't bite.'

'So you're saying now...' Wendy says in a sing song voice.

'Jesus, I had to try and convince everyone it happened, we had to split them up. That's what the Lady wanted.'

'Two years running though. You get the scarlet woman gig. It's like your special skill.' Wendy laughs, the moon illuminating her face in the folds of her hood.

'Okay, look, it was only because Lynn couldn't finish the job. She had the history, should have been able to walk in and snap up Patrick just like that. And I didn't actually sleep with Graham, it was just a honey trap, Lynn couldn't get him to do what we needed then either. I did what I had to do, same as we all do. I kind of feel bad about Patrick though, he wouldn't even consider it.'

'Not even for a minute?' Wendy looks shocked.

'Nope, still, he was one of the bad ones. Mel said he did awful things to that girl. I hope she can come round to our side. I like her. I'd like us to be friends.'

'I never met a man who didn't even consider sleeping with me before,' Wendy mutters. 'Must be something to do with you. I'll give you a shout when I see the dogs.'

Susan goes back inside with a curt nod.

Wendy doesn't hear it coming. She is flat on her back before she knows it, winded and unable to cry out, after a perfectly executed roundhouse kick to the chest. Polly crouches over her, finger on lips. She looks at Wendy, eyes wide and shocked, years of self-defence classes failing to prepare her. Polly smiles, 'Nothing personal,' she whispers in her ear before cracking her head against the steps.

Polly gets up, looking down at Wendy on the ground before rolling her onto the porch out of the snow. Stupid mistake, she hit her too hard; questions first, then violence. But the violence felt so good. She is digesting the overheard conversation. Patrick never cheated on her, never had any intention of it. This has all been one big con. How far back does it go? She adjusts her clothing and shins up the drainpipe, watched only by the door knocker's unseeing eyes.

Upstairs, Kerry looks out through tall windows, jealous of the opulent surroundings. Silver candelabras set into the walls, oil paintings and tapestries so meticulously clean it is obvious Lady Melissa has people who 'do' for her. Kerry can't help thinking that what with all the things everybody else does for her, Lady Mel could maybe lend out some of her perks once in a while. She and Dan could do with a bit of help, especially with Dan's mum the way she is. How dare Mel involve her in all this! Still, she played her part well. It seems to have worked out.

Kerry hopes the ceremony will be complete soon. She needs her bed. These ceremonial robes might confer status but they are heavy, and itchy, and the blizzard has left them smelling damp and unpleasant. There's something about this particular aspect of the whole business that unsettles her – 'not in living memory,' was how Melissa described it. An ancient thing, circle of life, renewal and rebirth. The child is only a baby though, and some vague assurances it will be fine from a woman who just fed a man to a pack of dogs – again – are not all that comforting. There is a creak behind her. She turns around expecting to see Dan coming back from his guard inspection.

'Anyth...' the words die in Kerry's larynx as she is cracked back against the ancient wood-panelling, breath knocked away.

'Where is my daughter?' Polly hisses in her ear, snow-covered from the blizzard and still panting from the exertions of her climb.

'I... I don't know, not here, nobody's here,' Kerry stammers, recognising the righteous ire in Polly's eyes.

'Don't make me ask twice.' Polly pushes a syringe up against her throat.

'She's not here, I don't know where she is,' Kerry says. She may be worried about the child, she may not be certain of Mel's intentions, but she isn't going to betray her. The woman would know. There would be consequences.

'Don't say I didn't warn you,' Polly replies, pushing the plunger and emptying the syringe into Kerry's neck. She drops to the ground and Polly stalks off into the house, aware there will be more guards; instinct telling her Elizabeth is here somewhere. A dull pain spreading through her chest reminds her the baby will be hungry – Mel can't do everything for her yet.

She rounds the corner of the winding, disorienting corridor and sees Jack, sprawled across a chaise longue, perusing a volume of poetry. She raises a smile at his slack attitude, she's tempted to sneak past down another passage and leave him for Melissa to deal with, but she can't leave any help standing.

Hanging on the wall she sees an ancient longbow and a quiver of arrows. A team-building weekend with a long-forgotten city firm taught her to handle one of these, and she quite took to the sport. The elegance of the weapon called to her in the same way as fencing. She takes down the bow – pulling it onto the string, it is strong, it is powerful, it is very dangerous indeed – and straps on the arrows, nocking one onto the bow.

She leans out round the corner, sighting her target, the ceremonial robes that still billow around Jack too inviting an opportunity. She draws back and then lets fly. Two arrows in quick succession. Jack's arms are pinned to the oak of the walls and he gives a cry of surprise. She steps out and quickly covers the length of the tigerskin rug between them.

'Where is my daughter?' she asks, holding him by the throat. He gags, unable to speak, his eyes popping as he struggles to answer. She doesn't want to make the same mistake twice and loosens her grip.

'She's, she's...' he tries to speak.

'Don't bullshit me, I know she's here, try and lie and you'll end up the same as Wendy and Kerry back there.'

His eyes widen further in terror, imagination filling in the blanks. He nods, indicating that she should let go of his throat for him to speak. Polly relents, allowing him full use of his voicebox.

'She's... UP HERE! QUICK!' he shouts, bringing Dan sprinting around the corner.

Polly thinks on her feet, headbutting Jack hard between the eyes to leave him unconscious. With no time to nock another arrow she grabs a huge African ceremonial spear from the wall and fends Dan off with a deft spin of the shaft; leaving him in no doubt she's done this before.

'I don't know what you think you're going to do maid, but give it up. You can't win,' he says, keeping out of spear range, hands held out as if wrangling a sheep.

'Where. Is. My. Fucking. Daughter?' Polly repeats, executing a hand to hand spinning pattern in a terrifying display of spear-handling competence.

'Not here, you're barking up the wrong tree, now put the spear down, I'll make you a cup of tea,' Dan says.

Polly advances, heading for the staircase, Dan backs away from the flashing point of her clearly-been-kept-very-sharp-indeed spear.

'I don't believe you, and I don't want tea,' Polly spits. 'What's with the dress?'

'Wish Weekend, we're keeping up the traditions, you'll get it if you stay here long enough. You want to stay don't you?'

'Yes, I did want to stay, with my dog, my daughter and her father but you lot are making that increasingly difficult. Now tell me what I need to know.'

'Honestly, we're just having a party, I thought Mel would have told you about it now you're living here? Please, put the spear down.'

'Okay.' Polly lowers the point, Dan walks towards her with arms spread wide.

'That's better, now if you'll just...' Once inside the spear's radius he makes to grab her wrist, but Polly has anticipated this, her whole move a feint to draw him out. She moves her hand on the spear, getting a better grip for close contact, then whips it back up, and thrusts it towards him. It catches in his long robe, causing him to fall against the banister rail. Polly follows up, pushing him back against it so he cannot move, spear pressing against his gut, other hand twisting his wrist back.

'Daughter,' she says, her nose almost touching his as she pushes against him.

'Not here,' he says. His head leans further into space as his centre of balance moves in the wrong direction. His traitorous eyes flash to a door below.

'Liar.' Polly grins and pushes in just the right place, knocking him the rest of the way over the banisters where he lands in the middle of the tiled floor, limbs spread awkwardly.

Polly runs down the stairs in no time and makes for the door. She knows it leads to the wine cellars. She has wandered about down there during her convalescence, but no further than a longing gaze at the racks of dusty bottles she could not enjoy until the parasite was done feeding on her. She is struck with remorse she has no time to indulge for her former resentment of the child she has come to save.

Her way is barred. Susan stands at the bottom of the stairs grim-faced and armed with a pike from above the grand fireplace. Polly raises her spear and prepares to engage.

'I'm sorry about my affair with Patrick, he wouldn't let up, I'm not calling it rape, because I didn't say no, but he was very insistent – Lynn tells me he's got form for that.' Susan grins, planting her feet wide apart.

'You never got near Patrick, I know, I heard you talking to Wendy you manipulative bitch,' Polly replies, swishing her spear through the air.

'I don't know what you heard, but I want us to be friends, I feel sorry for you, I don't want to hurt you,' Susan says. 'Join us, let this happen. We have more in common than you think. You can help. We keep the secrets, you can too.'

'You're not going to hurt me, but what are we letting happen, and what secrets are we keeping?'

'They wouldn't be secrets if I told you would they?' Susan laughs.

'I suppose not. What makes you think you should feel sorry for me? This is my home now, Melissa wants me to live here. What are you doing? Throwing yourself at other people's men and getting refused? Desperate for approval and doing whatever she asks, cuckolding your poor husband. He wasn't happy about it, was he?' Polly knows about psychological warfare. It's the easiest way to downsize a company, make them question their very *raison d'etre*.

'He does what he has to, so do I. You're not from round here, you wouldn't understand.'

'Nor are you. Come on, let me through, I need to talk to Melissa. I know she's in the cellar.'

'You don't,' Susan retorts.

'She tells me everything, I'm her life partner, we're raising a baby together,' Polly lies, wagering Susan doesn't get told everything.

'Well that's not true. Otherwise you wouldn't have had to do that.' She points to Dan's motionless form on the flagstones.

'Fair enough, you've got me. Now cut the shit, she's down there isn't she?'

Susan gives an imperceptible nod. Polly strikes once, spear thumping off the side of the pike. Susan begins to think this might not be worth it. She doesn't even know the secrets she is supposed to be keeping. It's difficult trying to fit in in a new town. Especially when your husband grew up here, family going back generations. She only joined the WI to meet new friends, find a way to fill the days. Initiation into Lady Melissa's inner circle seemed like a good idea, and Clive was so happy she joined him. Polly's words have made her think she is being used. She is not some tart for hire, whatever Wendy says. Maybe it's time to give it all up, persuade Clive to leave, move somewhere they won't be controlled.

She is about to step aside when Polly sweeps at her legs with the spear, knocking her to the ground. Her resolve strengthens as she sees red, who cares about the rights and wrongs of this, she's been knocked on her arse. Nobody knocks her on her arse. She lunges at Polly with the pike, only for a nimble sidestep to save her and the consecutive parry to land on the back of her head, blundering her away.

'There's no sign of the dogs yet, or Wendy, I don't know where she's got to, but I reckon Mel will have something to say about it. Ooof!' Edwina says, coming back into the hall just in time for Susan's next clumsy attack to connect with her head. She drops to the ground, limp.

'Thanks for the assist,' Polly grins. 'Now give it up.'

Susan is torn between her mothering instinct telling her none of this is worth it any more; and her natural competitive streak urging her to carry out the job she has been given. She can't let this woman get the better of her. She pushes back off the wall to rejoin the attack, Polly easily ducking underneath the pike, her spear thrown to one side. Before she knows what has happened, Polly has disarmed her and has her in a lock. She cannot move as she is forced down to the ground, where Polly pins her with her legs.

'Is she in the cellar?' Polly asks.

'Yes,' Susan gives in.

'Where?'

'Right at the end of the line, last room.'

'Who else is there?'

'Lady Melissa has her, Clive is down there – please don't kill him – guarding the doors.'

'Thanks, and sorry,' Polly says, pulling a syringe from her pocket.

Susan senses the change of weight, and sees her chance. With a careful wiggle, she tries to shake Polly loose.

'Nope,' Polly says, slamming the needle into Susan's flesh much harder than intended. She shudders before lying still. With a sigh, Polly pulls herself up and heads down the ancient stone steps to the cellar door.

'It's okay, I'm back, I am on this, you shall not pass!' Edwina declares. She has regained consciousness and remembered her job. She will not be pulled up for shirking.

'Fuck's sake, stay down!' Polly says.

'We keep the secrets!' Edwina explains, picking up the spear Polly foolishly left on the floor.

'What are these secrets everyone is keeping?' Polly asks, her fingers finding Susan's lost pike.

'I don't know yet, but if I stop you they might tell me,' Edwina continues as she rushes towards Polly.

'All this and you don't even know why?' Polly lifts the pike to knock Edwina aside. Before she completes the manoeuvre, however, Edwina loses her footing on the flagstones, her face turning a ghostly white as she realises what's about to happen.

'Oh dear,' she says, resigned to her fate as her chest crashes onto the pike. She slides down to end in an unhappy pool of blood.

Polly pulls the pike free and shakes her head as she grasps the door handle. The cellar opens to her touch and she descends into darkness.

23

Then...

However much truth there is in any of Elias' words, and I doubt nearly all he has said, if only because of the obvious love between him and Sophia he denies so strongly, I still believe that Thomas loved me. Elias does not know of the trick knot, I pray he never does, I could not bear it if Thomas were to suffer this same fate. Thanks to him I could have made it safe away, but for you. I have lived my life entirely selfishly up until this untimely end, and nobody has been more surprised than I at this final, avoidable sacrifice. I regret nothing, I have pleaded for your life, and done all I can.

I will secrete this in my new edition of this fine medical text, a gift bitterly given and undeserved. Perhaps Lord Elias will happen upon it one day in the future, find these pages, think of me and pass them on to you. Perhaps he will relent and raise you himself, with Lady Sophia. Perhaps he will live openly as your mother, the Lady Melissa Dewer he was born as, and you will come across them yourself. In any event I hope one day you read these words and know you had a father, if only briefly, and that he loved you. I name you Charles, for my dead brother, and hope to see you in the next world.

I hear them coming, fare well, or at least fare better than I.

Your father, Nathaniel Harker.

Now...

On the other side of the door Polly stops, allowing her eyes time to adjust. Stock check: the longbow is still across her back, sword about her waist and she is using the reclaimed pike for support. All this action has taken its toll on her body and she wishes she had spent more time keeping in shape since the birth. She can't stop now though, the ache in her chest tells her Elizabeth is waiting. She can't let her down again, she needs to know her mother loves her.

At the bottom of the steps is a glowing light, there is electricity down here – in the areas nearest the house anyway – always kept to low wattage bulbs, Mel says it gives the right ambience for a cellar. Polly thinks it more reminiscent of a dungeon. She creeps her way across the floor, aware Clive is on guard.

The wine looks so inviting, she is tired. To sit, drink and forget everything is such sweet temptation. But she cannot forget the daughter she has ignored for so long. There is danger here. She prays she is not too late. As she rounds the corner past the last of the archways that give on to what could be infinite darkness, she sees it. The final door, massive, ancient, leather covered and iron studded. The heart of the Manor. The heart of Dourstone.

Clive leaps out from another of the doorways that fill these catacombs, wielding an old branding iron whose tip has long since snapped off. He knocks the pike away from where Polly leans upon it and she collapses, vulnerable for a moment, but only a moment, her fighting instincts returning despite the energy-sucking subterranean gloom. She has been wallowing in fatigue, feeling the effects of all this action. But no more – adrenaline will win the day. Her hand snaps round to draw the sabre at her waist, bringing it round in a gleaming arc cut short by the intervention of Clive's shining steel hand. He snaps it round, trying to pull Polly off her newly-regained feet, but she twists her body and wrists effortlessly to evade his trap.

They adopt the *en garde* posture. Clearly Clive has fenced before. This might be to her advantage. She starts the classic motions, thrusting and parrying with vigour, always keeping far enough back to prevent him landing a blow – remembering all the tournaments she won with her lithe, dancing technique, keeping just out of reach with only brief forays into the danger zone. The sabre's longer reach is a considerable advantage compared to his branding iron. She feints left, then quickly stabs back in to the middle, landing an indisputable point. Unfortunately there is no buzzer, and Clive merely stumbles backwards as the sword makes contact with his chest. She has not used enough force to pierce the skin, but has ripped an ugly hole in his robe. At least there will be a tailor's bill.

His hands graze the ground as he regains balance without landing and swaps his branding iron for the discarded pike, evening the odds with his new reach. The tip is sharp, deadly and still warm with Edwina's blood. Polly curses her stupidity at not thinking to get it back, or at least kick it out of reach. She begins a new, more defensive, technique, parrying his blows, moving backwards in a constant reverse lean, as if her back were attached to a gimbal – she knows she cannot hold this position long. He grins, sensing his advantage and starts to press. Polly allows herself to make mistakes, mis-stepping, stumbling, adopting a face of fear, and it appears to take all her effort just to block his blows.

Clive bears down, a victorious grin splitting his face, cocky now, whirling the pike up and preparing for the death blow. Polly spins, her blade a whirl of flashing steel that cuts the pike in half, ruining Clive's grip and balance; her foot a blur of expensive, heavy, designer snow boot that connects with Clive's groin, bringing him down in a pile of agonising limbs.

She reaches into her pockets for another syringe but only finds a pool of damp broken glass. They must have broken during the fight. She grabs his branding iron and brings it down on the back of his neck, rendering him insensible. She considers finishing him off with the sword – Highlander style – but there has already been more death than she anticipated tonight. He is a stooge and has suffered enough. She remembers his face as he told her about Susan's infidelities – she doesn't think that was acting. He has her sympathy so she steps over him to the door. It slams into her face, knocking her over Clive's prone body to the cold, earthen floor where her sword skitters away.

'I don't think so,' Delia says, stepping out. 'Well done though.'

'Oh come on!' Polly shouts. 'Can't I get a break here?'

'Nope, nothing gets in the way of this, not you, not anyone. It's important.' Delia shuts the door behind her and folds her arms.

'Is my daughter in there?' Polly pulls herself together, crouched on all fours now, trying to get back up, sweat beginning to trickle down her back as her temperature inexplicably rises. That last hit took what might be her last reserves, she didn't bargain with having to deal with anybody but Lady Mel, and she has a feeling physical strength will have nothing to do with that conflict.

'Fuck it, look at you, no point pretending. Yes, the girl is in there, and she's not leaving until it's done.'

'Done? What does that mean?' Polly, now removed from the act of actively pursuing Elizabeth, has a second to wonder what is happening. Why she is here. Her imagination goes into overdrive and she copes the only way she has tonight, with violence. 'Get out of my way!' She finds a new cache of untapped reserves and launches herself, now unarmed, at Delia.

'No.' A simple retort, as Delia lands her elbow in Polly's ribs, leaving her winded, wheezing and crouched against the stone wall. Rage is no way to win a fist fight, time to think.

'That's,' cough, 'my daughter,' cough, 'in there,' cough, 'please?'

'You can play hurt as much as you like, I've seen it all before. Dourstone needs a protector, and that protector needs certain sacrifices to be made. I'm not stopping this.' Delia is adamant. Polly doesn't like the determination in her eyes, or the sound of these certain sacrifices. Surely Melissa wouldn't kill her baby? She has been so attentive to her needs these last few weeks.

'I need to see her, I need to see she's alright, what are you doing?' Polly lurches forwards, leaning hard on the wall, back towards Delia, desperate now. What if she is too late?

'I can't tell you that.'

A glint from the darkest corner brings inspiration.

'Fuck you then.' Polly launches a fist. Delia easily blocks it, and counter-attacks with a knee to the groin, Polly folds up, coughing and flailing against the ground to prevent landing on her face as she hits the corner.

'Help me up, I won't fight, I'm sorry, I'll do whatever Melissa wants, I love her, don't you understand?' She crawls across the floor.

'You can do better than that? Surely?' Delia scoffs, throwing her head back in laughter.

It is the moment Polly hoped for, a tiny lapse in concentration. She brings up the snapped top half of the pike – Edwina's blood slippery beneath her fingers on what remains of the shaft – and rams it into Delia's exposed throat with all her strength.

'Yes I can,' she says, pushing the spluttering form down on top of Clive where their blood mingles together in the dirt. She walks back to reclaim her sword, gripping it tight before opening the door a second time, her head now swimming with fever.

She is unprepared for what greets her – after everything she has seen tonight she shouldn't be surprised by anything; and yet she is. Her baby, strapped to an eldritch chair atop an ancient dais. A high lightwell spills moonlight over the floor but it is candlelight that illumines the Lady Melissa Dewer, it seems impossible to think of her as Mel like this. Mel, her friend, her confidante, her lover, the one person she thought she could count on now engaged in occult ceremony that will take Polly's baby away from her forever.

Polly does not intend to let her.

'I know what you want to do, I know what you have done, and I know who you are,' she bluffs. Melissa knows nothing of what she has been through, this is her chance to find out what's happening.

'Do you think that matters?' Melissa laughs. 'Do you think any of you matter to me? Do you know what I do for you?'

'I know you mess with our minds, trick us into doing what you want, feed us to your damn dogs.'

'They are not my dogs, and you don't know why, you couldn't understand why.'

'Try me,' Polly says, spinning her sword idly around.

'Stupid children, all of you. I protect this place, this is my home. I did this for you, all of you... mankind, none of the others care one whit for you. I had to bargain with the dogs, win them to my side, they belong only to themselves – no matter what your twisted legends say. I have been here longer than anything. I love what you humans were, so innovative, so clever, so reverential of the trees and the rivers – and here I have made sure you never forget. Not like everywhere else, where you've stopped caring for the things you can see and begun to worship things you can't. I was, and am, prepared to do anything to protect them. So I have. I didn't want to take on this form.'

'You didn't take on any form, you possessed her.' A memory of a shining spirit and a scared girl from a dream suddenly makes sense.

'She wanted me to, it was voluntary, it was that or burn with the whole community. We couldn't have that. I had to do something, they conjured me forth, I took my place, I fought off my... brother I suppose you'd call him, for want of a better description. They called him The Devil, I had no mind to correct them, it's as good a name for him as any other.'

'So why stay?'

'He comes back, every year – when the cold thins the walls.'

'I don't believe it, I think you made it all up, to keep people scared so you can suck the life from them. You're some kind of vampire.'

'Stupid girl, vampires aren't real.' Mel laughs.

'No, but that photo of you in the library is. The fake beard doesn't fool me, I know you too well now. You put that stone circle up, and you were an old "man" then. You and your dogs are sucking the life from others to prolong your own.'

'No, my spirit keeps the body alive longer than usual. It is a small price for the vessel to pay, Melissa has seen such progress in her long, long life. We bonded back when there was a George on the throne – such as it is – I can't remember which, either the mad one or the fat one. I don't bow to any of them. Anyway, it's time to let her rest.'

'Yes, leave her, leave us all.'

'Oh no, I haven't gone to all this trouble just to give up in the face of some banker with a pointy stick.' She waves Polly away as if she were a fly.

'Banker?' Polly laughs. 'I'm so much more than a banker now.'

'Really?'

'Yes, I'm a mother, your plan has failed, I care, I love Elizabeth, she is mine and Patrick's. Your glamours haven't worked this time elf.'

'Elf! Where are you getting this stuff?' Mel laughs. 'And you're no mother, you've been glad to be rid of her while she's been with me. Every single day.'

'Better than you, abandoning your son just because he wasn't what you wanted.'

'How do you know that?'

'I've read Nathaniel Harker's diaries, Patrick had them.'

'Diaries? I was under the impression it was a single entry, designed to slander me from beyond the grave.' Humanity returns to

Melissa's face, concern, sadness even. 'Do you have them with you? I would dearly love to see them.'

'Give me back my daughter and they're all yours,' Polly bargains.

'I loved him you know, whatever he said, it was – complicated.'

'You fed him to your dogs.'

'They are not my dogs, how many times do I have to tell you? You know nothing, now get out. I have no more need of you. I can find them myself.' With a wave of Melissa's arm Polly is flung to the far corner of the room where she hits her head against the stone wall. She shakes it off and tries again, fighting off the heat of whatever this fever is.

'She is all I've got!' Polly shouts, leaping to her feet and running back to the dais, sword in hand.

'Me too, she is the last of the Dewer females. Dourstone needs this, and the world needs Dourstone Nymet. You can't possibly understand my work.' Mel waves her hand again, disorienting Polly so much she runs straight past her into the opposite wall. 'Ah, come in my dear, are the dogs returned?'

Lynn enters the room. She steps over to where Polly is sprawled on the ground and binds her arms and legs with bailer twine. Polly is unable to stop her and unsure as to why. She is held fast by an unseen force, dizziness preventing her from so much as focussing on Lynn's face.

'Yes Lady, the pack has returned.'

'Cronus?'

'Not yet, the dogs have what you need though, I'm sure he'll be back soon.' Lynn steps up from Polly's prone body, walking across to the dais.

'Of course he will.' Mel lifts her head and whistles. 'Sometimes the pack do what I tell them dear. When I really need them to, when they are quite themselves, and when I have given them what they need, the bargain still holds.'

The room fills with hot, stinking fur and the panting of dogs – their eyes still that unnatural blue. Polly watches as one of them drops something at Melissa's feet. She lifts it up to examine in the moonlight.

'The first for the new vessel, and an appropriate one at that.' She nods, opening a draw under the chair and pulling out a jar, then walks over to where Polly lies helpless and waves the piece of wet flesh in her face. 'Her father's heart, it will be a powerful charm.' She unscrews the jar and drops Patrick's heart in where it floats down through formaldehyde to join the others.

'I gave up my own heart, such as it was, to this place. These substitutes are nothing in comparison, but they stand for it.'

She lifts Elizabeth up and sits on the throne with her on her lap. Polly sees it for what it is: polished bone, carefully joined together, skulls punctuating the extremities. That is why it looks off-balance, it isn't finished.

'My previous hosts.' Melissa smiles, stroking a skull beneath her fingers. 'The Dewer line, all together. I will add Melissa's bones once these are strong enough for the work.' She looks gleefully at Elizabeth, holding her up to the moonlight.

'You fucking bitch,' Polly says – the pain in her chest reaching a new crescendo. 'Let me go.'

'Oh no.' Melissa grins. 'We'll need another next year – and family is always best. The changeover is gradual, I shall need to inhabit both this body and hers until she is grown enough to take on the Manor. You'll be living down here now, until we have need of you.'

Melissa straps Elizabeth to the throne, her little face gazing back in wonder, not even a flicker for Polly. But why should there be? She has spent as little time with her daughter as possible.

Mel busies herself with the ceremony, drawing symbols on the floor and arranging her jars in the circle of candlelight. Her supernatural grip is loosened now there are physical bonds to hold Polly, giving her that most awful thing, hope. The walls are rough and she rubs bailer twine on stone to no avail. The swirling dogs hide her movement so she wriggles along the wall to where the sabre still lies. She cuts the cord from her wrists, wriggling inelegantly on the ground under cover of stinking fur before sitting back up as if still bound.

'I need water,' she cries. 'You can at least give me that, you need me alive yes?'

'I suppose – Lynn!' Melissa commands. 'Give her water.'

Lynn brings her a glass of water, there is a plentiful supply in a jug in one of the many alcoves – no doubt it is needed for some part of this ceremony. Polly gulps it down in hopes of lessening the heat of her brow and the throbbing headache that numbs her thoughts.

'Help me Lynn, you're a mother, Patrick was helping you, she killed him, just like she killed Graham,' she whispers. Patrick trusted her, they had history, surely she would help. 'Please?'

'Helping me?' Lynn scoffs. 'You still don't get it do you?'

'Get what?'

'You've been played from the start. I helped kill Graham, I was glad to, it was necessary to keep Dourstone alive. We planted all that stuff to get Patrick on the trail, he had to come willingly or it wouldn't have worked. We needed him, we needed his child. We don't need you, you're no Dewer, you're not Dourstone. You were just an incubator.'

'But, you...'

'Are an excellent actress,' Lynn gloats. 'I hated Graham, he was weak, he was useless. I never loved him. He wasn't local, he was vain, lazy, living off my money, he was an investment in the future of the town. Like you and your...' The word seems to taste bad in her mouth as she says it. 'Partner. Expendable.'

'My partner? The man you lost your virginity to? All that history? And you don't even care that he's dead?'

'Is that what he told you?' Lynn laughs. 'I've always been an excellent actress. Patrick was a bet, I won twenty quid and a bottle of vodka off of Debbie for deflowering him. He fell for it, I mean, who the fuck is a virgin still at sixteen? Losers, that's who. Poor, stupid boy.'

Polly has no qualms about this, this woman has not been manipulated, not brain-washed, she is responsible for getting them into this. She hops up and silences Lynn with one smooth jab of her sword, covering her mouth to hide the scream. The malamutes increase the volume of their constant moaning to further mask the sound. Melissa is crouched in front of Elizabeth, chanting softly, her closed eyes level with the skulls at the front of the throne.

The dogs part, allowing Polly to walk through. She reaches the dais as Melissa rises back up and turns, too late to see her adversary. Polly immobilises her with a hug, sword tip held to her throat.

'Stop what you are doing, and give me my daughter.'

'Are you quite mad?' Melissa cackles, now in full pantomime villain mode. 'Surrounded by the pack? You can't win.' She gives another whistle and Cronus lopes in, head down. Polly redoubles her grip.

'I'll take your head off before they can get to me.'

'I'd like to see you try, you're quite surrounded.' Melissa smiles, her face glowing with youth and glamour. 'Kill her,' she says, looking Cronus in the eye.

The dog makes no move, but sits in front of them, head still down. He shuffles uncomfortably then lifts his muzzle and lets out a mournful howl, Polly braces herself.

'You still understand so little, poor girl. This is just a vehicle, you can do what you will with this flesh, I shall endure, as I always have done,' Melissa gloats, unafraid of the sharp steel at her neck.

'But you've said yourself, you need a new vessel. The ceremony is not complete, not even begun as far as I can see. All I have to do is cut you off here, and that's it. Nowhere left to go.'

'You know nothing.' Melissa's face betrays doubt, worry clouding her eyes. 'Cronus! Bring the pack, take her down!'

He does not move, but continues to stare at Melissa and Polly.

'The dogs aren't working for you any more are they?' Polly smiles. 'Something's gone wrong, I think. Am I right Cronus?' The dog averts his eyes, looking back over his shoulder.

'Now!' Melissa screams.

There is a bark from outside the door and Fenrir enters, head and tail held high. He walks over to his mistress, dismissing Cronus – who rejoins the rest of the pack – with a look.

'I think you'll find the pack is mine now,' Polly leers.

'No.' Mel's face drops, still in the glow of whatever magic is working on her but no longer triumphant. 'The pack will never belong to anyone.'

'Maybe not belong, no, but I think they'll do what Fenrir says from now on. Up to you boy,' Polly says, stroking his ears. He gives a short bark and the pack move forward as one. Polly lets go and jumps back from the fray. The dogs turn on their former mistress, knocking her out of the circle and pinning her to the ground. There is a blood-curdling scream and Cronus pads out from the melee. He stops in front of Polly and Fenrir and drops something on the ground at their feet. It is a finger, with a macabre ring still on it.

Polly picks it up, sliding the ring from the finger and idly trying it on her own, as she walks to where her former lover lies in a pool of blood, held down by dogs. She does not notice the moonlight ignoring all laws of nature to follow her across the cellar.

'What should I do with you,' Polly laughs as the dogs part to let her stand over her vanquished foe. She likes the look of this ring, though she has never suffered from fits. She found the idea of a ring made from coffin-nails repugnant at first, but it feels good. It feels right. She may keep it, after all she has been through she deserves something.

'Please, please, thank you, let me go, let me go.' A familiar voice comes from this broken figure. Lines of age return to her skin, her face sinking.

'What?' Polly is stunned, she had forgotten the night Melissa lost her ring. This is that same childlike voice, those same startled, frightened eyes.

'I'm free, now let me go. The dogs, let them take me. Join the circle, it is our way.'

'Okay. As you wish.' Polly's eyes harden, she nods to Fenrir, who nods to Cronus who looses the pack. With a terrible, enigmatic crumbling smile, the real Lady Melissa Dewer vanishes in a thrashing whirlpool of fur. She does not struggle or cry out.

EPILOGUE

Wendy wakes to find herself underneath a bench. She shakes snow from her cloak and runs into the house where she finds Dan and Susan. Dan mutters something and, after a quick check, Wendy rearranges his body into the recovery position before moving over to Susan. The only thing she seems to have hurt is her pride.

'I think she got past me,' Susan says. 'I knocked Edwina out, it was an accident though, I didn't... oh God.'

Both her and Wendy's eyes find Edwina's body slumped by the open doorway to the cellar. They cannot speak as they walk past her down the steps.

They stagger through the cellars, shell-shocked at this unexpected death. Unplanned, one of theirs, undeserving. Approaching the open doorway to the ceremonial room they see an awkward pile of bodies. Susan feels the bile rise in her throat as she recognises Clive's false hand.

'Clive! No,' she shouts, running.

'No what?' he replies, muffled by Delia's arm.

'No scaring me like that you prick,' she says as they roll Delia off.

Wendy stifles a scream as the pike protruding from Delia's chin rolls into view.

'Oh God, Wendy, I'm so sorry.' Susan's relief is tainted with guilt as Wendy grabs at her wife, searching for a non-existent pulse. 'Maybe she's..?'

'No. She's gone. Come on, let's get in there,' Wendy says. She kisses Delia's forehead and closes her eyes before wiping her tears and scrambling to her feet.

The three of them enter the cellar.

'Glad you could make it,' Polly says. 'Sorry to knock you all out, but needs must. I didn't want anybody to die. I had no choice, it was self-defence.'

They survey the room, neat ranks of malamutes, headed by the Irish wolfhound, alert and guarding their new mistress. An almost inaudible wheezing comes from Lynn, curled up in a pool of blood. A neat pile of ancient brown bone in the middle of the room marks all that remains of Lady Melissa Dewer. And, sitting on the throne of bones, head haloed by the blond tips of her hair, caked in blood and gore with her daughter suckling at her breast is Polly. Kerry and Jack wander in, bleary-eyed.

'You've killed my husband,' Kerry says. 'You'll pay for that.'

'No, he's alive,' Wendy says. 'Which is more than can be said for my wife.'

'Or mine.' Jack folds his arms.

'It was not my intention, as I have already said. I am sorry for your losses, but...' Polly stands up and takes a deep breath. 'As the last of the Dewers – don't worry, we've got the paperwork – all of this belongs to Elizabeth now.' She indicates the baby, for avoidance of doubt. 'I will be administering for her until she comes of age. Which means I am Dourstone Nymet as far as you are concerned. Okay?'

They nod, agreement being the only option.

'Who was closest to Melissa? Who knows her plans, how all this works?'

All eyes move to Lynn, trying to crawl across the dirt floor.

'Oh for fuck's sake,' Polly mutters. Of all the people she had no intention of killing, that was the one she was least unhappy about. 'And after that?'

'Dan,' Kerry says venomously.

'Fine, we're going to need medical professionals and since you lot killed the doctor I'm hoping you can suggest something,' Polly replies, holding her nerve.

'Well, if you hadn't killed the vet I'd suggest she might be able to help,' Jack retorts.

'It was an accident.'

'Well, after Lynn and Dan, it'd be me. I know some things, I'll get the contingency plans.' Clive strides off towards the altar. 'Leave it with me.' He grins as he goes through a hidden door, accepting this change of regime as if he hadn't been trying to kill Polly where she stood less than half an hour ago.

Polly leans back on the throne, a smile playing across her face now the deed is done. She starts to feel content, as she hasn't since the baby was born. This is where she belongs, her and Elizabeth. The aching and fever lifted almost as soon as she held the child to her breast. Everything is going to be alright.

'Good, I'm sorry people had to die, and I wish nothing but the best for Lynn and Dan. You shouldn't have tried to stop me. Now clean this mess up, I'm tired.'

Polly sweeps regally out of the room, a sea of dogs following at her heels.

THE END

If you enjoyed this book then please, please please could you leave a review on Amazon as it's the single most important way for struggling self-published authors to gain visibility. You don't have to write more than a couple of lines, and I won't hold it against you if you say you hated it – as long as you're honest.

Leave a review here
Amazon UK
Amazon US

If you would like to delve further into Dourstone, then sign up to my mailing list at daholwill.com/sign-up/ to receive your free copy of *The Stalking of Lady Sophia*

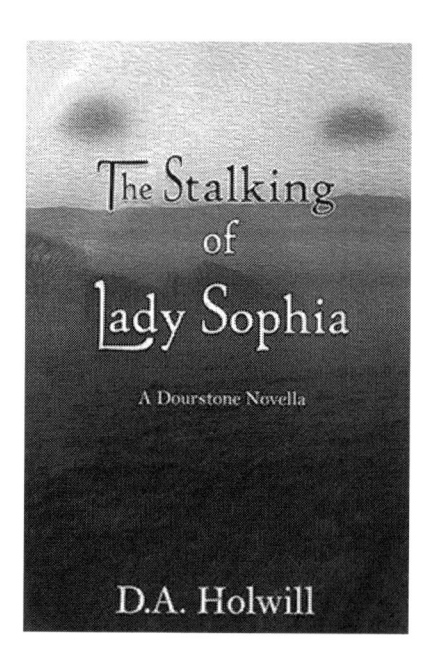

Long before Polly, Patrick or even Nathaniel Harker came to Dourstone, a young woman meets an enigmatic stranger at her father's funeral.

Sophia has lost her lover to an arranged marriage and her father to a drunken fall from Westminster bridge. When she sees a black dog from her bedroom window she does not believe the omen can make things worse.

Unfortunately for her they can, and circumstances force her and her mother to beg charity from estranged family in Devon.
With no way back to high society and her beloved, the only respectable person that will give her the time of day is the enigmatic Lord Elias Dewer.

Could he be her saviour, or the cause of all her misery?

Turn the page for a preview chapter of
Wicker Dogs Part Two:
The Bellever Hagstone

1

A fat moon illuminated the stone circle at the northernmost tip of Dourstone Nymet, white with the first snow of winter. It was midnight, the first Saturday of December. The sound of paws crunching through snow and hot, panting breath announced the arrival of an impenetrable wall of dogs, Alaskan malamutes. Their big grey faces so beautiful, so elegant, so loveable – so wolflike.

It is time. You must do it. A voice nobody but Polly could hear.

'The times they are a-changing,' she muttered, shaking her head.

Not for the better, you mark my words.

'Now see this,' Polly shouted. 'This is Dourstone Nymet, our Dourstone Nymet.'

She threw her arms wide, standing in the centre of the circle on a large, flat stone. She wore the purple velvet robes Dourstonian officials had always worn for the Wisthound weekend. Her hair – for so long hidden beneath bleach, hair relaxer and straighteners – now unleashed in all the glory of its African roots to hang round her shoulders in long natural curls.

A cheer went up from the people of Dourstone, all crowded round a bonfire outside the circle.

'And we won't let anything stand in our way, this is how we do things now. In the open, no secrets, no hidden figures. Do you trust me?' She turned about so all could see her.

'We do,' the crowd chanted in reply. 'We do.'

'Good, now, see this thing I do.' She held an ancient looking knife above her head, moonlight glinting along the teeth of its long, cruel serrated edge. Silence filled the space between beasts and humans until all had quieted. She would make sure this ceremony got the respect it demanded. 'We feed The Devil's dogs as the cold begins to bite,' she chanted. 'The first snows of winter stained with blood in the night.'

The second time round the crowd echoed her words.

The third time all were in perfect unison.

And the fourth, fifth and sixth.

She lowered the knife slowly before pulling it across her forearm.

Once satisfied the cut was deep enough she squeezed it to drip blood on the altar stone she stood upon. The stone that had spent the last century and a half hidden from prying eyes, carted between Manor and circle at need. But Polly had decided things must no longer be hidden. The cart fuelled the bonfire.

'Blood, see?' Polly's life force dripped from her hands, spattering on snow-topped granite. There was blood, there was seen to be blood. The stone had drunk so much down the years, yet its thirst remained unquenchable.

People nodded, dogs howled.

Polly's Irish wolfhound, Fenrir, stalked to the front, his eyes glowing the same blue as those of the malamutes. No longer the comical companion of her fireside, he was different, changed since that night a year before when he saved her life. He led these dogs now, and had to accept everything that went with being part of this most enigmatic pack. He nodded almost imperceptibly to his lieutenant, Cronus, the biggest and most scarred of all the malamutes, whose usually mismatched amber and sky-blue eyes glowed the same uniform blue.

'And food,' she cried, stepping down from the rock. Two robed figures hoisted a huge bag provided by Adrian the butcher into the pool of blood. They cut it open to reveal two whole pigs, as yet untouched. Polly nodded to Fenrir, who joined her. Cronus padded to his side, and at a signal from the wolfhound, raised his muzzle to the sky and gave a fearsome howl. The moon shone down between clouds as the dogs fell upon the carcasses: yellowing teeth and powerful jaws thrust aside skin intended to keep vital components inside like it was a paper bag.

The soft innards falling on snowy ground triggered a memory Polly would rather forget, when she had run for her life from this stone circle, chased by the dogs Fenrir now led and leaving her beloved Patrick to a gruesome end. As a result she had entirely given up meat, no easy feat when you unexpectedly find yourself the figurehead of a small farming community. But her final memories of Patrick's insides spilling out left her unable to consider even the most processed and unrecognisable of meats.

She hoisted a flaming torch on her shoulder and took her place at the head of eight figures in identical purple velvet robes. Where once their identities had been hidden, Polly's open door policy had reduced the tinner's masks hanging from their belts to props. The faces of Dan, Kerry, Clive, Susan, Wendy, Lynn, Jack and Father Hearne were visible. There was no other way. The people must know who it was that acted in their name.

'It is done, the town has its heart once more. We return to the Manor!' Polly cried, raising her torch to a cheer.

It's not, it hasn't, and you've really done it now girl, the voice in Polly's head said. The procession moved off down the hill.

'I told you, things are changing,' she replied, as circle and fire retreated from view. 'Nobody else need die, nothing is going to happen.'

You don't know how wrong you are.

'Why couldn't you just stay dead Melissa?'

Because you didn't know what you were doing when you tried to kill me. You want me here, you obviously need me or you'd never have taken my ring, the familiar patronising tones of Lady Melissa Dewer rattled round Polly's head as the townsfolk followed her away from the sound of tooth crunching through bone.

The next morning, an old-fashioned caravan creaked and clattered its way along the frosty moorside road to Dourstone, drawn by four hungry-looking black horses. Its much re-panelled and patched together sides, once a glorious black, had now faded to grey; the formerly magnificent black feathered plumes at its corners were now ragged stumps and the ancient sigils carved upon it had been rendered unrecognisable by the never-ending march of time and weather. A motley crew of mismatched mongrel dogs – their coats mingled to a uniform oily brown from the dirt of infinite roads – lolloped beside it, keeping easy pace with the horses. The bizarre procession came as far as the cross that marked the boundary of Dourstone proper, one of those markers they blessed every seven years when beating the bounds.

A black deadman's hat crowned the driver, while his face hid behind a beard that was hard to distinguish from his long, straggly, silver-streaked hair. His old-fashioned black leather boots crunched in the snow as he jumped from the cab and, before even untying his horses, pulled something from the folds of his well-worn black travelling cloak, ground it against the head of the cross, then threw it to his dogs.

'It's been a long time coming,' he said, lighting his pipe and looking across to the stone circle.

After he had taken a few puffs, an enormous black dog that could easily be mistaken for a small bear gave a gruff bark and nodded.

He took a few paces past the cross, into Dourstone proper, and grinned.

'Good boy, Wotan. We're home.'

The Bellever Hagstone Wicker Dogs Book Two Coming July 2021

DA Holwill is online at:-
www.daholwill.com
www.facebook.com/daholwill
www.instagram.com/dave_holwill
and @daveholwill on twitter

AUTHOR'S NOTE AND ACKNOWLEDGEMENTS

Firstly, before I am inundated with complaints from Alaskan Malamute owners, I am sorry for taking certain liberties with the breed. It was necessary for the story. Be assured Sky, an Alaskan Malamute I adopted five years ago, has forgiven me and so should you. With that said, she has insisted she be first on the thank you list for using her eyes on the cover. So thank you Sky, my life would be much easier and duller without you.

Thanks to my wife, Netty, who, along with creating the stunning etching of Cronus at the front of this book, has consistently reassured me it was worth writing to the bitter end. Thank you for your belief honey.

Also to the kids, despite being full-grown adults who continue to be surprised that my books are 'just like real ones.' One day I'll surprise you with one that really isn't.

Deb, for inspiring my monster, sorry she's not as terrifying as you, but I needed her to be believable.

Anita, for letting me steal your 'getting the round and pretending there's gin in your tonic water' trick to hiding a pregnancy from your alcoholic friends.

And so to my wonderful beta readers:

Netty, again, always first, usually right.

Tracy, for your endless positivity and cheerleading.

Lou, for making sure I stay (mostly) inside the bounds of medical possibility.

Kerriann, for not being afraid to point out glaring mistakes to a stranger on the internet.

Helen for suggesting the new pen name.

And anybody else who read this for me that I've forgotten, you're all invaluable in making Polly and Melissa the women they became.

Printed in Great Britain
by Amazon